THE LIVES OF OTHERS

OTHER TITLES BY ELLEN WON STEIL

Becoming Marlow Fin

Fortune

THE LIVES OF OTHERS

A Novel

ELLEN WON STEIL

LAKE UNION
PUBLISHING

Published by Lake Union Publishing, Seattle

www.apub.com

EU product safety contact:
Amazon Media EU S. à r.l.
38, avenue John F. Kennedy, L-1855 Luxembourg
amazonpublishing-gpsr@amazon.com

ISBN-13: 9781662527128 (paperback)
ISBN-13: 9781662527135 (digital)

Cover design by Mumtaz Mustafa
Cover image: © Robert Lambert / ArcAngel Images; © Linda Raymond, © Jennifer McCallum / Getty; © fotoak / Shutterstock

Printed in the United States of America

for my sister, Jennifer

CHAPTER 1

"You'll love it there, Radley. I promise." Alice's last words to me before I got into my cab to Incheon Airport, followed by a quick embrace I'd stiffened under.

I don't believe in promises anymore.

There are indeed no guarantees for anything in life. That is the only certainty I plan to count on.

The New England coastline summons me with every possible shade of cerulean waters; with each crash of a wave, I feel more compelled to stop and answer its call.

I pull the midsize SUV rental over onto a gravelly lookout to survey where I've chosen to temporarily transplant. On the nearly fourteen-hour plane ride over, I found myself questioning how Alice had talked me into taking her place. But as I take in my first deep breath of Maine air, I realize it was my own doing.

I feel as though I've escaped.

Cool ocean air whips around my neck, and loose strands of hair caress me as they fall. My eyes swell from the salty wind but even more so at the bold bursts of crimson and amber vying for attention among the serotinal green. My sight is assaulted by the beginning stage of this autumnal body that I find I need more of with each passing second. Slab after slab of Silurian rock castles reach out to sea, a black-and-white lighthouse perched on the farthest point, forlorn in its isolation.

The painted scene has been dropped. And I wonder if bonfires of color will ingest me in a few weeks before I even have a chance to explore them. What is it about the fall season that makes me feel ready to sunset, to dial down into stillness?

It's the seclusion that beckons me.

"There's something about that New England fall air. Something . . . curative even," Alice said in her ramblings about the beauty of the place. "Clark Orchard is a hidden gem. Far enough from the biggest muck of tourists but close enough to the ocean, near Fox Isle—that's the closest town."

I picture Alice back in Seoul, seated at her desk under the aggressively bright LED lights of SeoWoo Tech. Where I'd still be if it hadn't been for her promotion.

She'd bounced into my office that morning, her golden locks following suit.

"Can you believe this? Senior marketing director?" she'd squealed.

"Yes," I answered without looking up as I signed in to my desktop.

"I still don't know why you didn't apply for the position," she responded good naturedly.

I flickered my eyes with a wily glance. I wasn't naive enough to think I was liked by many, if any, of our coworkers. It's easier to be unliked sometimes.

It's easier to be alone.

I settled into my desk and slid the keyboard closer to my chest.

She put her hand to her mouth. "Wait! What am I going to tell my cousin, though? This director position . . . it's my chance to finally do something here. But I can't leave him high and dry during harvest season. I'd planned a sabbatical in a few weeks."

"Sabbatical?" I raised a brow.

"Don't you remember? My family on my dad's side—well, my cousin now—owns that gorgeous apple orchard in Maine. I visited often growing up, and he offered me a seasonal job. You know . . . get away from the hectic vibe of Seoul. Maybe have a few apple ciders. Spiked, of course."

She smiled excitedly, but with the look I gave her, it faded a little. And then I saw something in her eyes that made me turn away. Pity.

"I'm sure he'll understand," I murmured as I started to check emails.

She grew unusually quiet, and I felt her eyes on me. I paused from my typing.

Alice abruptly placed her hand on top of mine to halt my fingers.

"You," she said.

My eyes pivoted to her hand, and I slid my arm away.

"What?"

"You, Radley." She leaned in with a gleam in her eyes. "You should take my place at the orchard."

I oddly let her hold my gaze for a few more seconds before returning to my work. "No. I'm here where I need to be."

"The idea doesn't entice you? The fall season in Maine? Fresh air? You could use my plane ticket even."

"The ticket can be refunded or credited."

She sighed. "My cousin has a cottage I was going to stay in. It's so charming. And"—she lowered the top of her head—"you'd be left alone for the most part."

"I can be alone here."

Alice crossed her arms in a rare sulk.

"Radley. Look around you. It's been ten years since you came to Seoul. Two years since—"

"I said I'm good," I said harshly. I cleared my throat and adjusted my seat as I focused hard on my computer screen. The letters suddenly blurred together.

I waited for Alice to leave, but to my dismay, she didn't let up. "Is this really where you want to stay? For another year? Five years?"

I snapped my eyes up to her. "You may have gotten a promotion, Alice, but let me remind you that you're not that different from me in our positions in life. If I'm not mistaken, you're still single and working for the same company?"

Her eyes softened, and she shook her head. "Oh, Radley. You're really not this person."

I shut my eyes, and my jaw tightened. "I have work to do, Alice. And so do you."

When she moved to the door, I opened my eyes.

"Think about it, Radley," she said quietly with her back to me. "Offer still stands."

She was gone, but I was unable to move. Perhaps it was her out-of-character boldness or the fact that the idea of getting away for a while made my chest loosen in a good way, like stretching out a sore muscle until the pain was released.

You're really not this person.

By the time I returned to my screen, it had gone black; my office lighting bounced back an image that neither pleased nor upset me. A pale face stared at me with a puffy, round, closed mouth. I'd stopped wearing makeup long ago, but none of that would've helped the darkness under my eyes. I felt for the skin at the base of my neck where my hair hit bluntly, most days secured into a taut ponytail. The woman reflected in this screen looked shrunken.

Minimized.

A sabbatical would mean a break. A seasonal pause . . .

I rub my temples now, the many hours of travel taking their toll. I inhale the sea air once more before returning to the car. I left Portland three hours ago and still have another half hour to Fox Isle. But once I drive farther up the coast, the steadfast scenery starts to melt some of the tension in my head.

As I enter Fox Isle, I feel disarmed by the charming pastel-painted storefronts facing the placid inlet, shimmering in the afternoon light. Sailboats fill the marina, and wooden docks line the shore. Labor Day celebration flags from last week still hang from their posts. I keep going, past a saltwater taffy shop, corner pub, and souvenir store, its windows crowded with T-shirts featuring coastal prints and fish-themed tchotchkes. Toward the outskirts of the main drag is a combined gas station and general store. I stop there for directions, as I've lost GPS on my phone.

I'm halfway into the spot by a gas pump when a vintage teal truck blazes in, cutting me off. Slamming on my brakes, I grit my teeth and gesture with annoyance.

"Excuse you," I mouth.

But the driver in the truck takes no notice. He quickly gets out to fill his tank, sandy hair falling in his eyes.

So far, manners don't seem much better in Maine than in Seoul.

I reverse and pull into a pump closer to the front of the general store. By the time I get out, the rude sandyman has gotten back into his truck. I choose to ignore this incident of deep impoliteness and go into the store to pay and get directions for my final leg of the trip.

The store has maintained its old-fashioned allure of lacquered log walls and ceilings, creaky wooden floors, and shelves of candy jars behind the counter. I breeze past aisles of convenience items and sundries and wait in line to speak to the red-bearded cashier. He takes his time with the man in front of me, saying something about the tides and the cost of gas, and I do my best to suppress my impatient sigh. As I rock back on my heels, a woman enters.

I'm unable to look away.

Cascades of chocolate spirals are piled high on her head, and a rolled mint-green headscarf is tied at the nape of her long slender neck. The shape of her body is narrow yet athletic. She adjusts the strap of her purse, and I'm still watching her. Her presence demands a long stare, which she seems either completely unaware of or doesn't particularly covet. Her light-hazel eyes glance up, her thick curled lashes blink slowly, and she smiles at me. An ample pink upper lip stretches across an immense white smile as two dainty dimples appear in the light-brown flesh of her cheeks.

She glows with brashness. The dimness in every part of my own appearance and bearing fades with each second as I continue to stare. I'm a plain white paper crane encountering a bright burning bush, eviscerated by being in the same vicinity.

"Can I help you, ma'am?" the red-bearded cashier asks, leaning over the counter.

"Yes, pump number three. And I'm trying to get to . . ." I look over my shoulder, but the woman has moved elsewhere in the store.

"Need directions to Clark Orchard?" he finishes for me.

"Yes. How did you know that?"

He shrugs. "Cell service drops a bit on this end of town. People tend to come in here for help with that."

He tells me I have another thirty minutes to go. I purchase a bag of lemon drops near the register and thank him. By the time I step away, I don't see any sign of the woman from earlier.

Back in the car, tartness fills my mouth as I roll the tear-shaped candy around. The dirt road is lined with shimmery canary aspens guiding me along. Fiery maples like blood oranges preen in the background, and I'm soaring through a tunnel of watchful hues.

I slow down when I approach the gateway at the entrance. A low stone fence meets each side of the white-painted posts, an oval sign hanging between them with black steel lettering:

CLARK ORCHARD
Est. 1817

I pause before passing through, almost sensing the point of no return. What happens once I go through that archway? Will I shed my former self, a cicada leaving behind a transparent shell to wither?

There wouldn't be much to miss of that version. At least not for me.

The road grinds beneath the wheels as I cautiously cross over, as if going through too fast might somehow cause pain.

Farther ahead, atop a hill, I spot it—a great white farmhouse with black shutters, the base built with rocks that I imagine have been there as long as the orchard has. The house seems to observe me, this new occupant of the land, alerting everyone to my presence.

She comes silently. She comes with no past.

For a moment I'm distracted by the rows and rows of apple trees, dizzying in the geometric precision of their spacing, endless in their repetition, and I find I'm holding my breath.

The road dips, and I pass a charming garden surrounded by trestles and twinkle lights, dotted with light wood picnic tables and red Adirondack chairs. During busy hours this space must be fully occupied with visitors. A large, green-painted barn lies adjacent and looks to be the orchard shop.

It's empty now, as is the garden.

The orchard is also empty.

Shadows of late afternoon stretch out, and I park near another barn and stable. As I shut the car door, I hear mewing calls from an animal. At first they're faint, but the calls quicken and lengthen with each one.

They turn into wails. Painful wails that end sharply. I walk toward the sound and darken the entry of the pen with my stance.

I smell the sturdy scent of farmyard creatures and hay. A man forcefully holds down a sheep, her velvet black ears alert, her button eyes staring at me as if asking for help. One eye is fogged over with mucus and yellow crust.

"C'mon, Charlotte. Work with me, please," he grumbles.

Charlotte, assuming that's the name of the sheep, bleats louder.

"This is to help you, darling. I know you don't think so, but—"

She kicks her hind legs. The man grunts and then looks up to find me staring.

"Oh! Hello there. Any chance you could hold her back legs for me?"

I'm not sure how to even begin to answer that question. Something seems familiar about his face that gives me slight pause.

The man's navy eyes peer at what can only be a stupefied and disgruntled look in my own.

"My name is Beau," he says, as if that might pacify me.

His grip on Charlotte relaxes, and she immediately fights again, this time her head whipping under his arm.

"I'm here to see Edwin Clark. Do you know where I can find him?" I ask, pretending not to notice the straw that Charlotte's flung onto my clothes and hair.

Beau wrangles Charlotte once more. "Sure," he says in a strained voice. "As soon as you can please hold her for a brief moment."

I blink rapidly a few times and step deeper into the pen. After grabbing both hind legs quickly, I hold them tightly to my chest.

"Okay. Now what?" I ask.

He tilts his head, amused, and pulls out from the back of his jeans a small turquoise bottle of eye drops. "All right, darling. Medicine time." Swiftly, three drops go in the filmy eye, and we both let go.

"Baaaaah," Charlotte bleats before trotting away with a vengeful last kick of her legs at us.

I stand up and hastily dust off my pants.

He sits back on his knees and sighs. "Thank God. I never thought she'd take those drops." A bead of sweat drips down his forehead, and his closely shorn brown hair is almost damp. It's then I realize who he reminds me of. The appearance isn't identical—yes, the same eyes and perhaps the shape of his face and the strong cleft chin—but it's more his cheerful aura: just enough to hold you but not enough to irritate. A playful calmness that I forgot could be so reassuring.

My older brother, Jem. It's been so long since I've let myself think about him.

Beau looks up at me, and I wonder if he expects me to help him up.

"About Edwin Clark . . ."

"Oh, right."

"You see, my friend Alice Clark was supposed to work the season. But I'm here in her place. Her cousin Edwin is the owner."

He chuckles and shakes his head. "Edwin . . . now I don't remember the last time Alice actually called me that."

I step back. "You're—" is all I say.

"Edwin Beau Clark II. But most people call me Beau."

CHAPTER 2

I'm not sure why I assumed Alice's cousin would be older.

Maybe it's because she referred to him as Edwin. I had visualized an older man in his fifties, rough and wearing overalls, with a bucket of apples to hand me and a toothpick propped in the side of his mouth.

But Edwin, a.k.a. Beau, is none of that.

"You must be Radley," he says, smiling warmly. He stands up, ignoring the bits of hay and sheep hair clinging to his jeans and red flannel button-up.

"Yes. I'm here in place of Alice," I say again.

"Welcome to Clark Orchard." He motions his hand with sarcastic grandeur. "I hope this is better than what you expected?"

"I didn't really have any expectations."

He glances at me. If he found my response jolting, he shows no signs of it, and he walks us out of the stable.

"Why are there no other people? Visitors?" I check again, surveying the quiet around us.

"Ah. That's because the orchard is closed to visitors on Mondays," he answers as I keep up with his long strides. "And the crew is taking a break this afternoon. Labor Day weekend gets kind of crazy around here. You'll probably find them at the corner pub you passed in town."

We stop at my rental car, and I move to open the trunk before Beau waves me away. "I'll help you bring your things in later. First a quick tour?"

I nod and follow him back to where I came from, down the dirt road, and he points at the garden seating and barn shop.

"You'll find that's the hub of the orchard when open for visitors. We sell all twenty varieties of apples we grow in the shop, along with jams, pies, and cider. All the good stuff," he explains, winking at me. "Every now and then, a local winery does tastings here. I'll probably start you in the shop, and the crew can help you get acclimated to the orchard work."

I hear enthusiasm and pride in his voice, which makes me wonder what it's like to be born and rooted into what you do for a living. I gesture past the shop to a metal-sided structure. "What's that building for?"

"Cider building," Beau replies and hitches a thumb backward. "Already saw the stables and Charlotte. There are other animals for you to meet. We can save the main house for later. But this . . ." He puts his arm out and steadies me. I look down at where his fingers lightly touched my wrist and slowly pull my arm away, close to my waist. We've reached the crest of another hill, and any awkwardness I may have felt dissipates at the view.

"This is what makes it all worthwhile," he says softly.

A curtain of yolkish light hits the vast acres of apple trees, the shade cast by each single tree an abstract shape that can't be repeated. There's something gilded about the farmland framing thc orchard, stretching free out to the horizon, a smear of blue ocean a ribbon in the distance.

"All of this is yours," I say with my eyes still fixated.

"My family's."

His reply is nowhere near curt, but the words come out more evenly than anything else he's said.

"Six generations of fruit farming. One hundred acres of land that has seen so much." This time I think I detect a twinge of melancholy. But Beau quickly brushes past it and turns to me.

"So. Radley. You've traveled a long way. And the first person who greets you won't stop talking."

"Yes. But I'm here to learn."

He tightens one side of his mouth. "You know, the way Alice talked about you, I was expecting someone more . . ."

I wait for him to finish his sentence, but he thinks better of it.

"It's all right. You're not at all what I pictured either."

He laughs. "Are you hungry?"

"No," I lie.

The last thing I want is to give him any reason to think I require his company longer than necessary.

"My wife is making this amazing roast chicken tonight for dinner. She hates cooking, actually." Beau scratches his head, and a playful smirk appears. "Which is why I'm normally the one in the kitchen, but this chicken—"

"That won't be necessary."

"The chicken?"

I deliberately face him, my hands clasped in front as if to rope myself off. "I really don't want to impose. I'm interested in seeing where I'll be staying."

He doesn't answer, and I'm partially relieved that I've offended him, so he'll keep his distance. But instead, his eyes light up at the road behind me.

"There they are!" he calls out.

"Who?" I spin around and see a dark-gray minivan making its way toward us.

"Livia and the kids."

Kids.

"They've been so excited for your arrival."

Alice never mentioned there would be children.

"Maybe it's best you show me my room. I can stay out of everyone's way."

Beau flashes an incredulous grin. "Are you kidding me? You're the highlight of the week for these kids."

I don't smile back and shift uncomfortably as the minivan slows down. Before it can come to a complete stop, the back passenger door slides open with force, and two little legs pop out and plop to the ground.

"Nina! What did Mommy tell you about getting out before the car has stopped?" a voice calls from inside the minivan.

A little girl with light curly pigtails high on her head, bouncing like coils, marches at full speed toward me.

"Let me see her," she demands. She throws her unicorn backpack to the ground and stands toe to toe with me, my cognac leather ankle boots to her hot-pink sneakers.

I stiffen as she raises her head slowly until our eyes meet. Her curls still spring about as if they have a life of their own.

"Are you the new Cousin Alice?" she asks with wide eyes.

"No, I'm Radley."

She frowns. "You're smaller than I thought you'd be. Do you want me to teach you how to pick an apple?"

"Sure."

Beau moves in and places his hands lightly on her shoulders. "This is Nina, our youngest. She's also the family boss these days."

Nina smiles in that way children do, showing all her teeth. She grabs my index finger and places it on a bottom front tooth. "Feel that? It's getting loose. Maybe you can help me pull it later? My daddy says inflation doesn't apply to the tooth fairy—"

"Okay, Nina," Beau interjects, pulling her away.

Another little girl climbs out of the minivan, and I start to have flashbacks of clown cars at the circus. She's taller but undeniably has the same curly bronze hair, only hers is set free to wave in the wind. A lanky boy follows her, nearly the spitting image of Beau, and the three children stand before me.

"Six, eight, and twelve," Beau says, tapping each of them on the head.

"That's what you call them?"

"Sometimes. But if you want complete accuracy, we have Nina, Avie, and Tallan."

Tallan wipes his sleeve across his face and mumbles what I think is a hello.

"What are you all doing standing out there?" a voice calls from the minivan. The driver's side window rolls down, and the same megawatt smile from the general store flashes at me.

She's pulled the rolled mint-green scarf from her neck up over her hair. Her creamy-brown arm hangs out the window.

"Hi, Radley, I'm Livia. And I hope our beautiful little gremlins haven't already put you off," she says. There's so much effervescence in the way she speaks, each word a bubble floating out toward me. I find myself listening intently so I won't miss another one.

"No, it's all right . . . they haven't," I say louder than necessary.

Livia gives a nonchalant wave to Beau. "Babe, I picked up that spicy poultry seasoning you love so much at the store." She winks at me, and I feel my cheeks betray me by flushing. "Radley, you have to join us for dinner. Anyone riding with me back to the house?"

She flies over her invitation before I have a chance to respond.

Avie tosses her hair to the side. "Mommy, do you know how much carbon emissions we can save by walking?" She looks at me pointedly with round, bright, hazel eyes, and it's then I realize all three children have eyes the exact shade as their mother.

"You know, Avie, you're so thoughtful to think of the earth. Would you like to be Radley's personal guide to the house?"

She lights up eagerly. "Yes. I'll do that, Mommy."

"All right, my birdie," she says with a secret glint at Avie before turning to me. "I'll see you at the house then?"

I neither nod nor shake my head as she switches gears and rolls slowly before moving down the road. Beau scoops Nina up and hoists her up on his shoulders as she giggles.

A warm little hand clamps on to mine.

"Stick with me. I'll make sure you get to the house okay, Radley," Avie says firmly and proceeds to march us forward as I lean back from her speed.

"You don't have to do what she tells you, you know," Tallan murmurs quietly at my side.

Avie shoots him a sideways glare. "I'm only trying to help her. Besides, Mommy told me to."

"You lived in Seoul?" Tallan asks me, ignoring her.

"Yes."

"I know where that is. We just did a unit on East Asia. Fascinating region, but terribly sad about Korea. A country divided for that long?"

I nod. "Yes. A sad history."

"I'd love to study that someday. International relations, that is, maybe become an interpreter."

I nearly smile. "Are you really only twelve?"

"Thirteen next July," he answers.

Avie stops and stares at me with seriousness. "I want a gourmet fondue set for my birthday."

When we reach the house, I stop like a startled mare. A sense that if I enter this family's home, I'll break a seal that can never be unbroken. The front porch steps are worn in the middle from years of use. Proof of their lives, a family warm and living.

"What's the matter, Radley?" Avie asks, eyeing me attentively.

I realize she's pulling at my arm, but I've planted my feet. I say nothing to her and place my boot on the first step.

Their lives are not for me to be a part of.

"Please, come on into the kitchen!" Livia calls from inside.

Avie quickly leads me through the foyer, giving me little time to look around. But there's an immediate lightness from the scent of wood and spices. The floorboards creak with a storied past, and I'm encircled by sturdy walls that seem to whisper at me.

A merle-colored border collie mix runs up to inspect me. He sniffs my feet and then looks up with one ice-blue and one chocolate eye. I scratch his head, and his ears go back passively.

"That's Rabbit," Avie says with an air of explaining a complicated concept. "He's a herding dog and will herd anything. Kittens. People. It's a hoot."

"Watch out!" Tallan slides by on the wood floor in his socks, a stack of books in his arms. "Coming through." Rabbit barks and chases after him playfully, and we follow their lead into the kitchen.

Livia stands behind the pewter island, a cluster of copper pots and pans hanging above her head, as she cuts a lemon in half and stuffs it into a raw whole chicken.

"You're not a vegetarian, are you?" she asks, pausing with her hand still inside the chicken. "I mean, nothing against that. But if you are, I can—"

"I'm so sorry," I interject. "I don't mean to be rude. But I'm still a little jet-lagged and might not be the best company right now. It might be best if I head to where I'm staying."

I spot Tallan in the breakfast nook, pausing from the pages of his book to glance at us.

"Really? You have to be starving after such a long flight and drive."

"I'm okay. I stopped to eat something," I lie, feeling my stomach tighten.

"Are you sure you don't want to just sit with us and nibble a little?" Her eyes sparkle with kindness, and I almost agree.

"I'm sure," I say as politely as I can.

Beau closes the refrigerator door and places the milk on the counter. "Maybe I didn't talk your chicken up enough, Liv," he quips.

Livia laughs. "Don't let him fool you. He's not usually one to commend my cooking." She bumps him with her hip, and he gazes at her in a way that makes me unstiffen somewhat. She turns her attention back to me, holding the chicken in her hands. "Let me at least—"

"Mommy, you said you would help me with my fractions," Avie interrupts, tugging hard at her waist. Livia loses her grip on the slippery chicken skin, and it plops onto the floor with an unceremonious flap.

Nina appears like an apparition, wrapping her arms around her knees. "Hi, Mommy," she says.

I wait, expecting Livia to brush them off in the hurried rush for dinner, annoyed at their demands and in the zone of a weathered mother, when all romantic notions get pushed aside for practical ones.

But she doesn't.

She's the outlier. The motherly one-off.

"Hi, baby," she says melodiously down at Nina. "Avie, bring your fraction sheet to the counter while I get this bird to cook." She tips her head down to the floor.

"Ten-second rule applies to aviary creatures, right, Beau?"

Beau nods with exaggerated approval, bending over to scoop up the chicken. Nina nuzzles her face deeper into Livia's legs as Avie moves to retrieve her homework.

They are drawn to her, butter to bread. Her tenderness is natural with them, unforced, and I take a stuttered step back from the island.

"It looks like you have your hands full. Maybe it's best if I get out of your way here and head to my room . . . please," I say, my words and throat dry.

Livia pauses from washing her hands and then nods. "Of course. Beau, why don't you take over here?" She spins her finger around like a dial. "I'll show Radley to the guest cottage."

"Already on it," he answers, sliding the chicken back into the cast-iron skillet.

She dries her hands on a dish towel. "Don't forget to give Nina her evening dose before dinner." She places her hand on my lower back, guiding me out, and lowers her voice. "She's a little anemic," she explains, despite my not asking.

"Say good night to Radley," Beau instructs, seasoning the chicken with some pepper.

"See you tomorrow, Radley!" Nina shouts after us, soon followed by her siblings, the enthusiasm lessening by age.

As I reach the front porch, I suck in a deep mouthful of fresh air. Livia either doesn't notice my rudeness or pretends not to, saying something about how she remembers jet lag when she traveled during her college days.

The cottage sits behind the main house, a good forty yards straight back. We walk a flat section of grass separating the two dwellings. I look up at the cottage to see a single apex with an ocular window at the top. The front is squared and simple, covered in rustic shingles. A black modern door greets us, with gold fixtures flanked by narrow windows.

"We had to replace the door last winter," Livia says, as if reading my mind. "But the rest of it has good old bones." She opens the door for me and flicks on the light. "There's a kitchen in the back, a full bath, and the bedroom is up in the loft. Clean sheets and plenty of closet space up there too."

I run my hand over the white dinette table, a fresh vase of lilies placed in the center. A weathered green bookcase sits against the opposite wall; hanging next to it is a black-and-white picture of the orchard.

"This is perfect," I say, forgetting I'm not alone.

Her eyes focus on me, looking pleased, or perhaps relieved. I'm not sure. "We're so happy to have you here, Radley."

"Thank you."

"It'll be nice having another woman my age around the orchard." She rubs her arms as she looks around the cottage. "Sometimes I feel a little bit like I'm on my own island. Even with all the crew, visitors, and the kids . . . you know what I mean?"

Yes . . . I do know.

"I suppose . . . the kids are probably missing you right now. And the chicken."

I see a flash of disappointment in her face, but she laughs through it. "Right. The chicken."

After she's gone, I remember that my bags are still in the car, parked by the barn stable.

I wait until almost nightfall to avoid running into Livia or anyone else, walking the long way out, far from the house. The sky darkens, and I have the solace I've craved ever since running into Beau. The sound of grass under my feet is rhythmic and soothing.

Soon the rental is humming on the road, and my hands grip the steering wheel. I feel compelled to press on the gas and drive out to the sea. The recollection of the family's warm words and voices echo inside me. I pause from retreating.

And then I see it. The light from their house.

I'm tethered. Resistant. A scattered stone.

Back at the cottage, I lug my heavy bags up the loft stairs. I unpack a few clothes before abandoning the task and reaching for the bag of lemon drops, my dinner for tonight. I suck hard on one and roll on the bed to face the ocular window.

I press my face closer to the glass.

There they are. A clear dollhouse of a view. The back of the home full of windows for me to feast on. Here in my perch, I've been given a diorama of this family.

No move they make in the confinement of each square of glass escapes my sight.

Eyes finally open. Eyes drinking it all up.

They're not the first family I've watched. I don't mean to pry. I don't mean to be ill-mannered. It just . . . happens. The spy who only wants to mine secrets with her eyes she will never share.

That's all.

That's all I hope to gain.

It starts with a glance. A motion I can't help but stop to take in. This was how it began with the family in the apartment across from mine in Seoul. It was the mother I noticed first. Her hair gathered neatly at the nape of her neck as she slowly cut tofu into little cubes and scraped them from the cutting board into a boiling soup with her knife.

I watched them on many other occasions after that. A nebula of four black shiny heads, bobbing with unbridled contentment. Hands clapping for every possible celebration, a birthday or high score on a math test, countless meals with enthusiastic chatter and game nights where nobody sulked over losing. All taking place at their round kitchen table with a tribe-like synchronization.

They became a comfort to me each night, a reliable show I could turn on. I was rebalancing the equilibrium—settling the score from all the other times I'd been alone. I'd earned my viewing of this family from self-isolation.

Time with them became the only way I could feel anything.

And now here, with this family I've only just met. Perhaps it's too soon. I'm drawn to them despite my reservations. I move away from the glass as my face flushes with unease.

No. Not this time. This time you stay out.

I'm fully prepared to go to bed instead. But I catch a glimpse of the littlest one. So small and still.

The quiet of their house tonight lures me.

Nina sound asleep in her bed. Hot-pink sneakers from the day a lump on the floor. Her peacefulness stirs the disquiet in me. My eyes roam over to the room to her right. Avie is still awake. Twirling a lock of hair, her hand rotates and she flops to her side, closes her eyes, bringing her body into a fetal position. On the far left, Tallan at his desk, still with a book. He's hunched over, barely moving.

And then above them all in the highest bedroom.

She walks toward him. Long legs bare up to the only thing she wears. A T-shirt that covers all but the very bottom of two curves. He sits on the bed. Watching her. She arches onto her tiptoes before flattening one foot, her hands reaching for the edges of the cotton fabric of her shirt, drawing it up slowly and over her head.

She drops it to the floor.

I shut my eyes. The house is closed for tonight.

CHAPTER 3

I remember exactly where I am when I wake up.

The sheet slides off my body as I go to the ocular to see them. But the light isn't right this time of morning. There's enough of the sunrise to shield them from me.

I wrap myself in a long sweater and pull-on knee-high rubber boots to walk the grounds. The leaves of the apple trees brush against my arms, sprinkling me with morning dew. I close my eyes and face the sunlight, and I feel the seclusion that never leaves my side.

Left alone and I'm harmless. Left alone and I feel the indulgence of empty space.

But I realize I'm not alone. Someone is watching me.

Tallan jumps down from one of the trees. It shakes, and onc apple falls to the ground. I should be startled, but I'm not. He bends over with a book in one hand, picks up the yellow-orange apple with the other. He shines it on his shirt and takes a giant bite.

"Holstein," he says while chewing. "Great for cider, but it's actually my favorite to eat off the tree." He holds it out, offering me a bite, as a piece of his glossy chestnut hair falls across his forehead.

I shake my head. I'm more interested in the book. "What are you reading?"

He looks down at it, as if he's forgotten it was there. "*Lord of the Flies.*"

I raise my eyebrows. "Aren't you a little young for that?"

"On the class reading list. I finished *Crime and Punishment* last week."

I wrap my sweater tighter, wanting to guard myself from vexing memories of middle school angst.

"Do your parents know you're out here?"

He shrugs. "Maybe?"

"You don't think they're worried you're not at breakfast?"

"Since Nina was born, they've been pretty hands off with me." I sense a lingering glumness in his voice as his gaze drifts back to his book.

"I see. Well," I say, taking a few steps back toward the cottage, hoping to leave as I arrived. Alone.

"Why didn't you stay for dinner last night?" Tallan asks as he takes another bite of his apple and tosses it on the ground. "Whenever we get a new crew member, we have them over. Mom and Dad are really big on keeping it family-style around here."

Family-style.

"I was tired," is all I can come up with.

"The chicken was extra good."

"I'm sure it was." It comes out a little snippier than I intended.

"Another time then." He turns to leave and then quickly steps back as he shifts the book between his hands. "Why don't you come back to the house with me? Avie and Nina kept asking about you last night."

This is not setting precedent very well.

"Sorry, Tallan. But I have some more unpacking to do yet." I pull my sweater sleeves down over my hands, shifting the weight in my legs to give the impression of urgency.

"Ah. Okay," he answers. His hair has dropped forward until it's almost covering his eyes, and he slouches, moving to pull his hoodie over his head dejectedly.

He's doing what seventh graders do. This is typical; don't get involved.

I let him walk ahead of me and then turn back to enjoy the sunrise again. But somehow, it's not as pleasant.

"Tallan," I say.

Why are you still talking to this child?

"Yeah," he answers, tilting his face out of his hoodie.

Maybe it's because he reminds me of myself in middle school. Always in a book. Not really the favorite of the parents. A little more lost than most. Or more likely, I want more of a front-row seat. A moment of getting up close and personal to the details of this family I'm watching through my new window.

They deserve a visit from their watcher.

"Let me walk with you," I say to him.

When we reach the front porch, neither Beau nor Livia are in sight. Tallan drops his book right on the floor in the foyer, and I'm half tempted to pick it up. He walks past the kitchen and into a room I haven't seen yet.

The den is flooded with morning light, and I quickly realize it's also a playroom for the girls. The bottoms of three walls have built-in rows of bookcases and yellow fabric storage cubes. Sheer cotton crosshatch curtains flutter across the floor, each window cracked open, inviting a light draft.

In the center, a child-size table and chairs occupied by Avie and Nina, still wearing their pajamas.

Nina delicately holds up a powder-blue teacup, part of the pastel tea set spread across a scalloped tablecloth.

"Do you want a cup, Radley?" she asks and takes a small sip.

"Is that actual tea?"

Avie, whose back has been to me, turns with an adamant stare. "Of course. There's always real tea at our tea party." She points to an empty seat next to a worn stuffed rabbit; one of the eyes is missing, its sable fur matted. "You can sit next to Rabbit."

"Rabbit? I thought that's your dog's name?"

"It is," says Tallan, leaning in the doorframe. "This is who he's named after."

On cue, Rabbit scampers in with a long wet tongue hanging sideways out of his mouth. He circles the girls a few times before giving me a stare.

"Hi, Rabbit." The dog tilts his head. "Hi, Rabbit," I say, nodding to the one in the chair.

"They do this every day," says Tallan.

"The Rabbits sit together?"

"No. The tea party."

Avie nods emphatically. "And guess what, Radley? *I* set it up every time. I make the tea all by myself. It's the only way."

Nina rushes over and holds out an empty plate. "This is the lemon olive oil cake I made just for you, Radley," she explains. Today, her curls are piled on her head in the same fashion Livia's hair was yesterday.

"That's . . . pretty sophisticated for a six-year-old."

She lowers her head and whispers with a slight lisp, "I'm so-fist-eh-kaded?"

I struggle to suppress a smile.

Avie reaches over, picks up Rabbit, and squeezes the plush toy against her chest. "I've had him since I was a baby. He's so precious to me."

"As are you to me, Avie girl," Beau says, appearing in the doorway next to Tallan. He holds out a cup of coffee for me, and the smell makes my stomach growl. "Good morning."

"Good morning," I say, taking it.

"Hope you slept okay. I made a batch of corn bread muffins. Help yourself. They're in the kitchen."

This time I wouldn't be passing. "Thank you." I take a long, deep sip. "Where's Livia?"

He adjusts his baseball cap. "Weekly five a.m. yoga class. Also, what she calls her 'sanity session.' I'll be wrangling the kids soon for school and drop-off. When I get back, I can show you around more."

"All right."

The quicker I learn, the quicker they'll leave me alone.

"Can I stay and show Radley the orchard?" Nina asks, slicing another pretend piece of cake.

Beau shakes his head. "Not today, sweetie." He turns back to me. "*And* you can't be here for more than twenty-four hours without learning how to properly pick an apple." He squeezes Tallan on the shoulder and claps his hands once. Tallan seems to tense. "All right, girls, ten more minutes, and then it's go time."

Later, the sky grows overcast as I inspect the barn. I find Charlotte in the same spot where I first met her. Her eye seems the same, as does her attitude. She must remember me holding her down. With one look she's off to the other side, where another sheep and three goats gather around her.

On the opposite end, two horses stand in their stables. I slowly approach, trying not to startle them. The solid-black horse snorts once. The white-and-tan-spotted one seems curious and leans out to inspect me.

"That's Pepper. She's a sweet one," Beau says, carrying in two buckets of dry feed. "Do you want to feed her?"

I take one of the buckets and hold it under her snout. She's gentler than I expect, eating at a steady pace.

"Nice," he says approvingly.

When we're done feeding the horses, I follow Beau to the cider building. He points west behind it to another cottage, this one a little larger than mine.

"The Ruiz couple stays there. You'll meet them soon. The other two crew members are local and live in town."

He stops, noticing me walking double time to keep up. "Sorry. Livia says I never remember my height. I'll try to slow down."

"It's fine."

"We also have an ATV and a utility golf cart for rolling around the orchard. Lots of acres to travel. Don't worry, we won't always walk."

"I really don't mind."

"All right then," he replies with a grin and proceeds to push open the metal door into the cider building. The smell of fruit rushes at us, and the air is cool.

He places his hand almost lovingly onto a teal piece of machinery. "Just got this replaced a week ago. Brand-new brusher washer. Cleans the apples before they go into the press." He points to another contraption. "Stainless steel cider press . . . are you comfortable learning to work these? The crew tends to do a little bit of everything. I don't know how much Alice told you—"

"I can handle it," I answer quickly.

I study him as he proceeds to explain the steps and process of each one. He's patient and eager to share, and I picture him being the same way with Nina, Avie, and Tallan—the father everyone wishes to have. Virile but gentle, the protector who can answer every question, help with any task. But brooding enough for Livia to get into bed with each night. He, too, walks a careful tightrope of equilibrium.

It must be exhausting having to be such an ideal.

Fortunately for Beau, I'm a fast learner. He wipes his hand on a towel after running the washer and asks if I'm ready to finally learn to pick an apple. When we step outside, the sun has returned, and he leads us to the middle row of trees, which bear apples that look like the ruddy Holstein that Tallan ate this morning.

Beau halts at a tree he seems to find fitting and holds up one finger. "First rule of apple picking. Make sure it's ripe. There's nothing more wasteful than picking an apple that isn't ready."

"And how do you know it's ripe?" I ask.

His finger traces the top of an apple. "These are Holsteins, and early September, they're almost all ready to go. You see how it's golden at the top? Not immature green? That's how you can really tell."

I scan the branches and spot one that looks ripe. "Like this one?"

"Yes." He steps closer to me and holds the bottom of the apple in his palm. "Most people think you pull down from the stem. But that'll bruise the fruit and yank the spur away. We need the spurs to grow again next season."

I feel his breath on my neck. "Don't use your fingers. Gently cup it and flip."

He moves my hand to the apple. I let the underbelly of the smooth skin rest in my cupped hand and lightly move it upward. It easily pulls off, and I hold the apple in my palm.

"A natural," he says to me with satisfaction.

Somehow this small success brings a real smile to my face. He takes note, staring at me, and I hand him the apple.

"I think I get the idea."

"Try a few more," he instructs.

I turn back to the tree and find another ripe one.

He reaches to pick his own. "Alice didn't really tell me much about you. Other than you needed a change."

"You can go ahead and say it," I say, overturning the apple easily.

"Say what?"

"I'm sure there's more to how she described me. Alice isn't exactly ever short on words."

He chuckles. "She might have said something about how your bark is worse than your bite. But she also said that you don't even really bark . . . whatever that means."

I tilt my head. "Accurate."

"Where did you grow up?" he asks as we walk farther down the row of trees.

I look down at the apple in my hand. "I was born in Seoul. Adopted at eighteen months by a couple in Wisconsin."

"Midwest girl, huh?"

"I guess."

"Any siblings?"

I nod. "An older brother."

Beau sighs. "I always wish I had siblings. Maybe that's why Livia and I had so many kids. We're both only children."

As I hear him chatter away while he teaches me, the familiar kindness in his eyes and his seemingly altruistic motives send nostalgia washing over me. It's funny how the past can creep up when you aren't watching. The door I've kept shut to any emotions for my brother that I've stored away to avoid the sorrow has cracked open.

He's suddenly here. In this orchard. Showing me how to pick an apple, and my breath clips briefly.

"What's his name?" Beau asks.

"Jem," I reply quietly. "His name was Jem."

He's quick to catch on to my words, displaying his astuteness. "I see."

"It's okay. We were very close growing up, until we weren't. And then, when I was in college, he went into a diabetic coma. His passing was sudden and quick. Like it never happened."

"I'm so sorry, Radley."

He looks at me with such empathy. I don't say anything after that, as I've long realized I don't owe anyone any comforting when it comes to Jem. We walk back to the barn stable in silence.

Later, when it grows dark and hushed, I wait for them all to settle down for the evening. The house is luminous, an abundance of lights turned on for me tonight. I sit in the ledge of the ocular, hands clasped in my lap and still.

I'm less hesitant this time, watching with admiration.

The family's choreographed chaos gives me satisfaction, each member doing their part to bring life to this house. I wonder what it would be like inside with them. The love they all have for each other, igniting an energy that doesn't exist for me.

Would I be able to feel it somehow?

They are rowdier tonight.

The two little girls chase each other, their shrieks of delight so loud I think I can hear them. Their father playfully bursts through the door, fingers poised on top of his head like a monster, mouth roaring and scooping them both up in his sturdy arms and swinging them around.

The son, at his desk in his room, shakes his head, and a small smile spreads. He returns to his book briefly but then gets up and disappears for a few seconds before reappearing in the doorway of the girls' room, a secondary monster to teasingly chase his sisters.

But where is the mother?

Alone tonight. At her vanity, a robe parted low on her chest. Her hair in a tight turban, she tilts her head up in the mirror, eyes downcast at the face staring back at her. For a second, I think she sees me. But I know I only imagine this. She runs her hand down her throat, perhaps feeling for a woman she once knew.

What's it like? To have everything you want and love one story below you?

My own hand reaches up to my throat as I mimic her. I feel for what she grasps at; my skin feels cold, and I imagine hers is warm. Searching for what, though? Her youth? A life entirely different from hers? I watch her as she tightens her fingers, pressing deeper into her throat as if to check for firmness.

Be careful there; you don't want to leave any scratches.

I suspect it's rare that she gets these moments alone. She pauses and then reaches for her night cream. Smoothing it on her cheeks, she raises a brow as if resigned.

This family. This house.

The perfection is both waxing and waning on me. Like a dessert that's too sweet. Eventually it will taste nauseating.

And I will want to spit it out.

CHAPTER 4

"I think she's awake."

"Shh. Let her sleep."

"What do you think this is?"

Little voices, light and fairylike, enter my head, and I open my eyes to see Nina and Avie hunched over on the floor together, their halo of curls bouncing as they inspect the contents of my suitcase like airport security workers.

Nina spots me observing them and holds up a package of shrimp chips. "Can we try one, Radley?" she asks, as if it's perfectly normal for me to wake up to this.

"Are they from Korea?" Avie asks, grabbing the shiny red bag from Nina.

"Yes," I answer, trying to not sound too irritable as I sit up and slide down from the bed.

"Hey! I was holding it first," Nina whines.

I rub my eyes. *It's too early for this.*

Avie pinches the top of the bag. "So we can try one?"

I nod and yawn.

She rips it open and takes out a single fry-shaped chip and crunches on it. Nina takes one, too, and they're silent for a precious fifteen seconds.

"Mmm. Salty. I love shrimp," Avie ruminates. "What other snacks did you eat in Korea?"

I watch her reach in the bag for more. The shiny red packaging crinkles, and I feel like I'm back in Seoul, recalling the rows of gleaming processed goodies in convenience stores on every corner.

I stayed two hours late the day Alice got her promotion to avoid running into her. By the time I left, it was dark and I was famished. Eight blocks into my walk to the subway, the retro-colored stripes of a 7-Eleven called to me.

The ramen steamed as I gently blew into the plastic bowl, stirring with chopsticks. Up in the corner of the store, a flat-screen played a Korean drama. The female lead laughed on a boat with her enemies-to-friends lover, a miniseries from a few years back.

I slurped in a long string of noodles and chewed slowly and quietly.

The scene changed in the lovers' drama on the TV. The ocean turned stormy, and the female lead cried as the high waves splashed into the boat. She reached out a hand into the rain, calling out for help.

My appetite left me altogether, stomach fizzled with acid that climbed up my throat. I dumped the rest of my cup ramen into the garbage. Red broth splattered all over the black lining and dripped onto the floor.

I hear the cottage door open now, below the loft.

"Girls?"

It's Livia. She climbs up the loft ladder and puts her hands on her hips. "I'm so sorry, Radley," she apologizes. "Girls. What did I tell you about sneaking into the guest cottage? This is where Radley's staying."

"Sorry, Mommy. But we wanted to see Radley," Avie protests for the both of them.

"I see," she says evenly. "But you need to ask before coming over."

The girls half nod and return to the bag of shrimp chips, taking turns like little birds at their mother's beak.

Livia turns to me. "Really, I'm so sorry. When the cottage is unoccupied, they sometimes come in here and play. I hope they didn't wake you?"

She bites her lip in that knowing motherly way.

"It's fine," I say.

Her hair is in a loose braid that's lying down over her shoulder. "Beau says you're quick to get the hang of things."

I pause, realizing they've talked about me. Something I missed while watching them last night. It makes me wonder what else they've said. What musings they've had about this plain, new woman in their lives. The one who watches them from her window.

"He's a good teacher," I tell her.

An admiring smile plays out over her smooth lips, and I feel particularly worn in my morning stupor. "The orchard is one of the other loves in Beau's life. He tends to get overly excited about it."

I tuck my hair behind my ears. "Well . . ."

She studies me, maybe trying to gauge my mood. "Could I entice you with some coffee and quiche?"

I glance at Avie and Nina, who wait for my answer eagerly.

One morning in their house was enough.

"I actually made a little trip to the store yesterday."

Their shoulders sag, but their disappointment is short lived as Nina holds the bag of shrimp chips up. "Can we keep this, please?"

"If it's all right with your mother."

Livia gives me one more apologetic look. "Maybe next time then?"

"Sure," I lie.

Later, after watching the minivan dust up the road as she took them to school, I see the other crew members gathering in front of the store.

I'm surprisingly nervous as I get ready to go out and join them. Maybe they won't be as patient with my inexperience. A more-than-obvious fish out of water in this autumnal New England paradise I've managed to slip my way into.

I shield my eyes from the sun, regretting leaving my wide-brim hat behind as I approach them cautiously, as if they're a pride of lions, not to be disturbed.

A petite woman with brown eyes so large they take up a third of her face immediately steps toward me.

"You must be Radley," she says. She speaks with slow, rocking words that ease me. "I'm Andrea Ruiz. And this is my husband, Daniel."

She points back to a stocky man with dark curly hair and mustache. He holds his hand out. "So nice meeting you, Radley," he greets me. I reach out with my own, and his palm feels calloused and warm.

"We were just getting ready to open the store," explains Andrea.

"Where was she yesterday?"

A gravelly voice comes from the garden area. I follow it to a man wearing a flat, green herringbone cap, gray hair tied in a knot at his neck. He eyes me from one of the picnic tables before placing sardines from a small tin carefully onto a saltine. Seated next to him, a plump middle-aged woman with closely shorn dyed blue hair picks up a saltine and eats it as she stares at me.

"Hello," I peep, instantly annoyed at myself for sounding so weak.

Andrea shakes her head. "Come on now, Chester. She was with Beau learning about cider equipment." She turns to me. "We were pruning in the field yesterday, started pretty early. That's why we missed you."

Chester nods as if that satisfies him. He holds up a sardine saltine. "Want one?" he asks.

Sensing this as some sort of peace offering, I nod and walk over.

He slides it onto my hand and then licks his thumb and forefinger. "I'm Chester. Been working the orchards for over forty years. This is my daughter, Sidney."

Sidney doesn't say anything but gives me a slight smile.

"We work the fields mostly," says Chester.

"Thank you," I say, raising the cracker.

Daniel holds his hands up to his mouth and calls out, "That's the politest I've ever seen you, Chester!"

Chester bats his own hand down and grunts. "Nice to have you around then."

I return to Daniel and Andrea, who appear to be trying not to laugh. It doesn't seem to be at my expense but at their drollery with Chester and Sidney.

Andrea leans in, speaking softer. "Don't mind Chester. He's always like that but wouldn't harm a fly. And Sidney really doesn't say much. They live in town together." She inserts a key into the lock and slides open the massive barn door.

I look up first to the skylights, which pour in shafts of natural light, spotlighting the crates of apples in red, yellow, and green hues. The beams crisscross above in the high gable. Wood-grain musk and cider zests fill my nose. Daniel begins to flick on the glass pendant lights hanging from the rafters as Andrea steps behind the register. The screen lights up, and she waves me over.

"We can start with learning this system. It's pretty user friendly, but everything has its quirks, you know," she explains with a wink.

I've probably been in Andrea's presence for less than five minutes, and I'm not one to easily thaw with most people, but even I can't refute the instant warmth she radiates, as if she's an auntlike figure I've known for years. In this moment with her, I feel an unexpected comfort. I sense my shoulders relaxing, antennae I've had up ever since my arrival finally going down a bit.

I listen as she takes her time showing me the register. She slips on a pair of reading glasses. Her mouth moves in a methodical, pacifying manner, eyes checking in on me every so often with care. We move to the wall of jams, preserves, and apple butters.

"How long have you worked for the Clark family?" I ask, adjusting a mason jar so the label faces straight.

"Ten years, can you believe it?" she responds with a smile. "Daniel and I come here every fall. We work at a cannery in Portland in the offseason. We love it here. Beau and Livia are honestly like family to us. Our daughter, Luna, even watched the kids for them. Gosh, she's been coming here since she was eight."

"Oh, will I be meeting Luna?"

She shakes her head with a mixture of sadness and pride. "Luna's starting her freshman year at Emerson. Full-ride scholarship. She's the first one in our family to go to college."

"You must be so proud."

"I am. She's everything to us. We only wish we could live closer to her."

Her wistfulness is palpable.

"I'm sure you do," I say. "Are you able to visit?"

She shakes her head. "Frankly, we can't afford to. But we're hoping that will change soon." She doesn't elaborate, and I don't push for more.

By the afternoon, she's coached me on every possible facet of the store, and my stomach is full from the fantastic pork empanadas she cooked me for lunch. She refused to let me go back to my cottage alone and insisted on taking me to hers.

Daniel was pleasant and quiet while she whipped up the empanadas, all the while telling me about when the crew usually met in the morning, how we rotated, and that I should seriously consider investing in a wide-brim hat. I sheepishly nodded. This sort of pushiness usually would have backfired, but her breed of pushiness was that of a mother hen. I found myself tolerating it.

Maybe I actually needed it.

As the day winds down, I stretch my arms under the shade of a maple starting to redden, sipping on cider. Despite enjoying my time with Andrea and Daniel, I'm looking forward to being alone for the rest of the evening.

A cloud of dirt puffs up on the road in the distance. It clears to unveil a vintage burgundy truck, the wheels oversize and souped up. As it gets closer, I can tell it's a Ford Bronco. The driver lays on the horn with a hand wildly waving out the window.

"Isn't the orchard closed now for the day?" I ask Andrea, finishing my cider.

She laughs. "Yes."

"Why are you laughing?"

"Because." She pats my back as we stand. "You're about to meet Grandma Faye."

Why is she saying this like it's something I need to brace myself for?

The Bronco pulls up to the main house and parks.

A woman with a long white braid down her back throws her tan, knee-high boots out of the Bronco. It's as if Jane Goodall incarnate has entered the orchard. She lands sturdily and holds her hands by her mouth, leaning back.

"Where's my chickadees!" she calls out. She whoops once and plants two fists at her waist.

The front door flies open, and the three children, now home from school, come racing out, practically mowing the woman down until they all fall in a heap to the ground. Rabbit runs to join in, barking after them. Their squeals of laughter echo all the way to where Andrea and I sit.

I can see Nina spring up and whisper something in Jane Goodall's ear.

Oh no. No, no, no.

Nina excitedly nods and sprints toward us through the grass, the rest of them following her.

"Andrea, I think I might head back to—"

"Radley!" the woman yells out in our direction.

Andrea stifles another laugh, and I have a giant urge to elbow her. Her amusement makes clear she already has a proper grasp of my nature.

It's too late for me to walk away. It would be far too rude. Nina reaches me, out of breath, and grabs my hand. I resist at first, but she gives me a brief and confused glance that I can't contest.

"Come meet my grandma Faye," she orders. "Andrea! Did you tell Luna I said hello?" she chirps up at her.

"Hi, baby girl. Yes, you bet I did," Andrea responds sweetly.

Grandma Faye briskly marches over to us.

"I'm Faye. But almost everyone calls me Grandma Faye." She reaches for my hand and, as she takes it, grips it vigorously. Her eyes are eagle-like, sharp and focused, an electric blue that locks everything in her view. "And I know you're Radley," she says before I can utter anything.

"Yes. It's nice meeting you," I say, stifling a resigned exhale.

"I'm Beau's mother. I just returned from a sailing trip to Prince Edward Island. Ever been there? *Anne of Green Gables* fan at all? I hope you are, or at least that you like to read. I don't understand people who don't enjoy reading. It's like people who dislike dogs. Ungodly." She reaches down and strokes Rabbit on the head while he looks up at her adoringly.

I must have widened my eyes.

"Ah. I'm doing it. Chattering like a magpie. Aren't I, Andrea?"

"Maybe a little," Andrea chimes in.

Tallan and Avie catch up to Grandma Faye, and she wraps an arm around each of them. "Oh, I get so much strength when I'm around my chickadees. Helps me get energy."

"Get" energy? This is her without it?

"Grandma Faye owns a sizable sailboat," Avie states factually. "She named it the *Calypso*. That's a Greek goddess, you know. She's said to have healing powers."

"Well, I own it with the Shaws. I'm sure you'll meet them when you come for a sail. Sort of a time-share," she adds.

Sorry, Grandma Faye. I don't do boats.

Nina squints one eye. "Are you leaving us again soon on your sailboat?"

"I'm not sure yet, but most likely not, my dear. I just had it out for two weeks, and the Shaws are itching to take it down to the Keys."

"Wait. So you're not going down to see your boyfriend then?" Tallan taunts with a sly grin.

"Grandma Faye has a 'man friend' in South Carolina. That's what Daddy calls him anyways," says Avie.

I glance at Grandma Faye, who doesn't seem the least bit embarrassed. "Mr. Fairfield is an old friend. And yes, occasionally we may get silly when we have my famous peach margaritas." She shimmies and winks at me. "I normally take the *Calypso* down to the Carolinas mid-October. But alas, I'm thinking of skipping this year. These kiddos are growing too fast. Mr. Fairfield will just have to forgo me."

I clear my throat. "Well, it was so nice talking . . . ," I start to say.

"Oh no, you don't," Grandma Faye declares boldly. "You're not slipping away so fast. I'm cooking one of my big ole feasts tonight. I do that whenever I return from sailing—my crispy ribs, scalloped potatoes, and clams from a secret Clark family recipe you'll be begging me for after tasting!"

"And your apple-rhubarb crisp? With vanilla bean ice cream?" Nina asks with shining eyes.

"Yes, yes, and that, too, with extra vanilla bean, as you like it."

She pulls me in and clamps her hand on my arm, and I go rigid as she cackles lightly.

"No need to fight me, dear. Everyone still on Clark Orchard land is going to be eating with Grandma Faye tonight."

The last of the sunset burns out like a candle by the time we all sit down at the picnic tables in the garden. The twinkle lights sway soft and gentle above our heads. My stomach rolls as I smell the crackling meat and buttery juice of clam broth.

Beau opens a bottle of white wine and pours me a glass.

"Apologies," he says, handing it to me by the stem.

"For?" I raise my brows quizzically.

"Not warning you about Grandma Faye." He holds up his glass and smiles before pouring another one for Andrea, seated next to me. Daniel gives her a quick peck on the cheek before he pulls a clam out of its shell, and she blushes as if they were teen lovers.

Livia brings me a steaming plate. "New crew members get to eat first around here," she says, and her dimples appear. "Well, maybe I made that up, but you're going to never want to leave after trying these clams."

"So I've heard."

Nina appears, rubbing her head into Livia's side. "Mommy, I want to have the ice cream first."

"I don't think so, sweetie. There's so much other great food Grandma Faye made for us to try first."

"Nope. I don't like that," she whines as she runs off.

Livia holds up a finger. "Excuse me," she says. "There's always one who wants dessert first."

I spot Tallan seated next to Chester, who seems to have shed his grumpy demeanor, as the old man explains something to him with wild hand gestures. A story that makes Tallan laugh as he takes a joyous bite of his ribs.

The air is warm tonight. Crickets chirp melodically as the meal goes on, with Grandma Faye every so often urging us to eat more. The littlest ones start chasing each other with bell-like laughter. And for a moment in this joyous concert of welcoming voices, I feel a hum of pure tenderness and belonging.

There is no malice. My heart skips a few beats. Not from infatuation but from the feeling that I've been placed in an unfamiliar dome. Suddenly, I picture myself banging against glass to get out. My heart races, and my throat feels dry. Hands numb.

"Are you all right?" Andrea asks me, her voice echoing.

The garden lights no longer seem charming but overly bright, and I excuse myself quickly.

The dead silence of the store settles me slowly. I inhale and exhale with purpose.

Andrea finds me and quietly takes my hand.

"I know what you're feeling. I've been there," she says gently to the side of my face. "I had episodes this whole summer before Luna left for college."

I turn to face her, afraid to look her in her eyes for fear of something else escaping me.

"There are people you can talk to. I did. There's a wonderful woman in town. She deals with both children and adults. Maybe something to think about . . ."

She leaves me to myself as I listen in the shadows, their cheerful banter no longer harmful.

CHAPTER 5

Livia's cheeks are flushed as she holds up a deep-purplish apple. The sunlight reveals flecks of gold in her irises. I find myself pausing, searching for more in her eyes until she rises from her crouching position to bring the fruit closer to my face.

"You haven't really eaten an apple until you've had a Macoun."

I take the apple and hold it as if weighing it.

She stands fully and brushes a curl out of her eye, her elbow out as if in a salute. "An heirloom variety, cross between McIntosh and Jersey Black. Try a bite."

How very Snow White of you.

I bring it to my lips and take a tentative nibble before sinking in deeper. I feel her gaze on me, waiting for my verdict.

"Sweet and also . . . tangy. Almost like a berry," I say through slow chews.

"Exactly," she says with approval. "Isn't it marvelous?"

I take another bite. "Were you always this into apple farming?"

She laughs. "No. I married Beau. So I married the orchard."

Nina skips up with a basket low to the ground, a few green apples bobbing into each other with her unsteadiness. "Are these enough, Mommy, for our pie?"

Livia glances down and nods. "Nice work, baby girl." She shields her eyes as she looks out for Avie, farther down the row of trees.

"You doing all right, my birdie?" she calls.

Avie waves emphatically and goes back to picking her apples.

Livia turns to me. "We do this most Saturdays during peak season. The girls love being out here and gathering a few apples to bake something."

Nina's basket lands on the ground with a thud. She sits down hard on the grass.

"What's the matter, Nina?" Livia asks; her gleeful expression turns into deep worry, day falling to night in an instant.

"Nothing," Nina replies quietly. She picks at the grass and doesn't look back up.

"Are you sure?" Livia moves to sit down next to her.

"I'm sure."

"Nina." Her voice is patient but fixed. "Remember, just because you're not feeling the best doesn't mean we have to go to the hospital. Mommy needs to know if we should take a break."

"I don't need a break," she pouts.

"All right. How about I sit with you then."

Nina looks at her out of the corner of her eye. "Okay, I guess."

Livia pats her knee and looks up at me.

"Do you mind taking Avie back to the house? We'll meet you in a few."

I waver briefly. It was enough to spend time picking apples with them, although I can see the energy drained from Nina, normally so spry and bouncy. She's withdrawn and hushed, her knees brought in close. A twinge pricks at my chest.

I can at least help out with the older one.

"Sure," I answer.

I leave behind Livia and Nina huddled together as I walk with Avie. She hangs her basket on one arm and takes my hand and clasps it softly. The wind picks up, and I use my other hand to hold my brimmed hat. Along the path of trees, a lone patch has started to turn colors. Fiery red leaves shake on the branches. If I focus hard enough, their agitation flickers like flames.

"She gets like that sometimes . . . well, it's been a while since the last time it happened," Avie says, swinging our arms together.

"*Gets* like that?"

"It was maybe a year ago. Nina started getting really tired. And then she fell asleep at school. So Mommy and Daddy took her to the doctor."

Livia mentioned she's anemic.

Avie stops to pick a lavender wildflower, inspects it, and tosses it in her basket.

"But she got better?"

"Mm-hmm. She had to go to the hospital a few times. Nina hates the hospital. She says they don't let her play too much, and the food isn't yummy."

"I'm sure that wasn't fun."

"Nope. But I did get to visit her. The nurses gave us supplies to play doctor. And we had Popsicles. Tangerine. Have you ever had that kind?"

I shake my head.

She seems satisfied by this Popsicle memory and brightens. "You're going to help bake today, right, Radley?"

"I'm not much of a baker."

"Neither is Mommy. But she tries."

I stifle my amusement at the child's bluntness and press my lips together. "Well, I'm sure she's better than me."

It doesn't take long for Nina and Livia to catch up with us at the house. By the time we've settled at the kitchen counter, washing apples, Nina hops in and immediately tells Avie it's her turn to wash.

There's a worn appearance to Livia's expression, the skin around her eyes wilted.

"Are you all right?" I ask her.

"Oh . . . yes," she answers distractedly. She fidgets with the oven before looking over her shoulder at the girls, who giggle as the water splashes on them from the faucet stream hitting the apples. "Girls, that's a great job washing. Why don't you dry up now and go to the playroom? I'll call you back in when it's time to bake the pie."

The girls continue their cyclone of horseplay, poking each other as they loudly exit the kitchen, like two pinballs hitting every angle of the room. Rabbit appears, barking, then eagerly follows them with a contented pant.

I expect Livia to start cutting apples. But instead, she goes to the refrigerator and pulls out a chilled bottle of rosé.

"Care for a glass?"

"Uh, okay," I find myself saying.

She pours each of us one and takes a deep sip.

"It's Saturday, right? Happy hour?" she half laughs.

I take a drink and set my glass back down on the island. "Nina is feeling better then?"

Concern flickers across her face, but she brushes it away with another sip. "Yes. I think so." She leans her elbows on the counter. "She's on medication for anemia. I think I told you that, right?"

I nod.

She exhales at almost the same time. "We don't usually tell people . . . I mean, I'm sure everyone knows she's sick. But we wanted to give her privacy. Keep details only among family."

Only among family.

"But I feel like I can tell you about it, Radley. Right?"

"I mean, only if you're—"

"It helps," she interjects. "To talk out loud about it. Otherwise, I feel like it's not happening to us."

I give her an encouraging glance.

She shakes her head. "A year ago, it was so awful. She had to be hospitalized twice. The doctors aren't quite sure why it happened. They ran all sorts of scans and tests. But . . . she recovered."

She grows quiet. Merely bringing it up must have brought the apprehension from that time back. She sighs. "Parents. Mothers. The worry—it never goes away. Always there like a wet rag above our heads, ready to be wrung at any minute with something else to fuss over."

I don't say anything as I slide my glass around the island top.

"You ever think about having kids?" she asks. "You're so good with the girls. They adore you."

"No," I reply and take a longer sip.

"I swear I'd have a dozen if I could."

"You should then," I say half sarcastically.

She doesn't respond with the mirth I expect. The wine seems to have sobered her in an odd way.

"Nina actually would have been our fourth baby."

Would have been.

"Oh . . . I didn't realize."

She shrugs. "You couldn't have."

A shriek rips through from the playroom, and she pauses with a mother's ear, tilting one side of her head up. A ripple of giggles follows.

"I lost her fairly early . . . it was a 'her,' we found out later. The blood-screening results came a week after I miscarried. I don't know if it made things easier or worse knowing. I was only ten weeks, but . . ."

I cast my eyes downward, as if to give her privacy.

"But then having Nina. The baby of the babies . . . it really helped things. Especially with Beau and I." She places a hand under her chin, rubbing it and looking lost for a few seconds before she shoots a quick smile at me.

"I'm sorry. You probably don't want to hear all this. I don't know why I'm going there today."

"It's all right."

She studies me and I feel exposed. As though if she stares at me too long, she will see me for what I really am.

"You're easy to talk to, Radley. It's like you aren't judging anything."

I want to tell her that she's wrong. I want to tell her that she shouldn't be telling me these things. But I force a grin—the kind that bantering women are supposed to give when they have wine together—and I finish my glass.

"I'll take a little more, please, if that's okay?"

"Oh, sure."

She reaches over with the bottle and gives me another pour, this one more generous. "You seem like someone who never gets rattled."

I shrug with the glass to my mouth.

"Do you ever get rattled?"

"Of course," I say as breezily as I can.

"I'm sure not over much." Her face looks warm, either from the wine or the oven preheating.

"Well . . . we all have our moments, don't we," I say, raising my glass.

She does the same. "Cheers to those moments." The rest of her wine disappears. "And possibly for more moments alone." She catches me looking at her quizzically.

"Motherhood rough these days?" I can feel the question hanging above her head as soon as I've posed it. I wait for her, taking in every movement in her face. Her cheekbones, the lines by her mouth, the slightest lift in her forehead as she deliberates over this.

"Rough? There isn't a word strong enough to describe how rough."

There. She's said it. Even in all her flawlessness, she's said it.

"That terrible?" I give her a sympathetic frown.

"Don't get me wrong. Most days I'm so grateful for our family. And our three babies. But sometimes . . ."

I make sure to keep her gaze. "Sometimes what?"

"Sometimes even in moments of happiness, there's always this sadness. Sadness that everything comes to an end. You know?"

Yes. I do know. I've known that for a long time now.

I start to feel flushed and lightheaded. I don't know if it's the extra wine or Livia's continued chattering that's now growing faint. My head hurts like it did in the barn with Andrea the other night. I'm beginning to wonder if talking to the woman in town she recommended would be worth considering.

To ease these spells . . .

Later, I have a perfect view of them, their windows glowing like fire. Feverish glass panes, the light trying to escape into the pitch-black night. I place my chin ceremoniously onto turned-up palms, a bowl of dark chocolate raspberries sitting next to me in the windowsill. I am eager tonight. Willing more to happen for my eyes to absorb.

Bath time has ended. The two little girls scoot like penguins into Avie's room, their hooded towels topped with animal ears. Beau follows behind them, carrying pajamas in each hand. He isn't playing his usual "fun-loving dad" role very well tonight. His motions seem forced, his face flat with tiredness. I drop another chocolate into my mouth, the bitter cocoa melting as my anticipation increases.

I turn my attention away from them as they dress, focusing instead on Tallan's room. He's lying on his bed, fingers pressing in his earbuds, head bobbing to music. He flips onto his stomach, restless, perhaps even upset. He sits up and stares at the wall, unmoving.

I shift my eyes back.

Livia has entered Avie's room. I'm surprised when she walks by Beau without a single glance. No touch of the arm or lingering, knowing smile between parents, partners, *lovers*. What's happened to my lovely married couple? What spell has been cast, what landscape disintegrated? I feel my stomach drop a little at this first sign of a fissure.

Maybe they're both simply tired.

He shows the same indifference to Livia as he directs Avie to her bed. Livia moves by him to take a clingy, pajamaed Nina to her room.

The weariness the child exhibited earlier in the day has appeared again. She's limp in Livia's lap as she rocks her, singing to her and closing her eyes with such pleasure. An indulgence that I can sense even from where I sit. I zero in on them, my mouth open as if to drink it all in.

Thirsty for more of this pureness. To cleanse, to soak it in with greed.

CHAPTER 6

I stare at the framed picture of a sailboat. On the shelf below, a silver sailboat is nestled in a wooden rest. Next to it, vintage books are stacked between sailboat bookends.

"Do you sail much, Radley?" Dr. Edair asks, looking at me and then the wall of shelves.

I shake my head. "What did you say your first name is again?"

"Mia. You can address me in any way that makes you most comfortable."

The camel chaise I sit in is positioned diagonally across from Dr. Edair's chair. She sits in front of a window with a view of Fox Isle's marina. The ocean is calm today, with controlled waves.

"I think I'll call you Dr. Edair, if that's all right," I say to her.

"All right then."

Her soft amber eyes remain neutral. Everything about her demeanor is gentle. No sudden movements, gray wispy hair to her shoulders—even the way she takes her glasses off is careful. She reminds me of an English teacher I had in high school in the way she speaks, all her consonants loose and forward on the lips.

I like her so far.

I suppose because Andrea trusts her so much, I came to this first session with less scrutiny and more resolve.

"I take it you're big on sailing?" I wave at the sailboat decor.

She kindly nods and crosses her legs. "My wife and me. She got me into it when we met. She decorated my office, actually."

"Oh, so you're not from here either?" I point at her, for some reason hoping she's in the same club as me.

"Not Fox Isle. But a Maine native." She shifts in her chair and changes the subject back to me. "I understand you saw a psychiatrist back in Seoul, is it?"

I pause with a lifted chin. "Yes. How did you know that?"

"It showed up in your chart."

"Oh." I stretch my fingers out on the arms of the chaise. "So, you know why I'm here."

You know why I'm so tangled up inside. Why I'm better off being alone.

"I only have the record of who your psychiatrist was. Unfortunately, international electronic records don't go into as much depth as we'd like."

Seagulls squawk outside, and I watch a fishing boat take off from a dock.

In the silence, Dr. Edair pulls a notepad out and places it on her knee. Her pen clicks, and she starts to write a few notes.

"I'm an old-fashioned gal. Many of my colleagues I meet at conferences can't believe I still handwrite my notes. But there's something about the computer that doesn't really get the information the same in my head. Something about the keys." She wiggles her hand by her ear.

I nod politely as if agreeing with this, even though my head is now elsewhere.

She pushes a little dish of peppermints on her desk toward me.

"Have one."

I hesitate.

"I find it helps my patients to focus when they have something in their mouth."

I sit up and reach for the dish. The peppermint is square shaped. I toss it in my mouth, and the sugar starts to dissolve, the menthol spreading in the back of my throat.

She watches me, and I give her a clenched smile with the mint between two molars. "Good," I say.

"I don't tend to get into the heart of why a patient is here right away. We take it very slow. A toe dip in the water, if you will. The more I get to know you, the more we can explore your reactions and emotions. Most importantly, how to help you get the most out of them. We're all unique in how we're wired, Radley."

The mint is halfway dissolved, and I shift it inside my mouth.

She adjusts her glasses and looks over the top of them at me.

"Why don't we start with some easy questions? Questions that you're more certain of, as far as the answers. Sometimes when we have to answer more abstract questions, we can clam up. But questions about your health history, for example. Those are more direct. You don't have to give me all the specifics, but providing basic information may get us warmed up. Are you okay with that?"

"I'm fine with that."

"All right." She glances down. "You're thirty-two years old. Nonsmoker. Do you drink alcohol?"

"Yes."

"How often, would you say?"

"Socially."

"So, one to two drinks a week?"

"I'm not a heavy drinker. That sounds accurate."

"Any chronic physical ailments?"

"No."

"How about in your family?"

I pause. "I'm adopted. Any genetic health history I can't provide."

She stops writing. "That would be a great segue into your family history. You'd be surprised how much we can uncover there. We're rooted in those early years. Seeds are planted that sometimes don't expose themselves until adulthood."

Very Mother Earth of you, Dr. Edair.

"Okay." I play with a loose thread on the chaise cushion. "What is it you want to know about my family?"

Her head dips with her arm. "The beginning. As far back you think you can go."

I stare straight at her. "My birth mother didn't want me."

"I see," she says, staring right back. "How do you know that? Have you met with her?"

"No. I've never met her. I don't know if she's alive anymore or what became of her. I don't know her name even. The only fact I have is she was sixteen and didn't want me."

Please don't ask, "How does that make you feel?"

"But you've acknowledged this." She's firm for the first time.

All right . . . so there's a toughness underneath it all. I can respect that.

"Meaning?"

"You aren't in denial of the facts surrounding your mother putting you up for adoption."

"Yes . . . if you want to look at it that way." My gaze drifts down to my hands.

"Have you ever considered that maybe your mother did want you?"

I look up at her slowly. "No."

"And why's that?"

"For the simple logic that if she did want me, she would have done everything she could to keep me."

Keep me. The words sear a bit in my mouth.

The lines in the corners of Dr. Edair's eyes crease with kindness. "Would it be a bad thing if she had wanted you?"

"How would that have been possible?"

She shrugs. "She was very young. Perhaps she was pressured by her family. Or extreme poverty can force people to make the most difficult choices. My point is, Radley, you have selected a reality that isn't certain."

But it doesn't matter. She didn't keep me. She didn't want me.

Dr. Edair leans closer. "Radley, did you and your previous therapist ever discuss the higher risk of mental health issues for adoptee children versus non-adoptee children? I don't like speaking in broad strokes, but I also want to understand what prior knowledge you bring here."

"Yes. I have been counseled and read up on this myself. But I can tell you that I don't really buy that. At least in my circumstance. There was no real trauma. I have no memories of Korea. I was quite young when I was brought over, and I will flat-out tell you, my family was fairly normal."

She smiles almost sympathetically. "'Normal.' That's a choice in words for sure."

"I get it. There is no such thing as normal."

"There is if it's what you consider normal. The ideal you hold."

"In that case, they were normal. Although normal does not equate to happiness."

I can tell Dr. Edair wants to expand on that, but she passes it by maybe for another time.

"So, you were raised by what you consider a normal mother and father?"

"Yes."

"Any siblings?"

"An older brother. Jem."

She chuckles. "Someone really liked *To Kill a Mockingbird.*"

I roll my eyes. "Believe me, I've heard it. Jem and Radley. Our dad would tell me his favorite character was Boo Radley and that he was the true hero."

"I might have to agree with your dad."

The way she seems to admire him irritates me. "They loved that about our names. Making everyone think they had to be intellectuals. Innovative thinkers."

"Were they not?"

I scoff. "Far from it. My dad melted into his recliner after dinner and watched game shows. My mother read trashy romance novels in her room."

"What about you and your brother? Where were you two?"

"Left alone in our rooms. If there wasn't anyone around to parade us in front of, we weren't needed. At least I wasn't."

She raises a brow. "Needed?"

"My parents reveled in being seen as saviors. The poor little foreign adoptee rescued and brought up by a loving couple. They put me in ruffly dresses at church, showboating me around like a doll. But I saw right through it. Jem did too . . ."

Her hand moves on her notepad, and I wonder if she's writing this little anecdote. "Were you close with Jem?" she asks, still writing.

"Yes."

I don't say anything further.

Her hand stops, and she looks up. "Are you still close?"

"No," I answer with a scratchy throat.

"Why do you think that is?"

I stare at the sailboat shelves again. This time I spot a figurine of a little girl on the very top right. She stands on a glass beach with blue porcelain waves crashing up against her; she's bending forward with her hands poised delicately, as if she's kissing the ocean. I want to tell her she's too close to the water.

"It's all right." Dr. Edair's voice floats in around the top of my head. "We don't have to open and look inside every door today."

I find her face again and focus. "Do you think it's possible, Dr. Edair?"

"What's possible?"

I lick my lips. Everything is so dry. My eyes, my mouth. I reach for another mint and suck on it quickly.

"To be a worthy adversary to your own pain."

I look down and realize I'm twisting my fingers together. She looks at them and then back at me.

"Radley. Why did you come here?"

I came here because I relish the pain of others.

She peers at me. "What is it you want help with?"

Because I can't confront my own.

"There's this family," I say louder. "This perfect, beautiful family."

"What is it about them that you find so perfect?"

"They just . . . are. I can't stop thinking about them. I can't stop watching them. Wondering if all the exquisiteness they live in will ever stop."

She puts her pen down and stares at me.

"I think I want it to stop."

CHAPTER 7

Morning clears my overindulgence from watching last night. I sip coffee and towel dry my hair after showering. Dark strands cling to my neck.

Through the playroom window, I see Avie intently pouring tea for Nina. The girls clink their teacups. Avie pauses to look out, peering up and pointing at something. I turn to see a cardinal. She stares at it for the longest time. Hand over hand precisely, elbows out like she's mimicking wings. Her precious Rabbit sits with her, button eyes watching.

What are you thinking about, little girl?

She breaks away from the window as Livia arrives, corralling them to get ready for school. I slide out from the windowsill.

Dawn breaks, and I feel an urge to go for a walk before meeting Andrea in front of the store. My energy has surged.

I run my hands against the row of apple trees, fingers tapping at glossy leaves. The horizon of the ocean appears darker this morning, sun barely cresting, and it all disappears as I stroll downhill. I pause to admire the tree line in the distance, an army of mixed sage, orange, and buttery blazoned pompoms, each globe-like explosion of brilliance growing larger the closer they're rooted to me. I don't stop, chasing their hues. My pants are damp at the knees, boots dripping with morning dew.

Eventually, the edge of the Clark Orchard property appears, a low wood fence marking the border. But I want to keep going.

I like the space behind me. It grows and takes me farther away.

There's nothing but brush for a while. The entry to a path emerges, and I make my way through; the trunks of tall lean birches surround me, the bark peeling off in rolls.

The path ends and turns into a gravel road. I crunch along with each step, satisfied by the silence it comes against. A deep bend unveils a lemon-painted farmhouse. A woman sits on the front porch swing, rocking it with her feet planted. She notices me and stops.

"Can I help you?" she calls out. There's more curiosity in her tone than alarm.

She stands as I approach her. The bangs of her straw-colored pixie haircut drop across her forehead, and she shakes it back. Her figure is robust, an admirable hourglass. The fabric of her plaid dress is taut against her skin.

"I'm sorry. I didn't mean to wander onto private property."

This far anyway.

"Oh . . . that's all right. Didn't take you as a threatening intruder or anything." She smiles.

"I was going for a long walk and—"

"We get lost tourists here and there. Happens more than you'd think."

She has the kind of voice that rings deep, like a speakeasy broad's.

I must look tense because she steps down from the porch and puts out a friendly hand. "My name is Grace Jean. My husband, Vaughn—Mr. Jean, I like to call him," she says with her hand by her mouth as if it's a secret between us, "and I own this farm. Mostly dairy but . . ."

A cow moos from the nearby grazing field, long and as if on cue, and I crack a grin.

Grace does also, and her mouth splits, revealing large teeth. We both laugh, and I realize it's the first time I've truly laughed in a while.

Maybe Alice was right about the air here being curative . . . maybe.

"Can I offer you coffee?" Grace asks, pointing to the table on the porch set with a narrow metal kettle and two mugs. "I was waiting for

Mr. Jean to get back from fixing part of a fence in the north field, but he's taking longer than I thought."

I hesitate at first, wanting to move on with my walk. But then I realize she's alone like me. Not only in the literal sense; there's something melancholy hidden in the jolliness of her voice, like the undertow of an ocean wave.

"I'd like that, thank you."

She looks pleased, and she raises once on her toes. "Great." She leads the way up the porch steps with a swoop of her skirt, and I sit carefully on the swing.

She pats her hands on her thighs. "I'm realizing I never asked you what your name is."

"Radley," I tell her.

"Ooh, I love that. I've always thought 'Grace' is so common and boring."

I observe as she pours me a mug and carries it over with both hands.

"Do you take any cream or sugar?"

I shake my head. "Black."

Grace nods approvingly. "You seem like a black coffee gal."

The coffee is strong and incredibly flavorful. I let out an involuntary sigh.

She gives me a playful glance. "Won't give my brewing secret away, but I can show you the beans I buy. They're local to Fox Isle."

I drink more. "How long have you and Mr. Jean been farming?"

"Ah," she says, looking out into the field. "Mr. Jean was born in this very house. Generations of dairy farmers I can't even count. Even before the Civil War. One of the oldest farms in the region. You might hear stories even of the Underground Railroad passing through our land."

"Stories?"

She shrugs. "Land has stayed the same. Other than Mr. Jean adding a field of potatoes a few years ago."

"And you?"

"Former photographer," she says. "I'm a Maine native also. From a small town a few hours north. I did the wedding and newborn photography thing for a bit after college. But it never took off. The truth is it didn't fulfill me like I thought it would. And then I met Mr. Jean at one of the weddings I photographed."

I nod, listening.

"Don't worry, he wasn't the groom," she says, laughing hard.

I laugh and set the mug in my lap. "You're lucky. Your land is beautiful."

"Yes . . . she is," she murmurs proudly. She turns toward me. "What about you, Radley?"

"I moved here from Seoul not long ago. Worked there for ten years after teaching English post-undergrad."

Her lips form a slight circle. "Now that's a drastic change in scenery!"

"Yes . . . but a needed one."

She studies me. "What is it that you do now that you've moved?"

"A former colleague of mine couldn't help this season at her cousin's orchard. I took her place on a whim."

"Good for you," Grace says chummily.

"I guess. It's not like me to do something like this. I was pretty set where I was."

She shakes her head. "Sometimes change can be the boost we didn't know we needed."

"Perhaps."

She goes quiet and then pivots her head to me slowly. "What orchard did you say you're working at?"

"Clark Orchard. Beau and Livia Clark? I'm sure you know them, being close by?"

Her face drops like a curtain. Her mouth tightens into a scowl.

"I see," is all she says. She finishes the rest of her coffee and sets it on the table.

I don't ask about her abrupt change in mood. I slide my mug next to hers and stand up.

"I'm realizing I need to head back to get to work on time. Thank you so very much for the coffee, Grace."

She pushes out a hasty smile that dips back into a frown. "Yes, it was nice meeting you."

I exit the porch and turn back to see her scurrying inside her house and shutting the door.

CHAPTER 8

Andrea slowly runs her hand down Pepper's leg, the shiny tan-and-white hairs lying flat against the horse's hindquarter. Pepper snorts twice, and her tail swings wildly, narrowly missing my face. I step away as Andrea stands up.

She looks concerned. "I think something is up with her leg. She's been putting less weight on it," she says.

"I've seen her limp a few times even," Chester huffs from the barn entry. Sidney nods next to him with her arms crossed.

"Maybe we should have Dr. Fin take a look at it?" Andrea suggests, her eyes still lingering on the leg.

"I'll mention it to Beau and Livia," he says.

He doesn't wait for a response and motions to Sidney to follow him.

Nina pops her small head in from the side of the barn door. "There's something wrong with Pepper?" Her face scrunches with worry.

"Hi there, Nina," says Chester in his gruff voice. "Nah. She's just got a bum leg. Vet will fix it."

She comes out from the door. "You're sure? Don't tell Salt, but Pepper's my favorite horse."

"I'm sure. And I won't," he solemnly tells her, swiping a cross over his chest with a finger. He pats her on the head before leaving with Sidney.

Nina still appears forlorn. I'm not sure if it's her low energy or her deep worry over Pepper. She goes over to stroke the horse's hind leg, whispering that it will all be better soon.

"Aren't you supposed to be in school today?" Andrea asks with a grin.

Nina shakes her head. "Mommy said since I'm so tired, I can stay home and rest."

"Then shouldn't you be resting?" she continues.

"Maybe." Nina shoots me a mischievous glance and smirks. I find myself giving her one back. Her curls are piled high on her head, making her look more angelic than usual.

"Tell you what," says Andrea. "I won't get your mom right away as long as you promise to stay out of trouble."

"Okay!" she chirps.

"Nina," Andrea warns knowingly with her fists on her hips. "I'm being serious, little lady." She reaches out and tickles her side.

Nina giggles. "I am too!" She runs off to the opposite end of the barn.

Andrea turns back to me. "Feisty, that one," she says, shaking her head. "All right. Shall we get back to our favorite task of cleaning out the hay?"

The menial tasks I actually enjoy. There's something about mindlessly working, keeping my head busy and away from other thoughts. But I don't share this with Andrea. She looks like she's about to get a root canal.

I pick up my rake and begin pulling out the older sections of hay.

"Have you had a chance to explore Fox Isle much?" she asks, head down and raking at a much faster pace than me.

"Not much. But I did go for a long walk the other morning."

"Oh? Where to? North or south of the orchard?"

"North."

She goes still. "You didn't happen to wander onto the Jeans' farm, did you?"

I stop and lean against the handle. "I did. I had coffee with Grace Jean, actually."

Andrea snaps her head up. "You're kidding."

"No. I'm not."

She throws her rake down and comes closer with wide eyes. "You've got to tell me what that was like."

"She was pleasant. We didn't talk long. Because once I mentioned I worked for Livia and Beau, she got very cold."

Andrea whistles. "Wow. Still bitter . . ."

"Bitter?"

"Livia and Grace used to be such close friends. She was always over here. Grace would show her recipes, they'd have wine. Sometimes I'd even join them. I can remember bringing Luna over when she was a little girl. When Tallan was just a baby. That's how long ago they became friends."

I can hear Nina humming in the distance. Andrea tilts her head, listening hard.

"You better not be up in the loft, Nina!" she calls out.

The humming continues.

She rolls her eyes. "I've told her so many times to stay out of there. It's so high up." She pauses again before shouting, "Nina! You better get down now!"

"I will!" Nina's voice echoes back.

Andrea waves her hand as if giving up. "Where was I, Radley? Sorry."

"Livia and Grace used to be close . . ."

"Oh yes. Well, it wasn't a secret that Grace and her husband Vaughn had been struggling for years to have children. I think it was Grace's dream to have a whole lot of them on that dairy farm of theirs. You know, to help out and carry on the family tradition. But it wasn't happening for them, sadly. You'd think Vaughn would be more understanding, but he was all about his lineage. Opposed to adopting even. You know she calls him Mr. Jean?"

I nod. "Yes. She did reference him that way."

"Livia went on to have Avie. And then Nina. You can imagine how that made Grace feel. Of course it's not Livia's fault. But it certainly didn't help."

I lift my brow. "That's why they don't speak? Seems ridiculous."

She holds up a finger. "Not exactly. While Livia having all those kids didn't help matters, something else must have happened. It happened a little bit before Nina was born. Because one day Grace just stopped coming here." She snaps her fingers. "And stopped speaking or even acknowledging Livia altogether."

I shake my head. "Grace seemed so . . . lovely. I can see why they were friends. But when I mentioned the name Clark, she changed just like that."

Andrea picks up her rake. "I would love to know what really happened. But Livia doesn't talk about it with anyone."

What could have caused such hatred?

"All I can say is, don't expect Grace or Vaughn Jean to be coming over for dinner anytime soon. That would be—"

A scream pierces the air in the barn.

"Nina!" Andrea yells.

The two of us run to the far end where the cry rang out from.

The loft. Nina is playing in that high loft.

I look up, and my throat closes with alarm.

Dangling like an ornament ready to slip off and shatter at any moment is Nina. One hand grips the wooden railing.

"Help me," she says in a quiet voice. As if saying it any louder will cause her to fall to the ground.

"Madre de Dios," Andrea utters, covering her mouth.

There's no time. I have to get to her. I have to save her.

"I can't hold on," Nina whimpers. A cry begins to shake in her belly. Her arm trembles.

I can save her.

"Nina," I whisper. I move beneath her with my arms out. "I got you . . . I got you!"

She cries harder, and her hand slips. Fingers curl, barely holding on to the wood.

"Oh God!" Livia screams from the barn entry.

I got you.

Her tiny body seems to float down. I feel the weight of nothing as I shut my eyes.

CHAPTER 9

"Are you all right?" Dr. Edair asks me.

It's our second session. I face the sailboat shelves instead of her window.

"Not particularly."

"Do you want to talk about what happened to the girl? I know it's been only a few days but . . ."

"No . . . not today, anyway."

"All right."

She taps her pen a few times. The pointed end makes a *plop, plop* sound against the notepad. I find it soothing. She stops.

"I'd like to try something a little different today, Radley."

"Okay. What, exactly?"

Her clothing is dressier than during our first session, when she wore comfortable slacks and a sweater. But today she wears a navy blazer with lined edges, white wide-legged pants, and kitten heels.

She sees me looking over her outfit and shrugs as if she's been caught. "Dinner with Harriet tonight. It's our anniversary."

"Congratulations. How many years?"

"Ten . . . it's been ten years." Her cheeks are tinged, and I believe I've made the good doctor blush.

"You seem to make each other happy. Or at least she makes you happy. I can see that. You're lucky," I tell her.

Her mouth forms a lopsided smile. "I'd hope so. Marriage is never easy. But Harriet, well . . ." She shakes it off and touches the rims of her glasses.

"Back to me, huh?"

"Back to you," she says without irritation. "Instead of me asking you a series of questions, this time I want you to visualize and describe."

I let my head fall back in the cushion of the chaise. "Okay. What would you like me to describe."

She puts out an open palm. "You mentioned being adopted. But you also described your family as being normal but not happy. You started to tell me about this last session. I'd love to know more. What did you mean by that?"

"Isn't that a question?"

My snark doesn't faze her. "I want you to think back on a typical morning with your family. You're eight years old. Tell me about it. What do you see?"

I stare up at her office ceiling's sand-swirl texture.

"Well, it's 2001, so any decent sense of decor is out of the question."

There's no affable chuckle from Dr. Edair. She's serious today.

What did our kitchen look like back then?

"There's a small box television tucked in the kitchen counter," I start.

She nods and I take a breath.

"The antennae are pulled out and hang over the counter. They always hit me when I walk by them. Dad is making his over-easy eggs like he does every morning. He flips one of the eggs. The grease splatters on the counter, and Mom nags him. She puts on her big gold bob earrings and fans her face, complaining about how hot it is. Then she pours herself coffee and taps in an insane amount of NutraSweet."

"And where are you?" Dr. Edair asks.

"Sitting at the kitchen table. Coloring. I liked to color in the mornings."

"What's your mood on this particular morning?"

I feel my brow twitch. "Indifferent."

"Why is that?"

Most of my childhood was neutral. A great big wall of beige and neutral.

"There was no depth to anything my parents did with me. It's like there was a shell carefully placed over me the second I arrived. And in trying too hard not to cause any cracks, they ended up . . ."

"Did they ever hurt you?" she asks directly.

I shook my head. "Thinner. They made the shell thinner." I sit up. "I don't want you to think I'm ungrateful. Yes, they were a bit artificial . . . self-serving, even. But they aren't bad people. They meant well and did everything parents are technically supposed to do. But I could always sense a different way about them with me. They weren't like that with Jem."

She points her pen up in the air. "Let's get to Jem in a minute. But I want to get back to your parents. How were they different with you?" She looks down to write another note, seemingly expecting some time for me to deliberate.

"I wasn't worth conflict," I answer bluntly.

Her glance up at me is a confused one. "Could you please clarify?"

"When a parent cares. An invested one. You can sense their frustration. You can sense their longing to do everything they can to make sure you become a good person. But with me? I was brushed over. The child that didn't require additional care."

"You sensed this? How?"

Our eyes meet and my jaw tightens. "Certain childhood memories are like stained glass windows. Dark and saturated. These ones you don't forget."

"And the one you didn't forget?" she asks softly.

"I decided to test my father one time. I was seven. He took me to the gas station with him, and I deliberately stole a package of bubble gum. I remember unwrapping it in the car loudly. Staring up in the rearview mirror to see his reaction. And he just . . . looked at me for a few seconds in the mirror before turning around. I could see it in his eyes. I could see the recognition I had done something wrong. But he simply turned back to the steering wheel, and we drove home. He didn't even say anything to my mom."

"This angered you?"

I shook my head. "No. I felt . . . empty. An absence of any emotion. Because they never felt anger. Because I wasn't *worth* it."

She grimaces. "'Worth.' That's a tricky word, Radley."

I don't answer, and she taps her pen a few times.

"You've never mentioned their names. What's your relationship with them now?"

"Kathy and Jim Asher. So American. So corn belt, right?"

"Do you still speak to them?"

"Occasionally. After I went overseas, it became less and less. They never visited me over there. It's like they knew it was better the way it was. Left plain and folded, like a bed made permanently. And then with what happened with Jem . . . well."

She doesn't press about what happened. Not yet anyway.

"Can you tell me about when you and Jem were children?" she asks instead.

I sigh.

Happier times. Happier times that fade so quickly.

"He loved explaining things to me."

Even though I can't see her from the chaise, I can practically hear Dr. Edair smile at this.

"No matter how busy he was, or even if he was hanging out with his friends, he'd make sure to teach me. And he wasn't afraid to get into it with me. We fought, as siblings do. Maybe that's why I latched on to him. He didn't see me as someone to treat any different in our family because I wasn't blood. I was his little sister. He was my older brother. And that was that."

"And that's what made you two close, instead of with your parents?"

I arch my back. I've barely moved and feel stiff.

"Maybe. Or maybe it's because he never put up with bullshit."

She lowers her head at me. "Meaning?"

"Meaning he wasn't willing to partake in the game my parents were playing . . . that nothing was ever wrong, and we were happy. And neither did I."

I catch myself half grinning. She peers at me.

"Something you want to share?"

"Jem liked to pull pranks on our parents. It was his way of evening the score, shall we say. He knew how I felt. He saw what it was like for me. So, he did these pranks. For me."

A swell of nostalgia, regret, and grief rolls around in my throat.

"There was one that sticks in my mind. Not because of how good it was. But because of what happened . . . after."

She grows still, and I think I detect her holding her breath.

"My mother and father were obsessed with the Powerball lottery. Always thinking they would hit it big. Jem was clever enough to tape a drawing one night. He was such a smooth talker. He used allowance money to get the cashier at the corner gas station to let him buy a ticket with the winning numbers. I watched him throughout all this, his little sidekick. Always wide eyed at his boldness. He didn't give a damn what anyone else thought."

He was going to help his little sister.

I stop. I look down to see my fingers gripped together.

"Radley?" Dr. Edair asks.

"I'm fine." I swallow the lump in my throat. "He switched Dad's ticket with the one he'd bought. When they sat down to watch the drawing, he played the recording. He had me in on it, distracting them in the kitchen, asking for an evening snack. After the numbers were called out, you can imagine our parents' reaction. They thought they had it made."

"But they didn't," she says.

"They didn't."

I rest my hands at my sides. "When my father saw Jem laughing . . . when he saw him rolling on the floor and then taking out the tape, well. I'd never seen rage like that."

"Rage?"

"He slapped him across the face. But Jem didn't flinch. He looked at me and nodded as if to let me know it was okay. That it was all worth it."

"Was physical violence a recurring theme in your house growing up?"

"No. It was only that one time . . . but it was enough."

"I see," she says.

I turn my head and watch Dr. Edair uncross her legs and lean in.

"During our first session, you didn't answer when I asked if you and Jem were still close. Are you okay with talking about that now?"

I look straight at her. "He became a bit of a loner once he went to college. Like he wanted to free himself of anything that was from his old life. That even included me."

Best to give it to her straight.

"We became distant, and then it was too late. He's dead, you know."

We both are silent for a moment. Like she's letting what I've said dissipate a bit before moving on.

"What caused this distance?"

"It wasn't one thing. It was both of us. Him wanting to be on his own for once. Me fighting that and then resenting it. I shut him out when I felt slighted. Childish, but a reaction I couldn't control. I was so angry at him for having his own life. I'd depended on him for so long. And then I stopped answering his calls. Ignoring texts. We were both young adults. Both foolish. Both completely unaware of how precious life can be."

She opens her mouth and then closes it. She hesitates, and I brace myself. "Radley, I'd like you to tell me about when you lost Jem."

"You mean when he died? You can say it."

It's Dr. Edair's turn to take a breath. "All right. When he died."

I fold my hands across my belly. I'm fully reclined now. "Jem was a type 1 diabetic. One of my earliest memories is watching him get an insulin shot in his arm."

She doesn't speak. She simply allows me to get it out.

"He was very responsible about his condition. Never once heard him complain. That's why it was such a shock when he was found unconscious."

"Who found him?"

"I did."

She says nothing. I can tell she wants to say she's sorry, but the psychiatrist in her staves it off and lets me continue.

"I was still in college. He wasn't answering his phone. And even though we weren't speaking that much, I thought it was unusual. If I called Jem he would answer no matter what. When I went to his apartment to check on him, the front door was unlocked. Isn't that strange? I knew he was gone when I saw him."

"Why is that?"

"Because no one's face should look the way his did."

She doesn't stop there. She presses on. "Did you call for help?"

"Yes. He was in a coma for weeks, but that wasn't Jem anymore. His body, technically kept warm by machines, was what was left."

I straighten my arms to my sides.

Dr. Edair presses a hand against one cheek as if cooling herself. "Radley. What you experienced. That is traumatic. I want you to acknowledge that."

"Yes, it was traumatic," I say obediently.

"But do you realize this may be a root of your anxiety? Your panic attacks?"

"It's all under control. I haven't really had one since the one when I first arrived here."

She presses her hands together. "My point is that it's not under control."

"Okay. Then consider the fact that I'm sitting here speaking to you about this."

It's like I've pained her. She removes her glasses and folds them carefully. "Do you think this is why you tend to distance yourself?"

"From who?"

"From people."

The more space the better.

"I had a thread with Jem. But that's broken now. It never existed with my parents or anyone else."

I'm still searching for that thread.

"I'd like to stop talking about Jem, if that's okay with you," I say to her with softened eyes.

She nods. "Of course."

A horn blasts from the harbor. Her office windows are closed today, but that does little to mute the sound. It feels like a warning. A warning to let it be and forget the past.

If only it was that easy.

"The family I was telling you about . . ." I don't look at her face anymore. This time I look back to the ceiling.

"Yes."

"I've discovered they're not as perfect as they seem."

"Does that please you?"

"Sometimes."

She clears her throat. I fixate on the ceiling swirls harder. So hard I think I see them moving.

"They seem like a family everyone wants to be. The kind you see on social media that gives pause. You stop and you think, 'Now, there's a family who has it all. There's a family we all admire.' But we look for the flaws. We obsess over the flawlessness. We're all obsessed with other people's lives, you know."

"And why do you think you have an obsession with this family?"

I tilt my head back down. "I like being on the outside. I like seeing them for who they really are. There's no hiding. No secrets. It's raw."

I hear her write something down. The halt in our conversation makes me want to tell her everything. Everything this family means to me.

They need me to watch them. They need me to make sure the rug isn't pulled out from under them. That they know exactly how fragile happiness can be. An easily breakable piece of glass.

We wouldn't want it to shatter.

"The truth is, Dr. Edair, I think it's easier to live someone else's life."

CHAPTER 10

Beau hands me a pair of clippers and gloves.

"Start with the damaged branches. Wind got this row of trees pretty bad last night."

I slip on the worn padded gloves and spot a thin wilted branch. I lift it like a broken wing. "This one looks like it could go soon."

He inspects it thoroughly and nods. "That could be pruned."

I grit my teeth and squeeze the handles together against the branch's brief resistance as he points along the tree line.

"These outside rows don't have as much protection. You'll see they need more pruning than the inside rows."

The branch falls to the ground, and I pick it up. The very inner core is a bright white.

He leans in and shrugs. "It's okay. The rest will grow back. We can't always be so certain."

His reassurance calls up a familiar memory, abruptly bringing Jem back to life, and for a second I think I see him again. Standing among the row of trees, grinning back at me. I feel dizzy and placated all at once. I can hear Jem, telling me to keep going. A recollection of how he teased me for being so logical, while he was a free spirit. *"Not everything has to be justified, Radley."*

I shake my hands out, taking myself away from this mirage of Jem. I adjust my gloves and check the rest of the tree. I find a bent outer branch at the top and cut it off. We continue working side by side.

Unlike yesterday, there's little wind, and I wipe sweat from under my hat. Eventually I throw it off and let it drop behind my back on its strap.

Beau swipes at dampness on his chin. He's grown a slight beard since my arrival. He notices me studying it and grins.

"I always grow it out during harvest season. My father did the same."

I let the heavy clippers swing my arm to the side. "You've always known this is what you wanted to do? Other than birthright, I guess."

"Yes," he says emphatically. "Always. I even double majored in agriculture and pomology."

"Pomology?" My eyebrows knit together.

"Science of fruit growing. It's a real thing, I swear," he says, making a sweeping motion.

"Must be nice to be so sure of something."

He crosses his arms to consider this. "A blessing and a curse, I guess."

"Meaning?" I grunt, snapping off another branch.

"My father was so revered. Jonah was his name." He casts a gaze out to the rest of the orchard as if to honor him. "Everyone adored him. My mother. The crew. He was an amazing father and leader in the community. Fox Isle doesn't seem the same without him."

"I thought you were named after your father? Edwin Beau II?"

He chuckles. "No, that was my grandfather. Apparently, he was quite the stern man, which always amused my father because I was a very smiley baby." He swings a hand in my direction. "What about you? Something tells me you were a serious kid."

"I don't know the answer to that, actually. My parents really never told stories about me as a baby. Maybe it's because I was a little older when they finally got me."

"Nah. All parents love to tell baby stories."

Not these parents. But there are worse offenses.

"Was Jonah as energetic as Faye?" I ask, steering away from my own childhood.

"In a quieter way. There are few that are as robust as my mother."

"I've got to hand it to your mother. She's a lot. But she loves hard. Family. Life. I like that about her."

He shoots me a surprised glance. "Really? I thought she'd scare you right off the orchard."

"Takes a lot more than that to scare me."

"Is that so," he says quietly.

I move on to the next tree, and he follows. "It's been well over a dozen years since my father passed. And I still feel like he's watching my every move."

"Did you take over after college?"

He nods, picking a rust-colored apple and then a second. He tosses me one and rubs the other on his shirt, taking a large bite.

I look down at the apple in my hand and then back up at him. "How did he pass?"

"Heart attack," he says as he finishes chewing. "Working in this very field. How it should have been, I guess. Only too soon. He would have loved the kids . . . really loved them."

He gives himself a single exhale of wistfulness before patting his gloved hands together with a thump. "But we've done pretty well since. At least I'd like to think he'd think so."

I squint one eye. "Beau, you think of your father like a god."

This jolts him a bit, and his eyes flash. "I guess you aren't the first to point that out."

"Not surprising."

"You must think I'm a father-pleasing idiot."

"I never said that."

He smirks, and I realize I'm slightly relieved I haven't offended him entirely. He studies me and holds my gaze for a few seconds longer than I'm used to.

I clean the apple with my sleeve and take a few bites.

"Radley, I know I've said this before," he says quietly, "but I can't thank you enough for what you did for Nina. You saved her."

I keep chewing, hoping he will stop at that.

"I still think about it. What could have happened if you hadn't caught her. She would have been seriously injured or worse . . ." His voice wavers.

"But she wasn't," I say firmly.

Please don't get emotional on me.

He pulls his shoulders back and straightens. "Right. She wasn't."

"Besides, Livia has already thanked me enough."

It was true. She had hysterically cried for what felt like eternity, holding Nina tightly, even though she hadn't suffered a scratch. I'd let her embrace me, sobbing into my shoulder from relief. I stared at the wet stain on my shirt in the mirror when I returned to the cottage later.

"No, I haven't," Livia suddenly says, her voice sounding a few notes deeper than usual.

She stands with her hands behind her back, right between two trees. She looks at Beau and then me, and I can't imagine her looking any lovelier. Rays of sun backlight her outline, her hazel eyes a more glowing green today. Her tendrils cascade free and loose down her shoulders—an "in the wild" version of Livia.

"I'll never stop thanking you, Radley," she says, walking closer. "So you might as well get used to it." She winks and smiles at me.

Beau rocks on his heels with his hands in his pockets. "Need something, Liv?"

She moves her body so it's square in front of his. "Dr. Fin is here to take a look at Pepper's leg. Thought you'd want to talk with him too."

"Of course," he answers, reaching out to graze a few fingers on her arm.

"Radley, you should come too," adds Livia.

I hold up my pruners. "I'll finish up here."

"It looks pretty much done. Come on," she says, placing a full hand on my back.

The walk back is mainly silent. Beau leads the way, followed by Livia and then me. I admire the two of them, strolling nearly in step. Both statuesque, hard to miss. Like they belong in this real-life

Americana ad I'm watching. The enchanting fall trees all bowing to their king and queen.

As we approach the barn stable, I note a vintage teal truck parked nearby.

I've seen that truck before. A very rude man drove that truck.

I turn the corner into Pepper's stable to find the sandy-haired man who cut me off at the gas station down on one knee, inspecting her hind leg. She's calm and still, allowing him to apply pressure and run his fingers along her lines.

"Could be a bowed tendon. I'd avoid too much pressure on it. Let her rest. If that doesn't work, we could try cold therapy. It's nothing we can't help her with," the man says, still intensely focused on Pepper's leg.

He finally lifts his head up and looks at me. If he recognizes me from the gas station pump, he doesn't show it. He has striking light eyes that are hard to miss, and his classic handsome features make my plain ones feel even plainer.

"Dr. Fin, this is Radley. She came in at the last minute in place of Alice this season," Livia says. She's beaming, and I'm not sure if it's because of the good-looking vet or the fact that she's introducing us.

"Hello," I say quickly.

Handsome or not, you're still bad mannered.

"We've known each other long enough where we can drop the 'Doctor' part, right, Liv?" He smiles. "You can call me Shai." He extends a hand, and I take it, reluctantly making note of its softness.

Beau strokes the star-shaped spot between Pepper's eyes. "So, you're not too concerned about our Pepper here?"

"Not at this point, Beau."

"Good deal," he replies, patting her.

Livia glances at Shai and then me. "Shai, the roast I made for dinner is almost ready. Why don't we all have a glass of wine out in the garden while we wait? The kids love it when you stop by. Faye should be coming home with them soon."

He tilts his head, considering briefly, and then nods. "I would love that, thank you."

Somehow, I find myself seated next to Shai with a chilled glass of pinot grigio without the crutch of anyone else nearby. Beau is busy starting a bonfire, poking at it to get it going, and Livia went to fetch wool blankets, the evening air getting brisk.

I can feel Shai's quick glimpses at me, probably trying to figure out where he's seen this unassuming Asian woman before. Finally, I say it.

"Gas station. Pump number three. A few weeks ago." I speak in short spurts as if giving him clues in a game.

He stifles a chuckle. "Ah. Now I remember. That was the afternoon I had to take an emergency call up in Yarport. Cattle dog had swallowed a rubber ball, and it was lodged. Time was of the essence. Unfortunately, my tank was empty."

I can't help but frown and consider this explanation.

"And I completely cut you off, didn't I?"

I nod with one swooping exaggeration. "Yes. Yes, you did."

He puts a hand to his chest. "Well, Radley, I'd like to formally apologize for being so incredibly rude. No excuses."

I twist my mouth to the side and give him a glance.

"Did he make it?"

Slight relief washes over Shai's face as he sees my inquiry as somewhat of an acceptance of his apology. "Yes, he did. Managed to dislodge it in the nick of time. He's likely herding cattle as we speak. And you had a hand in it."

I hold up my glass. "Well then, I guess it was all worth it."

He does the same and then leans back in his seat.

Livia appears with blankets and offers us each one. He declines, but I take one and place it over my shoulders.

"I see you two are getting acquainted?" she asks brightly.

I say nothing as I take in my wine.

"Believe it or not, Livia, we've actually met before," says Shai.

"Really!" she exclaims as if it's some miraculous event.

"It was at the gas station," I say flatly.

Shai's brows raise briefly, a glint of intrigue in his eyes.

Livia watches me, and I pull the blanket tighter over my shoulders.

"Well, dinner should be ready soon," she announces.

Later, inside the house, which is toasty from the roast in the oven, Tallan and the girls clamber inside, a jubilant Faye ushering them. She gives Shai a big embrace like they're old friends. Tallan's face lights up upon seeing him, and he immediately begins to ask questions about his latest vet cases.

"Dad says you did surgery on a cow last week. Is that true?"

Shai grunts and laughs as Avie and Nina squeal, trying to climb on his back while he answers. "I did. And I can tell you all about it while we eat the beef your mom cooked." He winks, and Tallan grins widely.

The chaos continues until Livia officially calls everyone to the table. Nina tugs at my arm and motions for me to come closer.

"Radley," she whispers sweetly.

"Yes?"

"I made name cards for everyone tonight. Well, not for Dr. Fin because I didn't know he was coming. Grandma Faye helped me."

She pulls me to the table and points to a seat. A yellow piece of construction paper is folded with the name RADLEY scrawled in crayon.

"Do you like it?" she asks, her eyes round and expectant.

I feel something give way in my chest. Like the first bit of soil to erode from spring rain.

"Yes, Nina. I very much do."

CHAPTER 11

September is nearly finished.

I feel like my routine has started to take form.

Rise to watch the family get ready for the day. Nina and Avie, their faces in the window and their tea party ready to commence.

Down to the shop to meet Andrea, field, apples, work.

Field, apples, work, repeat.

This morning, the girls pull me into their tea party. I'm not entirely irritated by this. I don't even have to pretend to be interested. I sit in one of their chairs in the playroom, my knees up high, chin rested in a fist as I observe their banter.

"I'll take three sugars today, not two, please," Nina orders.

Avie pretends to dump three spoonfuls into one of the pastel teacups. She pours a light-brown liquid and stirs with a tiny silver spoon, the handle enameled with painted rosebuds.

"Can I ask? What kind of tea is that?" I point to the pot.

"Today it's Darjeeling."

"And your mother doesn't care that you're having caffeine?"

"Of course she does. That's why it's decaffeinated," explains Avie, her focus now on pouring tea into her own cup.

"Right. Decaffeinated," Nina repeats. But something tells me she's not certain what that means. Half-moon shadows puff under her eyes. She takes a few sips of her tea and then holds it quietly in her lap.

"You okay, Nina?" I bend closer to her.

She doesn't respond.

Avie pours her more tea. "She's getting tired again. Like she used to."

Rabbit suddenly pops his head under her arm, panting, and she gives him a nibble of biscuit. He turns his attention to me, and I stroke the silken top of his skull, his eyes closing with pleasure.

"Mommy is going to take her to the doctor if she doesn't get better. The medicine usually helps, but not this time," Avie goes on, setting the pot back in its place.

Nina shakes her head. "No."

"Yes, Nina. Mommy says," she shoots back bossily.

A pout forms over Nina's mouth; she scowls and then reaches for Rabbit, throwing her arms around him. He patiently lets her squeeze him and then lowers himself to the ground.

"Besides," says Avie, inspecting her nails, "Mommy is happier now. You don't want to ruin that, do you, Nina?"

Happier now.

Nina buries herself deeper into Rabbit's back fur.

"What do you mean by . . . her being happier?" I ask carefully.

Avie, still looking at her nails, raises her gaze to meet mine. Her curls are layered down over one shoulder, similar to Livia's hair yesterday. I'm struck by how adultlike she appears right now. "There was a time Mommy was unhappy. Daddy too. They . . . fought a lot. They were louder then."

Louder. Unhappy.

She looks me dead in the eyes. "But they're better now. Mommy is happier now."

I pull back, sitting deeper in the little chair. "What was it that Mommy and Daddy fought about?"

A cognizant glimmer flutters across Avie's face. A tale of knowledge that she isn't going to pass on to me.

"They're better now. We're all better now."

Nina leans her head into Rabbit's, and her eyelids grow heavy as she pets him with one finger.

Neither of them says much after that. Another cup of tea for them both, and they leave the playroom to get ready for school as the faint clamors of Livia making breakfast in the kitchen echo between my ears.

I choose not to leave right then and make my way to the kitchen. Livia pours me a coffee and points to a seat at the island. I'm answering all her questions and being pleasant. She, too, looks a little wearier, mirroring Nina's lack of energy. Worry has started to creep across her forehead, the lines by her eyes a little deeper.

I watch Avie, on call for any need Livia might have, her face dutiful. A puppy ready to serve her master, wanting to please in every possible way. Her admiration shines as she follows Livia around, nearly bumping into her three times. Livia, tolerant and serene and never scolding, places a soft hand on her head, redirecting her to a different task. Avie holds up the spatula she was looking for. A quick wipe of spilled milk with the red dishcloth. She sets three places at the counter for her and her siblings.

Tic-tac-toe, three in a row.

There's a delighted swelling in Avie's face, like a pump filling a tire. The air pressure increases with each thank-you and compliment her mother sends her way.

If ever there was a middle child.

Part of me feels sympathy for her. She thrives largely on her mother's approval. I only hope it's something she can eventually outgrow.

The information I was fed at the morning tea party makes me eager for the day to rise and fall quickly.

Later, as night takes over, anticipation tingles in my fingers as I take my place in the window.

What unhappiness lingers?

There's no sign of Beau tonight. He's been gone since midday, but I find myself enjoying watching Livia in action. A solo performance.

The three children climb up the stairs in reverse order, Livia holding Nina's hand to assist. She drags her little feet. Head down like a rag doll. They disappear as they round the landing and reappear in the window at the top of the stairs. Nina has stopped altogether at the very last step. Livia scoops her up, and the others follow.

Avie obediently draws a bath. As if she were the mother, she checks it with her elbow as it fills. Livia has made her way into Nina's room, rocking her in the chair as they wait to take the bath.

I turn away to get a nightcap. I need something heavier for tonight. I can feel it in my bones, a vibration that tickles me with forewarning. Two large ice cubes clink into my glass. I give myself a generous pour of gin and cut a fresh lime. The citrus wakes me up even more, and I feel fresh. Equipped for the second act of tonight's showing.

Tallan does not say good night to his mother or sisters. His room is dark. I missed seeing him enter his room. He lies in bed so still I briefly wonder if he's maybe somewhere else in the house. But an arm moves to go behind his head. The mood coming from his room is so strong I can smell it from my post. Restless. Troubled.

The gin brings heat to my throat and cheeks, and I set my glass down. The bath has finished for both girls, and Livia leaves Nina in her bed to tend to Avie. After she tucks Avie in, she struggles to leave the room. Avie clings to her mother, pulling her in to stay. She's torn between giving in to this child's requests and returning to the ill one in the other room. I see her stroke Avie a few times, in a bent-over, cooing position. She kisses her, and Avie swings her arm around in one last attempt to make her stay.

This time Livia does not give in. She pulls back. I assume she whispers good night and closes the door. Avie lies motionless, frozen until she flips to her side, her back to me. I think I see a shudder of her shoulders. I press my palms against the window. There. Again, a shake of her small body. And then she is still.

Livia cradles Nina as she falls asleep. But she does not leave. She does not attempt to place her back in bed.

She stays there transfixed, watching her Nina. And I wait. Wait, wait, wait for her to return to another task or chore she needs to attend to. To give in to any other voice in her head telling her there's still so much left undone elsewhere in the house. But she doesn't. Gripped and strong is the night, latching on to her and her baby girl.

They are a glass sculpture, one torched and molded into the other.

I'm not sure how long I watch them. My eyelids grow heavy. And then it's darkness for myself.

I exhale, startled. I must have dozed off.

What's happened? Where have you gone?

She's no longer in Nina's room. The lights come on below in the kitchen. Beau has returned.

He walks up the steps, unhurried. Halfway up, he places a hand against the wall and pauses. It's a long pause that makes me hold my breath. When he moves again, his hand drags against the wall with such heaviness. If I inspected that very spot tomorrow, I'm sure I'd see streaks.

She waits on the bed. All the lights are on, as if she wants to make sure he knows she's awake. The sconces on each side of their bed like stars as her backdrop.

I can feel her tense when he enters.

I can feel her heart race. The blood rise in her temples.

Are you becoming filled with passion or hate? Show me, Livia. Show me which one it is that consumes you.

He stands in the doorway and shoulders off his jacket. There is an exchange of words. Mellow and brief. She speaks first. He answers.

Her mouth moves quicker.

His follows even faster, open and shut, open and shut, a torrent of angry words.

She stands up, her arms flying as if she's ready to go into a rage.

His back is to me, but I see his face in her vanity mirror. Red. Raging red and flooded with more anger than I thought possible for him.

One more movement of his mouth. One more. But that is enough. What he's said is enough to throw her into a craze.

I see her nostrils flare. Her eyes are wide and wet. And she shouts. I glance quickly below at the children's rooms, but no one stirs. Her hands like a blacksmith's burn into his chest, and she pushes with all her might. Once. Twice. A third time.

Oh, Livia.

I don't like seeing his face after this. I don't like the way it's shaped. The reaction too much. It unsettles me.

They move out of view. A blind spot of their closet shields them from me.

My sweet, serene Livia . . . what have you done?

CHAPTER 12

She texts me early in the morning:

LIVIA CLARK: Can you meet me at the house for lunch today?

I read the text with a heart both bold and heavy. My hand grips my phone in the dark. It's not dawn yet, but she's already reaching out. Could it be about last night? Does she think I can help her?

I reply with a quick "yes."

LIVIA CLARK: Great, hop over around noon then.

I set the phone in my lap and stare out the ocular at the house. The children are still asleep. Beau and Livia's bedroom empty. They've both retreated from last night's scene. My body feels numb, still stunned from what I saw Livia do. So wildly different from her normal doe-eyed admiration of Beau. The line between lust and disdain is a watery one. I begin to wonder if it will wash out.

When I arrive exactly on time, she already has lunch set up out on the patio. It's slightly chilly, but I don't protest. She's placed two saffron-colored bowls of soup dolloped with crème fraîche and sprinkled with dill at each seat.

"I hope you like lobster bisque? Faye taught me this recipe. Almost fail-proof, if I can make it," she says sunnily.

If she's troubled, she certainly isn't showing it.

"This looks delicious," I tell her. "Thank you."

We sit down, and I slide my spoon out from the napkin ring. I slowly slurp some of the soup. It settles on my tongue, creamy and mildly sweet from the bits of lobster.

"Wow."

"Yup. Fail-proof. I can give you the recipe if you want." She grins and takes a large spoonful.

I wait until I've finished a third of the soup before putting my spoon down to ask, "What is it you wanted to talk about with me?"

Her thick lashes flutter, and she dabs at the corner of her mouth. "Oh. Nothing bad, really," she begins. She folds the napkin carefully into her lap.

"I assume that's why you wanted to have lunch?"

"Partly. But I also enjoy your company, Radley." She says this with such grace, I have to give her credit where it's due.

I give her a forced smile.

You can tell me. Go on.

"You see, Radley . . ."

Tell me about how you shoved your husband last night.

"I've really grown to trust you. We've really grown to trust you." She motions back and forth, as if Beau were there sitting with us.

Are you sure about that, Livia?

"And, well, our Nina. You may have noticed, I'm sure, that she isn't feeling all that well again. Her energy level is alarming. But she absolutely hates the doctor. Sometimes I think her dread of that is worse than her illness."

Nina. So, this is about Nina.

I feel my shoulders sag, and I realize it's from a surprising relief. Relief that she isn't divulging her deepest, darkest secrets. Relief that I haven't been caught.

"I don't want to make this worse by taking her in unnecessarily. But she's getting worse, so I've made an appointment with her doctor. She'll be having some labs drawn, which will take a lot of coaxing. And the last time this happened, she took so much of my attention and time."

Wait . . . what are you getting at now?

Her left hand curls in, and she slides her middle nail against her thumb a few times. "You know, as a mother, sometimes you have to know when to ask for help, right?"

She looks at me expectantly. As if she's looking for me to give her permission.

"Sure," I say and then nod a few times. "Of course."

Her eyes widen with self-reprieve, and she exhales. "After what you did for Nina, catching her in the barn, I feel an implicit trust with you. I can't explain it. If you're willing to . . . and Beau agreed, he would cut back on your other work around the orchard. But we would love for you to help with the other children."

You want me closer. You want more of my time.

"I'm . . . I'm not really the best with kids—"

She lowers her head. "Are you kidding me? These kids adore you." She smiles mischievously and her dimples flash. "I think it's your . . . brutal honesty, Radley. You're not disingenuous in anything you say or do. Kids pick up on that, and they love that about you."

Adore . . . the kids adore me.

"What exactly would all of this entail?"

She puts up two hands and waves them, rapid fire. "We're not asking you to officially nanny or anything like that. Don't worry."

This clarification intrigues me. I lean in closer.

"Maybe hang out with the older two when we get too busy with Nina. Very informal. Faye will be in and out taking care of them also. Plus, there's only one official duty we'd ask of you," she explains, holding up a finger.

"All right. And that would be?"

"The elementary and middle schools have different start times. Don't even get me started on that," she says, rolling her eyes. "But it would be a huge help if you could drop off and pick up Tallan? Beau can handle Avie."

"You want me to—"

"Only if you're willing, Radley. I really want to stress that. If none of this sounds appealing to you, then consider this just a friendly lunch."

She bends forward and takes a spoonful of soup. Her eyes remain up, examining me.

Would this give me greater access to them? The family that so far I've kept at arm's length so that I may watch them from afar, a proper audience member. Yet . . . is this something I'm ready to see? I've already seen too much . . .

"I can help," a clear voice says.

Where did that come from? Wait . . . is it too late to take it back?

I shift in my seat, panicked.

The sight of her pleased face tempers my fretting. "Oh, Radley, that's so great. Thank you! The kids are going to be thrilled. Beau too."

Thrilled . . . just thrilled.

She takes a bite of toasted baguette and cups her hand under her chin to catch the crumbs. "Do you think you'd be up for picking Tallan up this afternoon?"

—

I wait in my car just as Livia instructed, at the edge of the asphalt parking lot.

"This way you can avoid the chaos parade they call the pickup line," she warned me.

I search for Tallan in the stream of middle schoolers trudging out, most of them slouched forward with heavy book bags dragging them down. Lack of confidence is the school uniform at this age. Few can pull off any other look.

The car's getting stuffy, so I roll down the windows a little more. I lean back on the headrest and notice a group of four kids stopping to convene around a cluster of birches. Two of them look like jocks, the boy wearing a maroon football jersey, the girl a soccer shirt. The third is a boy in a bomber jacket with chin-length blond hair that he keeps flipping back. The other girl is hard to miss. She's all limbs like a young colt, hair to her waist. I realize I'm staring when she glances at me, and I look away.

Luckily, I spot Tallan coming out. He's not as slow as the other kids, actually walking at a reasonable human pace. The group of four stop talking as he passes, and he gives them a sideways glance. His cheeks are pink when he sees my car. Confused at first, I give him a contrite wave, doing my best not to draw too much attention. This causes his mouth to pucker with embarrassment.

For God's sake, Radley, be cool for the poor kid.

He nods and makes his way over, ducking in like we're in a getaway car.

"Hi, Tallan. Your mom wanted me to pick you up. She wants me to start—"

"I know," he inserts quickly. "She mentioned it this morning."

"So you do listen sometimes," I say, attempting to joke.

He shrugs and looks out his window. I see him giving one more glance to the long-haired girl. She looks his way and then quickly tucks her hair behind her ears. The bomber jacket kid reaches out to tickle her, and she squeals.

Tallan turns his cheek, but I can still see his entire face go red.

Red like his father's was last night.

He slings his backpack to the floor of the car.

"Was your . . . day okay?" I ask, keeping my hands square on the steering wheel and focusing on getting out of the parking lot.

"It was all right. We started a new unit on zoology. That was fairly interesting," he says, directing his attention out the window again.

"Middle school seems so long ago. I barely remember what we studied," I quickly add.

He raises his brows at me.

"Not saying it isn't important . . . to still pay attention," I say, faltering.

Tallan smiles a little. "I really enjoy random knowledge, believe it or not. That's what it all seems like to me."

"Random?"

"Yes. Entirely random to learn about trilobites for one part of the day and then trigonometry the next."

It's my turn to raise my brows. "You're learning trigonometry? It may have been a while, but I don't remember learning that at your age."

"I'm in advanced classes."

"Oh. So are you with older kids for those?"

"Yes. Eighth graders."

This seems to distract him, and he stares out the window again.

I think back on the group of four he dashed past. They looked older. I wonder if he has class with any of them. But I decide not to push it this time.

"You don't mind me picking you up?" I ask instead.

Prying for your own ego. Shame, shame.

"No," he answers. "I like you, Radley. I don't feel like I ever have to pretend in front of you."

"Pretend?" I question, making a turn onto the gravel road.

He twists one of the straps of his backpack. "Sometimes you have to pretend in order to keep things even and steady . . . do you know what I mean?"

I nod, pretending that I understand what he means by that.

"Well, I promise not to wave again like I did today," I say with a lighter tone.

He shakes his head. "It's all right. That's not what I was embarrassed about."

I remain silent, but he doesn't expand on what it really was that got to him.

"Mom's taking Nina to the doctor, huh," he says, more like a statement than a question.

"Yes. She thinks the anemia needs to be checked out further."

He sinks into his seat and crosses his arms. A troubled sag of his cheeks takes over.

"But don't worry," I say quickly. "I'm sure she'll get the care she needs and will be back to her old self soon."

"Yeah . . . that's what they said last time," he says flatly.

"Who said what?"

I glance at him and then turn back to the road. It's enough to see the deadened look in his eyes.

"Nothing. I'm sure the doctors will help her."

But there's nothing confident in the way he says this. He turns away again, and we spend the rest of the ride home in silence.

CHAPTER 13

"I won't take no for an answer, darling," Faye says, patting my cheek.

"Really. I'm happy to stay behind and—"

"This pale complexion of yours could use some sea air and sunshine," she presses on, practically shoving me into the passenger seat of her Bronco.

She shuts the door, and I open my mouth to protest but then stop.

There's really no fighting Faye, is there?

Livia positions herself to climb into the back. "Sometimes it's better to just accept it. She'll have her way regardless," she sagely utters near my ear as she passes, as if reading my mind.

Beau pulls up next to us in the minivan. "Ready, Mother?"

Avie waves frantically from the back. "Radley! You're coming after all!" She continues to cheer, pumping her fists into the air. I notice Tallan slouched next to her, shrugging at me.

The morning began with the girls excitedly announcing that Grandma Faye was taking everyone for an afternoon sail. Sunscreen was applied on every possible surface, and the girls rummaged for hats. I had every intention of staying behind alone.

"Boats aren't really my thing," I had pushed as my mantra.

But the minute Faye arrived, she made it clear that I was going.

She opens the windows fully, the wind blowing our hair as she sings at the top of her lungs to seventies rock music that I don't really recognize.

Livia squeezes my shoulders from behind and then leans back, one arm tucked behind her head. I see her in the rearview mirror, her scarf tied like a bandanna across her forehead; it whips with the rest of her wild mane. She tilts her chin up to let the sun hit her face.

Thirty minutes later, after a bumpy Faye car ride with her shouting "my hippie days" stories over the music and wind, we reach Fox Isle's marina. She parks in front of one of the end docks, and I already see the tiny figures of Avie and Nina skipping down the wood planks toward the row of sailboats.

As we make our way down to meet them, the dock seems to waver as the wind picks up. Livia nearly loses her scarf retying it. I feel my legs shake a bit staring at the *Calypso*, her cursive letters swirled in blue against the pure white hull. The sailboat is bigger than I pictured, a good fifty feet in length.

I watch the waves lap against the side of the boat, and my stomach does a slight turn. I take a sip of my bottled water.

"You okay, Radley?" Beau asks, putting a light hand on my back.

"Oh . . . yes. I'm okay," I lie.

You can still back out, Radley. You can still go back to the Bronco and wait.

Livia places her arm around my shoulders. "First sailing jaunt with the Clark family. Let's hope it's one of many," she says more into my neck than my ear.

Beau reaches out to help me into the boat.

I'm slightly startled to find three figures already standing at the bow, sipping on beers. One of them I recognize.

Faye slips in behind me as she pulls oversize orange sunglasses on top of her head. "Radley, I'd like to introduce the other co-owners of the *Calypso*, Pete and Jesse Shaw."

A herculean man with a buzzed auburn cut extends his hand first. I can see each vein in his titanic arms bulge with every slight movement.

"Welcome!" he booms. He places his arm around a short plump man, the top of his head shiny and bald. "I'm Pete, and this is my husband, Jesse."

Jesse shows a perfect set of white teeth. "Hello, Radley. Glad to have you on board. Help yourself to some of the charcuterie. The cheese is from our very own shop."

He points to a long board of various meats and cheeses.

"Jesse and Pete own a few delicatessens and cheese shops in the area," Faye explains, picking up a roll of prosciutto.

"You'll have to stop by our Fox Isle location. Triple crème from France just came in," Pete says to me eagerly.

"I'll be sure to. Thank you."

I flip my eyes over to the third figure. I must be giving him an unfair accusatory look, since he briefly smirks before feigning a serious expression. Shai then gives me a nod and raises his beer.

"And you already know Shai," Faye quickly adds. She slightly groans as she bites into the rolled meat and then picks up a square of white cheese. "Your cheese connection may or may not be the only reason why I chose to own a sailboat with you two."

Jesse bumps his hip into hers, and his small round tummy jiggles. "How do you know we aren't using you for apple butter and jams?"

"But I *do* know, Jesse," Faye retorts.

"Grandma!" Avie calls out, running up to hug her.

Beau stands behind Tallan with his hands on his shoulders, giving him a little playful shake, perhaps to liven up for the day. Livia holds a withdrawn Nina in her arms, her legs dangling and arms slack. She kisses the top of her head.

"I guess she almost fell asleep in the van. Do you think she could lie down in the berth?" she asks Faye quietly.

Faye strokes Nina's cheek. "Of course. But then maybe bring her up once we're out. I think the fresh air would do her a lot of good."

Livia nods and moves gingerly down a set of stairs belowdecks, Nina nestling deeper into her collarbone.

"What's a berth?" I ask.

"Where the beds are. There are two tucked down there in the bow. There's also a kitchenette, bathroom, and even a small desk area." Faye explains this heartily, but I can tell her mind is absent.

"Are you worried about her?"

"Hmm? You mean Nina?" She crosses her arms and sighs. "Yes. Liv told me yesterday that the doctors are going to run some additional tests. It's frustrating. We've been down this road before."

"I'm sorry, Faye."

She swats at me. "Don't be. Never say you're sorry unless an apology is truly owed." She slides her sunglasses back down and sniffs. "Doesn't make sense for her to be so sick again," she mutters with a dejection I've never heard before from her.

"But she got better?"

She sighs. "Yes, better . . . but to be honest, I've been losing sleep over this latest bout. And I'm already a bit of an insomniac." She chuckles. "Good thing I've upped my meds for it."

"Well . . . today she gets to rest on her grandma's sailboat," I say in a mild attempt to comfort her.

Her usual smile peaks. "That's right, Radley. Thank you."

Faye's bursts of energy return, and she masterfully gets the sailboat out of the harbor. There's something so natural about her fluid movement from one part of the boat to the other, her post at the helm almost regal, as the mainsail (as I've learned it's called) billows above her majestically.

The *Calypso* sails far enough where we can't make out the harbor anymore. Tallan sits at the table to play a game of cards with Beau. Livia relaxes at the stern with Avie in her lap, who plays with the ends of Livia's hair while looking up at her adoringly. Meanwhile, Jesse and Pete regale Livia with their latest customer encounters gone wrong at the cheese shop, making her laugh so hard she wipes at a few tears.

I stand near the mast and steady myself. The waves of the Atlantic are a deep sapphire, the endless possible depths beginning to dizzy me as I imagine them. A seagull screeches long and high, and for a second it sounds like a scream for help. My heart begins to pulsate like it did a few weeks ago.

Don't think about that . . . focus on the horizon.

I take a deep breath in through my nose but for some reason have trouble exhaling. The horizon starts to shape-shift into a squiggly line. I place my hands on the metal railing and stare down at the rolling waves. I think I hear another scream. Surely, it's another seagull.

That's not what this is. It can't happen here because it's already over.

I lean in more, straining to get a better look into the water.

It's just water . . . it's just water.

A cold metal can presses against the top of my hand.

"Ginger ale. The colder the better," Shai says.

I hold the can, confused.

"When I get seasick, it always seems to be the cure."

Seasick. He thinks I'm seasick.

But his abrupt interruption distracts me enough that I feel some panic in my chest start to dissipate.

"Thanks." I pop open the tab and take a small sip.

I turn my head to find him holding on to the rail with one hand. The sea air ripples his hair out of his eyes, and the reflection of the light on the water makes him look sun kissed, a top candidate for a Ralph Lauren ad. I nearly roll my eyes at this thought. I've come to that point in my adult life where the insanely good looking cause annoyance rather than admiration.

"Better?" he asks.

"It helped."

A piece of hair whips into my mouth, and I sputter it out. I quickly secure my hair back with a band, fully aware that when I wear my hair like this, I appear even more plain.

Yet I find Shai observing me as I finish pulling my ponytail through the band.

"This is interesting to you?" I say as I pull at the ends.

"Yes, actually. I grew up with two sisters. And I have to say, I never once saw one of them put their hair up with the expert speed you just did."

I feel a corner of my mouth tug. "We can't all be this talented."

He laughs, and I'm surprisingly pleased at this. I drink more ginger ale and then flip around with my back to the water.

"I didn't know veterinarians liked to sail."

"I didn't know veterinarians were precluded from sailing," he responds back.

"Only on certain days of the week, I hear . . . you're a friend of Faye's then?"

He nods. "Pete and Jesse too. Their parakeet and Himalayan cat are patients of mine. Their pets are actually best friends, believe it or not."

"What an odd couple."

I squint up to the top of the mast, the clouds passing above like a conveyor belt.

"Well, I hope my being here hasn't ruined your afternoon *too* much," he says with a twinkle in his eyes.

I raise a brow. "Ruined?"

"You didn't look all that happy to see me here."

"Oh . . . not unhappy. More like surprised."

"I see." He taps the railing a few times with his hand.

"But this"—I hold up my ginger ale—"was a very nice gesture."

"Shai," he says.

"What?"

"Shai," he says to me, grinning. "You can call me by my name, you know."

"Really? I've been having fun calling you 'the vet' in my head."

As he laughs again, I realize I enjoy hearing it. His presence somehow lets the seams out a bit on the stiches that repaired me once. A lightness in me has resurfaced that I haven't seen in so long.

I thought it had disappeared for good.

CHAPTER 14

Andrea shivers and pulls up the shearling collar of her jacket.

"October nor'easter wind. You can feel it coming in today."

She hands me a full bucket of Goldens, which I load into the back of the utility cart.

"I know everyone loves their Honeycrisps and Galas. The popular high-season breeds. But for me, these Golden Russets are a winner. Later to ripen but so sweet and worth the wait."

I softly grin. "I didn't know you were so poetic, Andrea."

She shrugs good naturedly. "Neither did I."

Daniel hauls in two more buckets and places them in the cart.

"Here, Ms. Poet," he tells Andrea, pulling off his knit hat. "You need this more than me. You're always complaining about the cold," he affectionately nags her. He tugs the hat on her head and gives her a quick peck on the cheek.

She lights up with a smile, mildly blushing. "That's why I've kept him around for twenty-plus years."

He gently pokes her in the side, and she rolls her eyes, playfully smacking him on the side of his arm.

"You see what I put up with, Radley?" Daniel says as he points his finger at Andrea.

I laugh a little and shake my head as I reach for another Golden to pick.

"Okay. You ladies need anything, I'll be a few rows to the right," he calls over his shoulder with two empty buckets in his hand.

Andrea and I silently pick apples next to each other for a while. I look at her as she hums, and she pulls down a branch to check for ripeness.

"You're in an especially chipper mood today, Andrea."

She smiles again, this time bigger. "Yes, I am."

"Daniel makes you that happy?"

She tosses her head back with a laugh. "If only."

"Then what is it?"

The knit hat starts to edge up, and she yanks it down closer to her eyes. "For years, Daniel and I have been saving every last bit we can. Our hope was to buy a small business and work for ourselves."

I stop picking and turn toward her. "Okay . . ."

"Well," she goes on excitedly, "a few weeks ago, Daniel heard through a former coworker at the cannery about a small laundromat for sale. Within our budget. But that's not even the best part."

She pauses and presses her hands together. "The laundromat is in Boston! We'd be near Luna at Emerson." Her eyes well up. "Finally, together again. And our own business."

"Andrea." I put my hand on her arm. "That's so wonderful. I'm truly happy for you and Daniel."

She wipes at a tear and laughs. "I can't believe I'm crying right now about it. In the middle of the orchard! But this is such a lifelong dream. Daniel and I have worked so hard. We've made so many sacrifices. Even Luna has sacrificed over the years. Do you know how many times we had to tell her no because we couldn't afford something? No to ballet lessons, no to the senior trip. Ripped at my heart every time. Probably more so for Daniel. He may not show it a lot, but he's a very proud man."

I nod. "I do see it. And I don't know a more deserving couple."

It dawns on me right then that this would mean they'd leave the orchard.

"This laundromat . . . when do you take ownership?"

"Oh! Not until the new year. We've signed the initial contract. And we have to wait for escrow and everything. The down payment's due at signing right before Christmas. With the end-of-season bonus Livia and Beau give us, we'll be able to make it."

"Sounds like a great plan," I say, a little relieved. I didn't like the idea of finishing out the season without Andrea and Daniel.

Not that I don't care for Chester and Sidney. But they aren't exactly chomping at the bit to be as friendly with me. Daniel—and Andrea especially—have made me feel not only welcomed but somehow that I belong in this foreign space I've landed in.

Andrea sighs. "You know, when it comes to Livia and Beau . . . without their generosity, I don't know if we'd even be able to think about any of this."

"Yes. They're quite the couple."

At least during daylight hours.

She rubs her arms and gets a far-off look on her face. "I'm so glad to see them happy again . . . like they once were. That's how it should be," she murmurs.

"Once were?" I probe.

She quickly snaps her attention to me, as if remembering she's speaking aloud and she's not alone. Her eyes widen.

"Oh . . . I didn't mean it that way."

"It's okay," I carefully continue. "The girls have . . . mentioned a few things to me."

Her brown eyes peer at me. "They have?"

"Avie in particular. Something about how they aren't fighting anymore."

She puts a hand to her mouth, taking in what I've said.

Don't do this to her. Not Andrea. She's been so good to you.

"I didn't realize the girls knew so much," she says quietly.

I follow her as she walks farther down the row and stay at her side, leaning in. Hoping that she'll let it slip, that somehow she'll spill something, and I'll get another drop of their secrets.

"I normally wouldn't say anything. Loyalty is very important to me. To Daniel. He'd be irritated at me for even speaking about it," she explains, her voice sterner than I'm used to.

I shake my head. "This isn't something I'm going to be repeating, Andrea."

"All right, well. Since the girls have already been telling you things . . ." She hesitates and glances at me for reassurance.

"Yes?"

That's it. Go on, you can tell me.

"When I first arrived at Clark Orchard, the Livia and Beau I met were so carefree. They had this vivacity about them, a contagious energy. Young, new parents who delighted at anything toddler Tallan did. It was easy to work for them. But the thing is, they never made Daniel and me feel like we worked *for* them. It was more like we worked *with* them—you know what I mean?"

I nod fervently.

She exhales. "That's how it was for a few years. Then Avie was born. And you could sense they were tired—parents always are. But now they had two children, and the tired turned into exhaustion. Nevertheless, they were happy with their growing family. The orchard was thriving, and Beau was even in talks to expand with a second location."

"Really?"

"Yes. I mean the orchard is certainly still doing well. But at that point, you could see how encouraged Beau felt about growing his father's legacy."

"So, what happened?"

"The deal fell through," she answers rapidly.

"Oh . . . that must have been hard on Beau."

"It was," she says, nodding. "Although he did a good job of hiding it. They always manage to rise to the occasion. A golden couple, through and through. A little after that, Nina was born. Juggling the three kids and operating the farm took up all their time. And then Nina's illness, of course, and the medical bills for that, I can only imagine. But they were still all so . . . content. Thrilling to watch, really, how they handled it all. But then . . ."

She stops walking then and turns her head to me.

"I won't say exactly what occurred. I respect them too much for that. Even if you do know there were problems." Her jaw is set tight and her expression stoic.

Dissatisfaction stirs in my throat, but I don't let Andrea see it. Truthfully, I wasn't going to press her any more. I like her enough not to do that. "I understand," I tell her.

She takes a large breath. "What happened was enough to crack even their blessed door. And when it did, it brought out a darkness in each of them." She locks eyes with me. "One I'd hope to never see again."

CHAPTER 15

There's an hour to go until I'm due to pick up Tallan. I drive down the dirt road and under the **Clark Orchard** sign to stop in Fox Isle's main square first. I'd promised Pete and Jesse a visit at their cheese shop.

The store is as bright and eclectic as its owners, with canary-yellow walls and miniature vintage chandeliers hung from the ceiling. I find Pete's robust frame behind the counter.

"Well, well. Look who finally made it in," he ribs.

"I've come to get that triple crème Jesse kept raving about."

He spreads his arms out over the case of cheeses. "You've come to the right spot. And might I add you're looking ravishing, Radley."

"Thank you," I respond but more as a question. Although I do feel a little more "kempt" today, having put on a dot of tinted lip balm and tousled my hair down in waves.

Pete pauses to put a finger under his chin. "'Ravishing Radley.' I like the sound of that. I'll be back. We've sold out what's in the case, but I know we have some in the walk-in."

I turn to peruse the rest of the shop. A center display houses specialty crackers and elegant jars of dried fruit. As I examine a package of dark sesame seed ones, the door jingles open and Grace enters. Her arm is looped with a man who rivals the burly size of Pete.

"Grace," I blurt out.

She pauses, and I expect her to turn away, my guilt by association from working for Livia and Beau a likely repellent. But instead, she gives me a thin smile that reads a little embarrassed.

"Radley. Hello." She lets the man, who I assume is Mr. Jean, step in front of her. "This is my husband, Vaughn."

He gives me a cursory nod, sniffs while rubbing his finger under his mustache, and makes his way to the counter.

Grace shoots a fleeting look at him and then gives me another meek smile. "He's not a big talker. I probably make up more than enough for the both of us. But once he gets to know a person, he can rattle on, believe me."

Sounds charming.

She shifts her weight in her legs and looks me over. "What brings you into town? I mean, other than cheese," she says, tilting her head to the case.

"Really, that's it. And to pick up Tallan from school."

What's left of her smile vanishes. "Livia has you taking care of the kids, I see."

"Not entirely."

Her nose wrinkles. "Doesn't surprise me she wouldn't be taking care of her own children."

I press my lips together before clarifying: "I'm not their nanny, if that's what you think. I'm only helping here and there since, well . . ." I stop myself as I consider if Livia would want this former friend, now enemy, to know personal details about her family.

"Since?" She steps closer, and it makes me lean back.

For someone who doesn't care for Livia, you sure are prying.

"Livia's especially busy this season. She needed an extra hand," I reply brusquely.

Grace searches my face, clearly unsatisfied with my answer, and I have an urge to tell her to mind her business, but I hold my tongue.

"It's the youngest again, isn't it. Nina?"

I narrow my eyes somewhat. "Yes—how did you know?"

She scoffs. "Everyone in town saw how sick that little girl was last year. She was pretty much a ghost. What with how pale and weak she looked."

"I'm sorry?"

"Listen, I hope she's okay," she says, bulldozing on. "I do feel bad for her. For all of the children, really." She huffs once with a miffed pout on her lips.

Her blatant rudeness doesn't have me entirely seeing red. But a cloud of pink has formed.

"The children are doing more than fine. You don't need to worry. Save yourself the trouble, Grace," I say with a cautionary edge to my voice.

Her eyes flash. "Perhaps."

"Livia is a very good mother. Perhaps you should focus on your own family."

I flip my eyes toward her skulking Mr. Jean. Right then, I take note that it's no longer just the three of us in the shop.

Pete has returned from the back with two wedges of triple crème in his hands and an open mouth. Next to him stands a very amused-looking Shai, who clears his throat.

Grace's face flushes. "I wouldn't know. I don't have children," she says, barely louder than a whisper. She straightens up. "Come on, Mr. Jean. I think we need to go to our next errand."

They exit the shop swiftly without another word. Once the door shuts, Pete blows out a long whistle.

"Can someone please tell me why she calls him 'Mr. Jean'?" he asks imploringly.

"I think she finds it endearing," I answer, holding my credit card out to him.

"You want both?" He holds the wedges up like free weights.

"Yes, please."

He takes my card and the cheeses to the register.

I angle my chin sideways to get a full view of Shai.

"And you. Do you ever actually work as a veterinarian?"

Shai gives me a rolling laugh. "Yes. I swear it isn't a cover-up. I'm a licensed veterinarian in the state of Maine."

"Then *what* are you doing back there?"

"I, too, was lured here by the promise of triple crème, Radley," he answers in a somber voice. "But unlike you, who's treated like a normal paying customer, Pete had me rummage in the freezing walk-in for mine."

Shai jabs a thumb in Pete's direction, and Pete shrugs as he places my cheese in a brown paper bag. "I never told you to go in the back, Shai, if I recall correctly. You're just too comfortable helping yourself around here."

He walks around the counter and hands me the bag. "There you go, sweetie. Come by anytime and give Faye a big kiss from us when you see her."

I leave the shop and stand outside looking for my keys, only to hear the door swing open and Shai departing as well.

"Don't you have more cheese to rummage for?" I ask him, putting the handle of the bag in my mouth and feeling around in my purse for the keys.

He gently pulls the bag out from my teeth. "Hold on a sec."

I stop and stand in front of him.

"Yes?"

"That was impressive. Seeing you hold your ground like that. Defending your friends."

"Decency isn't something impressive," I say flatly. "But thank you."

I step toward my car.

"Radley," he says. "Your cheese." He holds out the bag.

"Oh," I say, reaching for it. "Thank you."

"You know, there's a restaurant on the other end of the street that features Pete and Jesse's cheeses in pasta dishes."

"Interesting fact. Thank you for that." I grip the bag.

"Let's go there. Together. For dinner."

I stare up into his earnest eyes, and I start to feel that lightness again that I did on the sailboat.

There's no harm in one time. Just one dinner.

"Dinner. *Just* dinner," I mandate.

"Sure," he says with a lopsided grin.

I walk away with the bag and jingle my keys, my back still to him. "And no more popping up in random places. It's starting to get weird."

I'm a few minutes late arriving at Fox Isle Middle School. The crowds of kids are thinner today. Tallan sits with his legs crossed under the same group of birches the foursome usually gathers under.

He's alone.

I wait for him to spot my car. When he does, to my surprise, he looks pleased. My expression matches his as he slumps into his seat.

"Sorry for being a little late," I immediately say.

"It's okay. I like sitting outside. We're indoors at desks most of the day. And I know the orchard is getting busier."

"Right," I say, pretending to agree.

He smiles, and guilt chips at me.

"Truth?" I glance at him. "I stopped at Pete and Jesse's cheese shop before I picked you up. That's why I was late."

"Did you get the triple crème?" he asks right away.

This kid . . . he's listening more than you think. He's listening for everything.

"Yes. I did. Two wedges in fact. Want to try some with me when we get home?"

Home. His home, not yours.

"That sounds good, Radley. I'm starving."

"Perfect. Your mom is going to be home later with Nina. So I think dinner is going to be late anyway."

"Where is Nina?"

"Your mom took her to a specialist."

"Oh," is all he says.

The rest of the drive home is silent. I badly want to fill this space and ease his moodiness. But as we stop at a red light, the foursome from the birches pulls up along with an older teen, likely a sibling, driving the car. The waist-length-hair girl gives out a silvery laugh and music blares, the occupants of the car oblivious to Tallan.

Tallan slides down in his seat, deeper and deeper. Wanting to be invisible. Wanting to disappear.

CHAPTER 16

"Have fun, babies! And try to keep the sugar intake at least on the not-entirely-crazy level," Livia instructs as best she can over the excited clamor of the kids.

"I can't find my hat. I've worn it to the fair every year," Tallan announces.

"Bottom of the stairs," Livia says, pointing.

"Ah." He puts a finger in the air like a gentleman signaling a waiter.

"We want cotton candy! We want cotton candy!" Avie jumps up and down, holding Nina's hand. Her eyes look brighter today, but she drags compared to her sister.

Beau slides on his jacket. "Yes, yes. Cotton candy search is on as soon as we get there." He gives Livia a quick peck on her forehead.

I wait for Livia to smile or return his affection, but she rubs her temples instead.

"I wish I could go with you all. I love the county fair. But this headache today . . ."

"I know. But I can take this one," he says. He looks over at me as I lean against the bottom post of the stairs. "You and Radley enjoy the kid-free zone for a bit."

"Okay, Nina, take it slow, remember," Livia says, squatting down and pulling her into her arms. "And I want to hear all about the carousel when you get back," she says into her ear.

Beau claps his hands together once. "All right. Go time, kiddos."

As quickly as they created an uproar, the kids and Beau exit the house, and silence takes over like a switch has been flipped.

Livia stands up and stares at the closed front door. "The fair will be good for Nina. She's been so cooped up at home, resting. I know she doesn't show it, but she's restless."

"I'm sure. She'll have fun today." I lift myself from leaning on the post. "I can give you alone time. And your headache probably needs that."

"Oh. You wouldn't want to stay?"

"But your headache," I point out.

She points to the kitchen instead. "The kids and Beau are out of the house. I'm not wasting it with a nap," she declares. She doesn't wait for me and walks straight there.

I follow.

Livia tugs at the clip holding all her hair up. It falls like slippery silk ribbons, and she shakes it out.

"Ah. Much better. That clip was so tight on my scalp." She opens the fridge and begins pulling out items. An opened bottle of chardonnay. Bowl of mussels. Stick of butter. Bundle of fresh parsley. Garlic cloves. She moves to the cupboard and selects a shaker of red pepper flakes.

"You're making dinner?" I look at the kitchen clock, a white owl with eyes that swipe back and forth with the time. "It's only four o'clock."

She pops off the cork with her mouth. "Good. We'll start with this as an appetizer then."

The glug of the wine pouring sounds inviting. She swirls the glass and places her fingers on the base of the stem. "It's okay, Radley. It's only you and me."

I arch a brow, not quite sure what she means by that.

Only you and me.

"Have you ever had Maine mussels?" she asks, pouring another glass and sipping.

"I've had mussels," I answer and take a drink.

"No. *Maine* mussels." She drags the bowl closer to me. "Everyone always talks about Maine lobster. But for me, it's the mussels."

The gas range clicks as she turns it and flips a metal pan onto a burner. The flame roars and then relents.

"You're going to become as obsessed as me when you're done tasting them."

Obsessed. Tasting.

"You know—you never really talk about your life back in Seoul," she inquires, shaking a few pats of butter and melting them down.

She tosses a few cloves of garlic at me. I catch them.

"Mince those up, will you please?"

I locate the cutting board on the island and select one of the knives from the butcher's block.

"There's not much to tell, really. I taught English after undergrad and never left."

Livia turns down the heat. "Why did you stay? Were you curious about your heritage?"

I slice through a clove and begin dicing. "Yes and no. I enjoyed learning some of the language. The food. But I think it was the buzz of Seoul. It numbed me."

She looks at me with curiosity and then down at the cutting board. "A little finer."

"Oh. Yes."

I finish mincing, and she comes to my side and wafts the garlic scent to her nose.

"That. That right there is the key to this dish. Go ahead and dump it all in."

I slide the garlic into the pan with my knife. Livia follows by dumping in the mussels. She covers it with a lid.

"Do you plan on returning to Seoul?" she asks.

"I'm not sure. Technically I'm on sabbatical from work."

She shakes her hair back and stares up. "I want to travel again. See places like that. It's hard with the kids. I hate missing out on anything;

they change on a dime, you know. But it would be nice." Her glass is nearly empty, and she fills it again and tops off mine.

"What about you? You never really talk about college. Those years." I move my glass as if clinking hers.

"Oh. *Those* years." A sly smile grows across her pillowy lips. "Definitely had some good times in college. That's where I met Beau."

She moves back to the stove and turns the heat back up. She lifts the lid and pours in chardonnay and slams it shut again. "Whoops. Didn't mean to be that loud."

I sip deeply. "You were saying. You and Beau."

Her hazel eyes are glossed and tranquil. "He was the most beautiful man I'd ever laid eyes on." Her lips sputter into a laugh. "Sorry. That sounds so clichéd, right? But it's true. He was this Adonis on campus. And we were so intense in the beginning. The attraction was like an instinct I'd finally discovered."

She traces her hand down her throat and finds a curl to rub between her fingers. I swallow and turn away.

There it is again. The deep attraction to him. What is it that's made it wane lately?

"I love my babies." She speaks quietly. "I really do. But sometimes . . ." Her voice shakes. "Sometimes it's so . . . so very hard. And I wish . . ."

What is it, Livia? What is it you wish?

I look at her now, fixated on her eyes, not letting her stop this thought.

"I wish I could see what it's like. To be alone. The space all around me only for me and no one else."

Ahh. So you see, you aren't the perfect mother.

"You're a wonderful mother, Livia." I emphasize the words. "You shouldn't think otherwise."

Her eyes. Her beautiful eyes well up, and she blinks. A tear falls from her matte lashes, and she wipes it away.

"I'm sorry, Radley. You don't want to hear me lament about motherhood."

I smile softly. "It's all right."

The lid tremors. "Oh! The mussels." She throws the lid off and gives the shells a stir. "All of them opened. Lovely."

I let her take over, finishing my glass. She chops up the parsley and adds it to the steaming mussels with a few dashes of red pepper flakes.

We sit down at the island, the pan and a loaf of crusty bread between us. She tears off a piece and dips it in the buttery broth.

"Oh my," she says, chewing slowly. Her eyes close. "I swear they get better every time."

I dip in a piece.

"You lied," I say.

Her eyes fly open. "What?"

"You lied. That you aren't a good cook. This is incredible, Livia." I pull out the mussel from its shell and let it slide into my mouth.

She laughs. "I can cook only a handful of dishes. And this is one of them."

We continue dipping bread and finishing off the mussels.

I reach for another shell, and Livia's gaze meets mine.

"All right. You and Shai. What's going on there?" She playfully clinks her glass to mine and finishes what's left of hers.

I stare at her empty glass.

"Nothing. He's . . ."

"Gorgeous," she finishes and then giggles.

I nod toward her. "Okay. I won't deny that."

"Radley," she says with a deadpan gawk. "If he were one of these mussels, most women would devour him."

Heavy on the wine. Heavy on the words, Livia.

I scoff. "I'm not most women."

She winks at me. "That you aren't. That you aren't, Radley." She fills her glass again, and I scoot closer.

My turn.

"Come on, Livia. It's not like you're married to an ogre."

She wiggles back and forth on her stool. "Beau is attractive, yes."

"Didn't you just call him the most beautiful man you'd ever laid eyes on?"

She holds up a finger slowly and pauses. "Yes. Yes, I did."

"Most women would do anything to be in your shoes." I take a bite of bread and wait for her to respond, but there's nothing but silence. I look up at her face, which has turned blank.

Oh dear. I've malfunctioned the poor woman.

"I mean—"

"It's true. Most women would."

Something has changed in her voice. It's not tender like before. This time there are thorns attached to each syllable.

"But that doesn't mean our marriage hasn't had issues."

"Issues?"

"Yes. When someone in the marriage steps outside the line."

An affair.

But she never says the word. Even though I can see it traced around her mouth, ready to puff out like a smoke signal.

I expect her to say something else about what she means. But she doesn't. Instead, she reaches out and traces the top of my forearm. "Your skin, Radley."

My spine tingles with alarm and curiosity.

"So flawless and smooth. You're like a doll. A porcelain doll."

CHAPTER 17

I stand and stare at myself in my car's side-view mirror, wondering why I agreed to dinner with Shai.

My appearance admittedly seems to have improved since I arrived at Clark Orchard. Maybe it really is that New England air, as Alice said, or getting out of the rat wheel of the corporate office. I have traded dull overhead lights for seaside sunsets and dewy orchard mornings. Whatever it is, my complexion looks rosier. My tresses are fuller, and I've let them grow out some.

I had only one or two items in my wardrobe to even consider wearing to dinner. I selected the forest-green knit dress. I'd be comfortable and look somewhat feminine in it.

Shai had asked to pick me up. But I declined, wanting to make this as far from a date as possible. Meeting at the restaurant would be more like what friends do.

As I adjust my coat and open my car door, I hear yelling coming from the main house.

"Radley!" a voice calls.

I peer in the glow of dusk to see Avie running over the hill. Behind her are Nina and the rest of the family minus Tallan, Beau with his hands in his pockets, and Livia striding next to him.

"Wait! We have something for you," Avie calls out.

I hold the door open and wait as instructed. Avie reaches me first. She breathes in and out quickly.

"We wanted to see you off. On your date."

"It's not really a date," I correct her.

"That's not what Mommy said."

The rest of the family members have caught up. Nina leans against Livia and smiles faintly. Her fading demeanor cuts at me in a way I wasn't expecting.

"Nina. You didn't have to walk all this way," I say to her.

She comes over and takes my hand, squeezing it once. "I like your dress," she says weakly.

I glance up at Livia and Beau, who look at her with concern but then wipe their expressions away once Nina turns back to face them.

"The girls wanted to make sure you had something extra special for your date," Livia explains. She reaches into her pocket and pulls out two turquoise stone studs.

"I picked them out," Avie boasts proudly.

I take each one carefully and place them on my ears.

"So pretty," she says.

"The color accents your dress well. You're such a beauty, Radley," Livia adds with admiring eyes.

I want to correct her. I almost do, feeling the protest rise in my throat. I've been called many things in my life. But a beauty wasn't one of them.

I notice Beau then inspecting me as if searching for any evidence to support Livia's assessment of my appearance tonight. But then he looks away as if embarrassed to be gazing at me.

"You look . . . you look very nice, Radley," he says quietly.

He gives me a small smile, and I nod.

"I'll return these tomorrow." I rub the studs.

Livia waves it off. "Wear them as long as you want. Besides . . ." She pauses slyly. "After seeing you tonight, I'm sure you'll have other occasions to wear them with Shai."

Beau turns his head at Livia, the two of them sharing a brief exchange of looks I can't decipher. A subtle grimace tightens against his jaw, and he clears his throat like a disapproving older brother. And I wonder right then if Jem would have behaved the same way.

As the final hints of light hit the surface of the water, I meet Shai at the restaurant at the end of the wharf. He stands under the hanging wood sign painted in nautical white and navy: **Blue Dahlia**. In his hands are three . . . blue dahlias.

He grins and holds his hands up as if defending himself. "Before you roll your eyes."

I groan a little but take the flowers. The stems are fresh and stiff.

"I know. This is too literal. But I thought we could get some skepticism out of the way by starting out with some true cheesiness."

My lips, which had been straight and pressed together, tilt up a little.

"I'm starving," I tell him. "So there's that to contend with. And yes. This is ridiculously corny. But," I say, sniffing the dahlias, "these are lovely. Thank you."

His eyes are wide and innocent with relief, and I can't help but insert another little jab.

"Let's go see how good this pasta is. It might be your one saving grace."

He opens the door for me and chuckles. "Yes, ma'am."

The restaurant is small, candlelit, and cozy, with a view of the waterfront. Thick tablecloths drape petite round tables.

I place the flowers on our table as he pushes my chair in and takes a seat across from me.

"Okay. The wit about the flowers I can manage. But the undoubtedly romantic restaurant. This is only a dinner. Remember?"

"Yes." He deeply nods, and when his head comes up level, his smile thaws me a little. "You're absolutely correct. Two people. You. Me. Having pasta that I pushed on you as delicious. Dinner."

I eye him suspiciously and place the napkin on my lap. "All right, let's eat then."

We order pasta and drinks from the server, me a pinot noir, Shai a club soda.

"It's not that I can't or won't drink alcohol," he says, taking a sip, "but it never appealed to me. I love a clear head."

I shrug. "It doesn't bother me either way. Your choice."

The server places a basket of steaming garlic knots in the center.

Shai reaches for one, and I do the same. "Okay. I've got to get something straight first."

I pull mine apart, and the steam rises like a butter facial. "All right."

"You left the modern metropolis of Seoul and what I can only imagine was an exciting life to work at a small apple orchard in Maine. Why?"

The soft piece of bread in my mouth melts. "For starters? It wasn't so exciting. My job wasn't fulfilling. And secondly, I did something I hardly ever do."

"What's that?"

"Make a move on a whim."

He tosses the rest of his garlic knot in his mouth. "You're brave."

"Brave?" I question.

"I've never lived like that. Every move I've made has been as careful as chess. Planned. Safe."

"That doesn't mean you're not brave."

"Fox Isle is only forty miles from my hometown," he says pointedly.

"Born and raised in Maine?"

"Yes. And yes, I've always wanted to be a veterinarian."

I grin. "How did you know I was going to ask that?"

He fans his hands out. "For some reason, people always ask me that question. Curious as to how I became committed to animals, I guess."

"Animals are better than people most of the time," I say, taking a drink of my wine.

"I won't argue with that." He folds his napkin again on his lap. "If I'm being completely honest, it was my little sister that wanted to be a vet first."

The usual good-humored sheen to his eyes fades a bit.

"She was a gentle soul," he says. "She would have been amazing at it."

"Would have?"

He tilts his head quickly as if bitten and in pain. "She passed when we were kids. It's been a long time."

"Oh . . ."

"But sometimes it does feel like yesterday."

"I'm sorry, Shai."

I take a moment to observe him. We've certainly joked about the cynical wall I've built, which has made me take him less seriously. But perhaps I've never given Shai a chance, assuming he couldn't possibly be more than a handsome face with a pleasant demeanor.

But I could be wrong.

I'm beginning to sense a spool we share, that maybe a thread from it has managed to wind its way around me. Because of a lightness he's brought.

"I know what that's like," I tell him.

He gives me a gentle gaze. "I'm sorry to hear that's also the case for you, Radley." He doesn't press further, and for some reason that eases me even more.

The pasta arrives, glistening fettucine speckled with grated cheese and black pepper.

"The pecorino romano in this cacio e pepe is from Pete and Jesse's store. You'll never want to eat any other pasta again."

I raise my brows, twirl my fork, and take a bite.

Well, he's definitely not a liar.

"Okay," I say once. I go in for another bite. "Okay." I point to him. "You are absolutely right about this dish."

He looks pleased with my response and finishes his bite. "I feel like you're not the kind of woman to say 'I told you so' to."

I laugh. "Most likely."

"It's just as well. It's not my favorite phrase in the world."

As we continue to make the pasta disappear from our plates, I learn more about Shai and how he was once married to his high school sweetheart. That they realized they weren't really the same people five years in, when she wanted to move to Los Angeles, and he wanted to build his practice here. How he isn't afraid to admit he likes being alone sometimes and that caring for animals is his fuel.

I realize that I've laughed more in the last hour than I have in months—perhaps years—when my midsection aches a bit from the hilarity of his stories of vet calamities.

Shai has a way of making it all seem not so damn serious.

And whether I've needed that doesn't matter. I feel like I'm floating for once.

After the candles have burned down low and our plates are long finished, Shai walks me to my car, which I don't object to. The sound of ocean waves lulls me, and he turns to face me. It's this movement that wakes me up again.

"Shai . . . I enjoyed—no, that's not even true—I loved our dinner."

His lips curl softly. "Me too."

I make sure he is listening. That he doesn't miss me looking at him. "But I'm not someone you want to know. I mean, in that way. You know what I'm getting at? Believe me. I'll have spared you."

He shakes his head. "Radley. I'll spare you the time." His eyes shine with kindness. "And believe me: You are someone I want to get to know."

CHAPTER 18

"Buckle up. It's the busiest time of the season," Faye warns me with a cackle. "And it's happening next weekend."

She pulls a string of tangled lights from a box. "Here, dearie. Help me unravel these suckers. I like to up the amount of twinkle lights each Harvest Festival. I want to hang so many around the store we create a blackout in Fox Isle." She holds her hands up and wiggles her fingers.

I start to pull another end out. "Harvest Festival?"

Andrea pats my shoulder before placing another box on the ground. "Second week of October. Finale to peak season before the weather gets colder. It's a lot of excitement, but Faye isn't joking. Next weekend is going to be hectic."

I loop out a knot, the pointed ends of the bulbs poking me. "Will Luna be visiting for it?"

She shakes her head wistfully. "Not this year. She was thinking about it, but her midterms are coming up, and she wants to really focus on that. I understand. But . . ." A dreamy look spreads across her face. "The Harvest Festival does mean we're getting closer to the closing on the laundromat."

The return of Andrea's bright nature as she seems to think about the laundromat and Boston makes me smile a little.

"What's that grin about, Radley?" Faye asks boldly. "I heard something about the veterinarian. Dr. Shark Fin . . . Shai Fin. Whatever his name is."

I laugh at her blunder and then grow serious. "There's nothing to what you heard, Faye. Because there's nothing going on."

Andrea winks at me and opens another box of lights.

"Right!" Faye shoots back. "I may be old, but I'm not blind or deaf yet."

"I'm going to go bring in the rest of the boxes," Andrea tells us.

Faye gives her a thumbs-up. "Sounds like a plan. We'll keep working on these lights. Tame them one way or another."

After a half hour of mainly cursing from Faye, wondering "Who put these away like this?" and then finally making neat, looped piles of lights, she pulls at my arm, announcing a break.

"Let's go on over to the house, Radley. Have a little cider. This untangling has got me all heated."

We settle on the front steps with mason jars of cold cider. Faye leans back on her elbows and kicks off her work boots, revealing colorful, striped, mismatched socks.

"Like 'em? Got them at this funny little boutique in Charleston last year."

"They are indeed hard to miss," I reply, setting the glass jar down between my legs.

She gives me a playful scowl. "You may be a reserved one, Radley, but there's spice in there, I see."

I lift my chin up, not entirely denying this. "I'm not sure if 'spice' is the right word."

Faye bumps me with her shoulder. "How is Radley these days? You look good, from what I can tell."

"I feel like I'm standing firmer. Routine can be a very helpful thing."

She moves closer. "I hope the orchard has been treating you well."

I can feel her studying me from the side.

"Of course."

"Yes, well, one can never be too sure about outward appearances . . ."

She stops there and takes a rare pause.

"When are you taking the *Calypso* down south? Soon, isn't it?" I ask.

She smacks her lips from the cider. "I've decided to skip this go-around. Jesse and Pete are getting a turn."

"That's good then. We'll be seeing more of you."

"Yes. Plus, my cottage in the West Hills needs some sprucing. Too many winters spent away on the *Calypso*."

"You like living alone out there?"

She shrugs. "The orchard will always have my heart. But after Jonah died . . . it became too hard being here. It's enough to live close by . . . to see these chickadees of mine as they're growing faster than ever. And then of course, little Nina."

She grows quiet and then drinks her cider.

Beau and the kids burst through the front doors, Avie in a fit of giggles as he tickles her and carries her under his arm like a rag doll.

Faye squints up. "Did I conjure my chickadees? I was just talking about you all."

"Yes. You may have, Mother," Beau says before scooping up Nina and putting her on his shoulders.

"I joke with Beau that I'm actually part witch; sometimes I have scary intuition. A good witch, mind you."

"That or you're a mind reader," he grunts as Avie tackles his leg, falling to the ground in dramatic fashion. He carefully pulls Nina down from his neck and sets her next to him.

"Livia go into town?" Faye asks.

"Yes, picking up some supplies ordered for the Harvest Festival," Beau answers with a shrug. "She insisted on going in my place."

Tallan trails behind with his book at his side and silently sits on the front porch swing.

"How's my bookworm today?" Faye looks over her shoulder to ask him.

He opens the book and half smiles. "Hi, Grandma Faye," he says before turning his attention to the book.

She gives me a knowing glance. "Beau was like that at his age."

I look over at Beau, who's pretending to body-slam Avie as he places her on the ground with an exaggerated angry growl. Nina, with a rare burst of energy, reaches to him for her turn.

"I find that hard to believe. He's so upbeat and extroverted."

"He is now. But it can be tough when you're a young boy, facing becoming a young man, and you idolize your father."

"What do you mean?" I ask, despite having some inkling, based on what Beau told me when he was teaching me to prune. I don't let on that I'm aware.

Faye slides her empty glass on the step away from her. "Jonah was a good man. He really was, in all the ways a person should be. Honest, hardworking, intelligent. And he was charismatic as hell. Swept me off my feet, that's for sure."

I lean back into the step to listen.

"But he could be very hard to please. His Achilles was his inability to acknowledge when something was done right. It's not that he would criticize constantly. But for Beau, all he wanted was to hear his father say he was proud."

I shake my head. "That's not an easy way to grow up."

"It wasn't. And sometimes I worry if he still carries that."

The girls lie on the ground on each side of Beau, laughing with their eyes shut as he continues to play the role of a beast ready to attack.

I swing my legs to face Faye on the steps.

"Carries?"

She rubs under her nose with her index finger and sniffs a few times. I'm not quite sure if she's holding in tears or memories coming to the surface.

"When Jonah passed, I thought maybe he'd let go of all that. But in some ways . . . it made it worse."

"How so?"

"The perfection. The constant quest for perfection to make up for Jonah's permanent absence . . . one can only take so much, you know," she says bleakly.

I place my hand on Faye's knee for a few seconds. "But he turned out to be different from his father, though. I mean, in that way."

She nods. "He is. He's a very good father."

Her acknowledging smile fades slowly as we watch the girls and Beau. The corners of her mouth are forced and brittle, like two posts trembling to stay upright.

CHAPTER 19

It's raining today.

The hard stinging wind beats against Dr. Edair's windows. The view of the harbor has become a blurry painting.

I reach for her dish of candies and take a red one. Hot cinnamon burns my mouth in a way that livens me.

"Where did we leave off last time?" I ask her. She was out of town last week, and I feel like so much has happened since our second session.

Saliva pools in one side of my mouth, and I roll the candy to the other.

She doesn't answer me right away. Her greeting seemed a few degrees colder than usual today. Still pleasant, but the shade has taken over, and a solemn Dr. Edair remains. I try to think back on our last session—if I said anything that could have offended her. Could it be my probing of her relationship with her wife? But she didn't seem bothered at the time.

"Yes," she finally says to me slowly. "We were discussing that family . . . the perfect family."

There's something accusatory in the way she says this. But there's something else . . . some other note I can't quite put my finger on yet.

What is it? What is it she seems to be troubled by?

"Does it bother you?" I ask, staring squarely into Dr. Edair's face.

She squints her eyes as if she can't quite see me. As if the rain has an effect on not just the window but her sight.

"Does what bother me?"

"That I'm obsessed with this perfect family."

"No. No, it doesn't bother me," she answers right away.

"But something does seem to be bothering you."

The cinnamon candy has dissolved to the size of a tiny pebble. I crunch into it, and my tongue is briefly on fire.

She takes in a breath and then shakes her head. "Radley—let's focus on you. Go on. Please tell me more about this family."

She's switched her calm meditating voice back on.

She's evading my questions.

I decide to go with her direction, steering me back to what she wants to discuss.

"The mother," I start with. "I've been watching her more. She's troubled lately."

"Why do you think that is?"

"Her daughter. She's upset about her daughter."

"Have you tried talking to her about this? Consoling her?"

"No," I say, turning away to face the shelves. I notice Dr. Edair has added another sailboat to her collection. This one clear glass, maybe expensive crystal, placed on the center shelf.

I point to the sailboat. "That's new, isn't it?"

She glances over at the shelf. "Yes," she answers with reluctance at our veering away again.

"From your wife, Harriet? An anniversary present, I presume." I stand up and walk over to the shelf. "May I?"

She shifts her gaze to me nervously. She blinks it away and gives me a half smile. "That's fine."

I lift the glass sailboat. The underside is smooth. I place my index finger on the top of the mast, the fine end pricking me.

"It's very pretty."

She edges forward in her seat like she's trying to prevent me from breaking it. "Swarovski crystal. Harriet had a business trip to Vienna, so I tagged along."

"What kind of business does Harriet conduct?" I cautiously place the glass sculpture back on the shelf, making sure it's in the exact position I found it.

"She's also a doctor. She had a speaking engagement on urology."

I turn to face Dr. Edair. "How nice of her. To get you something so beautiful."

"Yes. Yes it was." She places her hands on her thighs and presses down. "Radley. I'll be direct here. Let's return to our discussion. About the mother."

The mother.

"All right. I can tell you more about this mother."

She motions back to the chaise. I oblige and lie back this time.

"I'm really interested in her. What is it you were saying?"

"She's troubled."

"Yes, troubled. About her daughter."

The mother and her daughter.

"What else troubles the mother?"

"She's troubled because she's no longer perfect. She's realizing that she might not be enough for her family. At least she thinks she's not enough. You see, that's the problem with being a mother. A mother is expected to be everything to the family, but they certainly aren't enough to be everything for her."

Dr. Edair rests her chin on her hand. She observes me before sitting up straight, and that's when I notice she's not writing notes today. "That's an interesting point, Radley."

"She's weary. On the inside," I go on. "She's worn down to the bone, even though on the outside, she looks like she floats, graceful and flawless from one task to the next. When no one suspects the storm that brews under her skin as they watch her. But she's become mush. Unidentifiable mush inside."

I stare up at Dr. Edair. "Because even she can't identify herself anymore."

My voice grows louder. At least I think it has. But it also seems to ring in my ears like an echo. "She thinks she isn't doing enough. For her husband. For her child. Can you believe that?" I laugh dryly. "Not enough."

Dr. Edair gets up from her chair. She wears a pleated midi skirt, flowing fabric that drops heavily the second she stands.

"What do you want for the mother then?"

"What?" I ask. I sound exasperated. I don't look at her.

"The mother. You find her to be unhappy. Lost."

"Yes."

"Then what do you wish for her instead?"

"I wish . . . ," I start to say. "I wish for her to see what she has."

Dr. Edair takes two steps toward me. I straighten, stiffening as she gets closer.

"What are you doing?"

She exhales with urgency. "Radley. Do you trust me?"

"Trust you? Why are you asking that?"

"Do you trust that as your doctor, I'm looking out for your best interests?" Her expression has changed to one of resolve and concern.

"Yes. I do."

She dips her head. "All right. Then I think it's time you start being honest."

"I am honest—"

"With me. With yourself."

I slide up until my head is raised above the top of the chaise. "Dr. Edair. What are you trying to tell me?"

She taps her fingers together. "After our last session, I felt the need . . . well, I had to look further into your records. They were sent to me from your previous psychiatrist's office in Seoul. I read them. The entirety of them."

Unidentifiable mush inside.

"Radley, do you understand what I'm getting at here?"

I focus on the crystal sailboat again. I imagine it dipping up and down with the waves. Water crashing everywhere.

Dr. Edair's words sound so far away now.

"I know what happened, Radley. What you've been through."

She can't identify herself anymore.

"Are you ready to start talking about this family? This perfect family?"

I feel the first and last hot tear. I'm not going to let any more escape. These eyes are dried-out wells. These eyes can't cry anymore. Not like that, not ever again like that.

"In their true context."

What do you wish for her . . .

I'm engrossed in Dr. Edair's lips. They speak at me, moving in and out, forming undecipherable shapes.

"Are you ready to admit that this family . . . is really your family?"

I had a family. I had a family of my own once.

CHAPTER 20

Nina sits quietly, wrapped in a flannel blanket. The fringed ends drift up with the breeze, feathering against her cheeks. The branches of the tree she's under quiver and then grow still. Her eyes flutter until she seems to go to sleep.

"The fresh air is good for her," Livia says as she watches her.

Rabbit pads up to us where we sit nearby. He nuzzles my elbow, and I stroke his ears a few times before he sits up dutifully and points his snout at Nina with a vigilant stare.

"Her doctor referred her to a specialist in Portland," Livia says, watching her. She crosses her arms, and I notice the dark circles under her eyes.

"What did the doctor say is wrong?"

She shakes her head. "He's not sure. She's clinically anemic. But all the iron supplements, steroid treatments, and usual medications that worked before aren't helping."

"Do they know what caused this?"

Livia tosses one hand up. "That's the thing. She's been anemic before. Last year her numbers were low, and her energy correlated. It's common enough in children, especially for picky eaters like Nina. So, we made sure she got more iron in her diet. The medication helped, and she seemed okay for the most part. But now . . ."

We both go still as Nina stirs, her brow furrows, and she yawns before turning to her side.

"Our fun-loving baby wants to nap all day. I've pulled her out of school temporarily. At least until we talk to the specialist."

"What will the specialist do?" I ask, bringing my knees into my chest.

"Rule out anything more serious," Livia says as sturdily as she can. "But her doctor is a little dumbfounded. Her other labs are fine."

"But she'll be getting care she needs."

Livia nods and bites her lip. "Yeah."

I find myself wanting to comfort her. "Don't worry, Livia. They'll figure it out. That's what the specialist is for. And then she'll get her energy back."

"Thank you," she whispers.

I nod and give her upper arm a rub.

"You're a godsend. You know that, Radley?"

"I'm not," I tell her quickly.

"I don't know what I'd do without you dropping off and picking up Tallan. He's so moody, and I know he's a preteen, but geez . . . it's all I need right now." She picks at some grass and tosses it to the side.

"He's a good kid. Incredibly smart. You don't need to worry about him."

It's true. I didn't tell her that only to ease her worries. Tallan has an introspective nature that's unusual for his age. A torment now but possibly a gift later in life.

She wipes at her nose with a tissue and gives me a halfhearted smile. "Yes. He is quite smart. Always mature for his age. I used to call him 'my little gentleman' when he was a baby. So serious even then."

"I could see that," I say, picturing Tallan as a stiff-upper-lipped infant.

Livia sighs. "I'll be taking her to Portland tomorrow before the Harvest Festival weekend. I want to get a lot of these tests and scans done before then, and they tell me they should be able to get everything done in one day. I feel so guilty not giving the older two my attention. You know what Avie asked me the other night?"

I give her a sympathetic lift of my eyebrows.

"'Mommy, why is it you love Nina more than me?'" She clutches her chest. "I know she doesn't mean that. It's what little kids do to get a reaction. But I can't help but wonder . . . Does she really think that? Feel that?"

I tilt my head. "I imagine it's tough, trying to keep it all on an even keel."

"Thank God you've been there for her more."

"Livia—"

"Stop, Radley," she says firmly.

My eyes flash at her sudden boldness.

"You being here. It's made our lives better. And I want you to know that. Really—"

"Okay, Livia." It's all I can manage to sputter out. To halt her glowing review of me that only makes me feel smaller.

A far-off look takes over her face. "And now with Nina and having to drive farther . . ." Her voice trails off, and she places a fist under her chin.

Around noon, Livia corrals the rest of the family inside for lunch. She doles out crunchy grilled cheese sandwiches and creamy tomato soup, dollops of sour cream in the middle.

Tallan eats slowly, examining each bite and keeping quiet as usual.

Avie pesters Livia, asking if she can help clear the dishes and clean the counter for her; Livia patiently reminds her each time that they're still finishing their lunches.

Nina nibbles on a crust as she rests in Livia's lap.

"Try to eat a little more if you can, baby," she coaxes her. "A bite or two more, and then you can go rest in your bed."

Beau strides in late, forehead glistening with sweat. He immediately goes to the sink to get a glass of water.

"How's Nina?" he asks as he catches his breath.

Livia doesn't look up as she answers, stroking Nina's hair. "She got some fresh air today. Spent some time under her favorite tree with me and Radley."

"That's good," he says, washing his hands and giving me a nod.

"I'm glad you had time to come inside for lunch," she says, looking over her shoulder at him. "Now I can share the news with Radley."

I pause from taking a bite of my sandwich half. "News?"

"Yes. We have some news," she says serenely.

Beau leans against the counter with both hands on the edge, seemingly unaware of what she has to say.

"Radley," she says, turning to me. "We would love for you to move into the main house."

My head grows warm and tingles. I feel blindsided. Yet I don't immediately protest. I don't squash this idea straightaway.

Avie exclaims that she loves the idea. I quickly look at Tallan, who at least doesn't seem dismayed by such a proposal.

I point to my chest as if still uncertain of who she's referring to. "You want me . . ."

"To live in our house," Livia finishes for me. "There's a spare room across from Tallan's and Avie's rooms."

"Are you sure you really—"

"Yes, Livia. Are you sure this is what Radley wants?" Beau interrupts.

He appears stunned and steps away from the counter and then looks at Livia. Nina slides down from her lap and finds her way into mine.

"Radley, please stay. Stay with us," she says in a faint voice.

"I'm not leaving or anything, Nina." I slip my arms around her. "I'm nearby in the guest cottage."

"You see?" adds Beau, giving Livia an inconspicuous glance.

"Radley, we need you closer," Livia retorts. "I'll be gone a lot with Nina and who knows how much more, depending on the results from this visit. The guest cottage is close, but it's not the same as having you here with the kids."

Beau's face hardens. "Livia. Why don't you let Radley decide for herself?"

His obvious reluctance pushes me to begin a polite refusal. I open my mouth to launch into one until a tiny finger traces my chin.

"Please, Radley. I want you here. I'm alone, other than Mommy," Nina whispers, her eyes half closed, and a face so pale and small.

Please, Radley . . .

Please, Mommy . . .

Another small voice calls to me briefly. I take Nina's hand.

"All right. I'll move my things."

The evening is quieter inside the house.

My view of this family will no longer be from afar. Their sounds, words, and flesh will all be there for me to be part of.

I live in this house now. I live in the middle of their lives.

I didn't have much to bring over. My move into the spare room didn't take long. Beau, despite his odd dissent to the whole idea, of course, in true Beau fashion, swiftly helped me without a complaint. He didn't chat with me like he usually does; instead he avoided any unnecessary time with me once I was settled.

I don't remember him making much eye contact. He hurriedly returned to work, saying something about the Harvest Festival.

The spare room is a decent size. I have my own bathroom, and the walls are thin enough that I can hear Avie and Nina giggling across the hallway. It's nice listening to both of them being silly. Nina's laughter has been missing from inside this house.

Their playful banter is a welcoming hum in the background as I hang up my clothes and once again unpack. After a while, I stop to cock an ear up like Rabbit would. There is such silence I step out into the hallway.

Whispers. Soft at first and then rapid, like a whirling windstorm.

I place my hand on the doorknob. It opens suddenly, and I fall into the room.

The girls sit on the floor, having a tea party. They must have moved their set from the playroom into Avie's bedroom.

Tallan stands in the doorway. His body unintentionally blocks me. His cheeks red and flushed, his eyes averted. I can't tell if he's upset or angry.

He doesn't stay long enough for me to find out, swiftly brushing past me with a guilty hunch of his back.

CHAPTER 21

I place a snack of apples and sliced cheese in front of Nina and Avie. They sit across from each other in the playroom and thank me simultaneously.

Avie gawks up at me with mischievous eyes. "Are you doing anything tonight, Radley?"

"Huh?" I kneel next to her. "*Doing* anything?"

"Yeah. Anything special?"

"Not in particular," I respond absently, leaning back to listen for Livia, who's taken a call in the other room. I'm assuming it's the doctor with news about Nina.

"Okey dokey then," Avie sings. She smiles, showing all her teeth, a squish of cheese between her two front ones.

Livia returns, her phone in one hand, the other on her hip.

"Was that the doctor?" I mouth quietly.

She shakes her head. "No. He won't be calling for another day likely. It's about Pepper."

"Pepper?"

"Her leg has been acting up today, and she needs more pain meds. Do you think you could please run over and pick them up?"

That would mean going to Shai's office.

I haven't seen him since the night at Blue Dahlia. He's tried calling twice, but I haven't returned his calls. I thought I said everything I had to say that night. At least that was how I was going to leave it.

"I know what you're thinking," she immediately inserts. "But his office closes soon, and you'll need to pick them up at the front desk from his vet tech. Poor Pepper." She sighs. "She's not herself today."

I look over at Avie and Nina, both watching me expectantly.

Poor Pepper indeed.

"I'll stop over there quick."

Livia puts her hands together. "Great. Thank you."

I rise to get my jacket and purse.

"Oh, and Radley. Beau and I are going to have a movie night with the girls. If you want some alone time, that is."

"Okay . . . I could use that," I say as I head out.

The Fox Isle Animal Clinic's windows appear dark when I pull up.

Maybe it's already closed.

I consider turning back but resolve to at least give it a shot. I knock on the entrance door, only to discover it's unlocked.

"Hello?" I ask as I walk inside.

No one answers, and I find the reception desk unoccupied.

Shai pops his head around the corner. I jump, startled.

"Radley," he says, holding up both hands as if surrendering. "I'm so sorry. Did I scare you?"

"Yes," I answer briskly. "Are you closed? Where's your tech? I came to pick up medicine for Pepper."

He grins sheepishly. "Pepper is actually fine. And my tech left early for the night."

"Pepper is fine? How do you know?"

He hesitates. "I thought this would be romantic. But now I see it's giving creepy vibes."

I scrutinize Shai's face in the dim lighting. "Romantic."

He steps forward. "Listen, Radley. I wanted to see you again. And at the risk of sounding even creepier, I enlisted Livia's help."

I cross my arms. "So, there is no Pepper emergency."

"No."

"And this was all a guise to get me here." I whip my finger around in the air.

"Yes," he answers tentatively.

"Why?"

"I . . . like you, Radley." His face pinkens at the childish nature of his statement.

"Shai—"

"You're undeniably frank. I feel there's nothing disingenuous in anything you do. And that's refreshing to be around," he says in a steady stream of words. "There. I've said it."

I wonder what he'd really think of me if he knew the whole truth.

"Sucking up won't help, Shai."

He settles with a slight grin. "I was hoping it would."

I shrug. "Shai, any woman would be flattered by this attention. That's hard to deny."

He casts his eyes on me with a more serious gaze. "I'm not sure why you think you're not worth knowing. But maybe let me be the judge of that, Radley."

I stand motionless, unable to come up with a rebuttal.

He steps closer and then points over his shoulder to the back. "Only if you're willing . . . there's a small surprise outside waiting for you."

I raise my eyebrows. "Another surprise?"

"I think you might like this one." He puts his hands out. A symbol for me to try to trust him. To maybe let go for a little while longer . . .

I put my hand in his. His touch is unfamiliar. Not because we haven't held hands before. But because it's been so long since I've allowed such a connection.

He doesn't let go. I follow him out to the back of the clinic, to find an unexpected view of the ocean, the sun beginning to dip into the horizon. A wicker picnic basket sits between two folded blankets.

"We can sit in chairs, if that makes you more comfortable," he says right away.

I look at him with amusement. "A sunset picnic. You went even cheesier."

"I had to raise the bar," he quips.

"The blanket is fine."

We settle on the soft ground. Shai pulls out sandwiches wrapped in parchment paper.

"I didn't know if you were more of a turkey or a ham girl. But then I thought, What if she's chicken salad?"

"I only eat tuna," I say starkly.

His face falls a little, and I hit his arm. "I'm kidding. Any sandwich is fine, thank you."

I sit back and watch as he lays out a fruit and vegetable platter, a large bag of salt and vinegar chips, and a plastic container of brownies.

"You also bake?"

He chuckles. "My vet tech. She also bakes wedding cakes on the side."

I shoot him a playful look.

"Not that I asked about one."

We both laugh, and I realize I love the way his mouth goes lopsided when he does this. When he really thinks something is funny.

I unwrap a turkey sandwich, and he relaxes back with a chicken salad one. We don't discuss anything serious—our voices held above a floating line that keeps us content. It's chatter between two people. Two people who could have known each other for ages, sharing a picnic by the sea.

I let myself pretend. I pretend that there can be more than this. That I'm capable of giving myself fully to this man who has given nothing but an open heart for me to see. To have faith that sometimes the world isn't here to swallow me whole. That he is here to try to ease me.

To maybe care for each other.

I look up into the sky to see a breathtaking swirl of deep rose and clouds.

When I bring my head down, I can see Shai also staring up and admiring. Maybe it's his ability to be present. His persistence in trying to make someone like me feel worthy. Worthy of attention, worthy of maybe a little something close to happiness.

I'm not sure what exactly. But I don't resist any urges anymore.

I reach out and touch his chin. Pulling it down gently, I lean in until our noses almost touch. He looks surprised for only a millisecond before moving forward. I meet his lips with mine, and for a moment, I wish that I could be someone who could fall for him.

And perhaps I did. Even for a little while.

I pull back and look into his eyes.

I'm sorry, Shai.

He sees what I'm trying to tell him, and he shakes his head once. But I stand up hurriedly to leave. I don't try to see if he moves to stop me. I think I hear him call my name, but it doesn't matter. My body has gone cold. It stays that way as I drive home.

CHAPTER 22

The long line of orchard visitors grows every time I look up from the register. I attempt to hand a receipt to the college-aged woman across from me, who snaps a quick selfie of the store behind her.

"Oh, sorry," she says through an exaggerated smile. She grabs the receipt without looking at me and pauses to take another picture.

"Your bag," I tell her, holding up her apples and jar of preserves.

"Thanks so much," she sings and saunters with swinging hips to examine her phone.

Andrea rolls her eyes at me from across the barn as she restocks the shelves with apple butter and proceeds to shake her head with a knowing wink.

The demanding nature of Saturday—or "Day One," as Andrea dramatically called it earlier—of the Harvest Festival was not an exaggeration. There doesn't seem to be one spot in the space by the store that isn't dotted with visitors. It's strange to see the usually peaceful orchard grounds become a drone of consumers' voices.

Tallan trudges by my side of the register with a crate of Honeycrisps. We already sold out of the initial stock in the store this morning.

"Is it over yet?" he asks me with a deadened face.

"Is what over?"

"The Harvest Festival," he groans.

Beau catches up behind him with two more crates. "Come on, buddy. We have more to fill the bins with," he says cheerily.

The drudgery of the festival weekend to Tallan contrasts with the exhilaration Beau exhibits on this busy day. He's in his element, hopping from one task to the next, making sure each visitor feels welcome, his attentive aura on high gear, greeting every face he encounters with a warm smile.

I give Tallan a sympathetic squeeze on his shoulder before the next customer in line assaults me with questions about where to find the kettle corn. Beau and Tallan empty their crates and walk out of the store side by side to go back for more.

"Next hayride to the field is in fifteen! Fifteen, that's one-five!" Faye yells from the entrance. She holds her hands up and then grins widely at me.

Most of the visitors in the store are too busy selecting apples or browsing to take notice, the noise getting louder and louder. Faye skips away, stopping to adjust a string of her prized lights by the entrance before moving on to yell out to the next group of people she comes across.

"I can take over for a bit if you want. You can go see if Livia needs help with anything," Andrea says loudly in my ear, trying to talk over the buzz of the crowd.

I gratefully nod at her and finish up the transaction I'm in the middle of before swiftly exiting the chaos of the store out into the open air.

Livia is camped out in the garden seating area, Nina sitting by her side. Her small face is tilted up to the warmth of the sun. She's so still it makes me hold my breath, waiting for her to make any movement. As I approach, her eyes open and she smiles.

"Radley," she says as she reaches for me, and some of the day's stress melts away at her sweet mannerism.

I slide next to her on the bench, and she nuzzles her head into my shoulder.

"We're taking a break," Livia explains to me. "Someone was getting a little overwhelmed with all the excitement."

"I bet," I say, patting Nina's small arm.

"I was actually talking about myself," Livia says.

We both laugh, and among the frenzied noise of passing visitors, our small unit sits close to each other on the bench, somehow managing to relax.

I know it will be a short-lived moment of peace, as I need to get up soon to help customers again. But before I have a chance to get motivated, we're unfortunately disturbed.

I feel Livia abruptly shift in her seat next to me.

I don't need to ask why. I follow her startled gaze to find Grace and Mr. Jean. They've made a rare appearance on Clark Orchard grounds.

Grace stands tall with her head up high, as if to shield herself from any scrutiny. A lurking Mr. Jean skulks to the store as she remains, unable to look away from Livia.

"Grace," Livia says as she stands. I can't tell if she's simply surprised or maybe aggravated by her former friend.

"Hello, Livia," Grace replies, taking three heavy steps forward.

I instinctively reach for Nina, holding her closer.

"Why are you here?" Livia demands.

Aggravated. Definitely aggravated.

"Am I not allowed to enjoy the Harvest Festival?" scoffs Grace.

"You haven't set foot on our land in years. And you certainly haven't spoken kindly about me and my family to everyone in town since then."

It was foreign to me, seeing Livia become infuriated. The mama bear in her wasn't afraid to come out when it came to anything related to her children.

"Who said I was talking about you or your family?"

"Please, Grace. Don't offend me even more than you already have. When it comes to my kids, keep your opinions to yourself."

Grace shakes her head. "I guess now is as good a time as any to actually start acting like a mother."

"You are so out of line, Grace," Livia says in a low voice.

"Don't worry, Livia. I'm only here to check out the apples. Not to shoot the breeze with an old friend," Grace jabs before glancing in my direction. "Radley, so nice to see you again."

"Yes," I answer quickly. "It is."

Livia turns back to me with confused eyes. "You two know each other?"

"She wandered onto our property weeks ago. That's when I learned she was working for you." Grace doesn't even try to hide the bitterness that stings with each syllable.

"You say that like it's a bad thing."

"Is it?" Grace arches a brow.

"You know, Grace," starts Livia.

Grace scowls and crosses her arms, and for a second, I think she's enjoying this.

Livia's voice grows sad. "I still don't understand why. After all the time we were friends . . . why you decided to turn on me."

Grace wears a sick smile. "Oh . . . but I think you do, Livia. You're too scared to say it out loud. In front of your brand-shiny-new friend."

I glance down at Nina, resting her head on my shoulder, half asleep, and I'm silently grateful that she isn't paying too much attention to Livia and Grace.

Livia marches closer to Grace. "I'm not sure you noticed, but my daughter is right over there. I think it might be time you end your visit. You and your husband need to leave."

Grace smirks. "You would do that, Livia? In front of all these people, you would show them how much you really care about your good old neighbor?"

"Please leave," Livia warns.

"Or else you'll what?" Grace asks, unfazed.

Beau suddenly appears at Livia's side. He takes her hand and pulls her back to the picnic table bench.

"Grace," he says to her evenly. "Thanks so much for stopping by. Be sure to tell your husband we said hello."

He gives Livia a look as if to warn her to let it be.

Grace goes silent. She makes eye contact with me before giving a quick nod to Beau.

But the scorn in her eyes at Livia. Boring straight through—something beyond hatred that thickens the air with one final look.

She disappears into the store to presumably look for Mr. Jean.

—

There is little fuss tonight at bedtime. The Harvest Festival did its duty in wearing out not only the adults but also the children. Even Avie does little to protest as she and the other kids drag themselves upstairs to get ready for bed. Yet I feel a shift—a veil that has covered the contented nature in this house dissolving.

The bones of this house . . . this family, have begun to tremble. A tremor that grows with each passing day I live inside.

I retreat to my room, turning in for the night. The house grows quiet again; the children must be falling asleep. I do my best to stay as silent as possible when I leave the spare room to get a glass of water.

Yet a whisper floats into the hallway. The whispering grows in length and volume. I stand in the middle of the hall, barefoot, with my hand gripping the collar of my robe. Another clip of whispering hits my ears. It's coming from Nina's room. Before I can reach her, the whispers stop, and her door opens.

Too late for me to go back.

Beau steps out of her room. He appears taken aback to see me standing in front of him.

I point to the stairs. "I was just going to the kitchen for water."

He barely looks at me. "Good work today, Radley," he manages to say.

What's happened to the older brother I'd manifested in him? The Jem I'd found in him . . .

He moves to leave, but I put my hand on his arm briefly to stop him.

I draw it back. He stares down at the spot where I touched him as if I've left a mark.

"If my being here is making you uncomfortable, Beau, it's okay to be up front with me. I get it that you want privacy with your family. I wouldn't be offended if you wanted me to move back to the guest cottage."

He doesn't look at me. Only listens.

"Have I done something wrong? Beau?"

He finally looks up with a pained expression. "No. No . . . you haven't, Radley."

His dark-blue eyes soften as he gazes at me. He opens his mouth to say something else. But he stops.

We both hear a shift in the wood floors. Livia stands at the top of the stairs. Watching us with glowing eyes full of attention, as if she wants to drink us in.

CHAPTER 23

"What's wrong?" I overhear Andrea mutter to Daniel.

"The tractor is acting up again," he grumbles. "People are getting testy having to wait so long for hayrides. And guess how nice Chester is when this happens? I swear he's going to kick people off the rides, he's getting so irritated."

"Tell Beau. You mentioned that it overheated easily last season. I don't know why he doesn't listen to you," she gripes.

The fatigue from Day One of the Harvest Festival has washed over into Sunday. Normally collected and cheery, Andrea and Daniel being snippy is certainly a sign of this.

"I'll go find Beau. Focus on what you're able to fix for now. We may have to pause the hayrides altogether," I say to them.

"She's right," Andrea tells Daniel. "Do what you can. Complaining isn't going to help."

Daniel nods.

"What are you doing standing there? Go, Daniel."

He sucks in air and blows out a whistle. "Okay, Mamacita. Whatever you say goes."

"Mamacita?" Andrea puts her hands on her hips.

With a playful quick wink, Daniel flees from the store before she can say another word, and Andrea sighs resignedly.

"That's right, you better run off," she says with a small chuckle.

"I'll go see where Beau is," I remind her.

But she's too busy to notice, lunging forward to stop a little boy from knocking over the display of stacked jams.

A male customer behind them makes me halt in my tracks.

Not because I'm startled but because seeing him produces a pit of remorse in my stomach. Even if I think that I did what was necessary, it doesn't help that he looks remarkably handsome in a tan sweater and collared jacket. And his sheepish grin brings back a flash of a kiss that now warms my lips.

Shai shrugs apologetically, a frozen apple pie in one hand and a jug of cider in the other.

"Need a hand?" I ask.

He sets the pie and jug on the counter. "I think I got it."

I shake a paper bag open and ring up the cider but then stop. I look squarely at him, pushing through any tentative stepping around each other.

"Shai. I'm not one to pretend everything is okay when it's not. I'm sure you're upset with me, and I get that."

"I'm not upset with you," he says. His eyes shine earnestly.

I lower the top of my head. "You're not."

"No. We had an amazing picnic. Even if you did run off before I could thank you."

"Even if there aren't going to be more picnics . . . or dinners, or—"

He shakes his head slightly. "I'm not here to rush you. I like having you in my life. That's enough for me, if that's all it is right now."

"Right now?"

He holds up two fingers. "Truth. Scout's honor. Veterinarian's honor. And I didn't come here to see you. I always come by during the Harvest Festival. I like supporting Liv and Beau."

I ring up the pie next. The total flashes on the screen.

"Despite not getting a friend discount and paying full price," he says slyly.

The pit starts to dissolve in my midsection. Shai has a gift for calming me down, intentionally or not. Grounding myself is easily achieved around him. But now I'm starting to feel a different kind of pit in my stomach. This one maybe of regret.

I hold up the bag.

"Well, as a paying customer, Shai, you deserve my ending spiel. Thank you so much for visiting Clark Orchard."

I give him a flippant megawatt smile, entirely too large to be real.

"Anything else I can do for you?" I ask.

He lifts the bag.

"Nope. That will do. For now, anyway," he answers.

My smile withdraws, and he gives me a small salute as he turns away from the counter.

It's right then that Livia storms into the store, with a fuming Tallan keeping up next to her. He rips his work apron off and throws it into a stack of baskets. His cheeks are flushed with emotion.

"Why do I always have to help Dad? I don't see Avie doing anything."

Livia shuts her eyes, collecting herself. "Tallan, Avie is your little sister. You're twelve, you should be taking on more responsibility."

"Responsibility?" he huffs. "You have no idea the responsibility I already take on, Mom."

"What?" she asks, confused. "What's that supposed to mean?"

"Nothing," he grunts. "Forget it."

The furrow between Livia's brows deepens. She seems to ponder pressing him for more, but she pauses.

"Tallan," she finally says, quieter now as she reaches out with her hand. Her fingers graze his shoulder, and he jerks away. "I'm not here to fight with you. Dad only wants you to help a little more. The Harvest Festival is busy, I know, but we're in the home stretch."

"I *have* been helping. I've busted my ass the last two days."

"Tallan," she warns him with wide eyes.

"Sorry," he replies, crossing his arms. "Can't I be left alone?"

"Alone to do what?"

"Anything but this," he grumbles.

Livia watches him as if any wrong move will make him combust. A look comes over her that I haven't seen before. A helpless one.

I come around the counter as Shai steps aside, clearing his throat—looking like he wants to blend into the barn walls rather than witness this mother versus preteen angst any longer.

"Hey, Tallan. Why don't you and I go for a quick walk? Take a break from all of this?"

He glances at me and then Shai, suddenly realizing *other* people are around.

He sighs and uncrosses his arms. "Thanks, Radley, but I'm okay. Grandma Faye is out in the field. I think I might go see what she needs help with." He doesn't wait for any of us to respond to him and walks outside with his head down.

His outburst seems to have defused for the moment. But the distress on Livia's face has not.

"He's okay." I move closer to her. "This is how kids his age act."

But my reassurance does nothing to placate her. Her expression has in fact gotten worse.

"Livia?"

Her hazel eyes open wide enough that I can see the gold ring around her pupil blazing with a fiery focus. She steps back, startled, and bumps into a bin, losing her footing.

"Are you all right?" Shai asks, concerned, as he puts a hand on her arm to steady her.

She starts to nod and then turns her head to one side.

"Livia . . . ," I say again.

She looks at me, panicked, and then back again. I follow her line of sight, and it's not Tallan leaving that she's surveilling.

A woman with icy eyes and a silken blond bob leans over to browse pies stacked on a table. She has a slender, gazelle-like figure—one long, lean line from head to toe that's hard to pry my eyes from, like an optical illusion I want to figure out. She has a wool blazer draped stylishly over her shoulders, and she turns to her companion to point something out, showing a dazzling set of teeth one size too large for her face.

I stare back at Livia. "Do you . . . know that woman?"

Her mouth falls open. "I . . . I don't understand why they'd come here . . . ," she starts. I realize the quivering in her voice is not from fear as her jaw tightens.

There's no time to get anything else out of her.

Beau appears in the entryway of the store. The sunlight is behind him, his brawny outline casting a shadow that hides his face. He remains in that position, not taking another step inside, as if he, too, has become immobile.

The icy-blond woman places a pie in her basket, seemingly oblivious to the reactions she's instigated.

The shadow over Beau's face disappears like a waning moon as he steps forward. He holds a crate against his middle. He glares in the direction of the woman.

His fingers grip the top edge of the wood crate. Tight. Shuddering.

The presence of this woman appears to madden him, like a pest that has returned—having thought he was done with it. A tantrum of fury flashes across his eyes.

I didn't know his eyes could get so dark. I didn't know a man's eyes could ever get that dark.

CHAPTER 24

Neither Livia nor Beau breathes a word about the blond-haired woman at the Harvest Festival. As rapidly as the weekend came and went, so does any unpleasantry she has dredged up.

It's business as usual the next day in the Clark family household.

Beau ushers Avie out the door for school, barely acknowledging me as he scoops up her backpack from the floor. His continued distance makes me feel like a nuisance. An unwanted guest he's being forced to host. An awkward swell that grows with each shuffled encounter.

Avie hops on one foot, trying to get her other rain boot on.

"Bye, Radley! See you after school!" she calls cheerily.

"See you," I say back, tugging at my sweater wrap, the opened door bringing in a wet draft.

Livia shuffles in and rubs her eyes, holding out a mug of coffee with a straight arm.

"Thank you." I take the warm ceramic handle.

"Love you, my birdie," she says to Avie between yawns.

Beau nods at us both with a tight smile and shuts the door.

"I can take Tallan today," Livia says immediately, turning to me with both hands on her mug, followed by a long sip. If she's at all bothered by Beau's distant behavior, she isn't showing it.

"Oh, really?"

"Yes. I want time to talk with him about how he acted yesterday. Harvest Festival or not, something is bugging him. I figure the car is the closest I'll get to making him my captive audience."

I hold up my mug. "Good luck with that."

She sets her mug down on the entryway table and twists her hair up into a bun, all the while keeping her eyes on me. "You're awfully quiet this morning."

"Me?"

"Well"—she tilts her head as she adjusts wisps of curls—"more quiet than usual. Something up?"

I shake my head. "Nothing's up." I begin walking to the kitchen, and she follows.

"Huh. I could have sworn I saw Shai at the store. Talking to you."

"Yes. He bought a pie and apple cider." I set my mug on the counter. "Nina's still sleeping, right?" I point upstairs.

"She is. And what's going on?" Livia presses. "From what I heard, you had a lovely picnic."

"We did." I stare at her blankly, hoping to end any further inquiries.

She heaves a sigh and grins. "You're a mysterious one, Radley."

A noise, sounding like a toilet flushing, causes us both to look up at the ceiling.

"She must be up," says Livia, turning somber.

Teasing me was an escape for her. The reminder of Nina instantly makes her lids sag, aging her in real time.

"What did the specialist end up telling you?" I ask quietly.

"So far, nothing is showing in her tests and scans. But he's tentatively diagnosing her with aplastic anemia. Her body simply isn't producing enough blood cells."

"Can they treat her for it?"

"They can try another transfusion later this week, but that seems to only be a temporary fix. Whenever she gets better, she declines again after that."

I stop asking questions when I see Livia's eyes well up.

"I'm sorry."

She swipes at the wetness and reaches for a tissue in her pocket. "No, no," she says as she blows her nose. "You don't need to be sorry. I sometimes wish I . . ."

She stops herself.

"Do you want me to go up?" I ask.

"Yes. That would be great. I look at her lately, and it just starts all over again. I don't want her to see me upset."

"Okay then. I'll help her get ready for the day."

"Thank you, Radley," she says. "I'll pull myself together and swing by the barn stable. Tallan is doing his morning chores."

I walk upstairs to find Nina standing on a footstool in the bathroom, staring at her little face in the mirror. Her hair is in a tangled lion's mane, curls every which way around her head. She holds up her clear pink toothbrush at me.

"Good morning, Radley."

I pluck the toothbrush from her fingers and open the toothpaste. "Good morning. Your mommy is going to take Tallan to school today. Mind if I hang out with you?"

She nods happily and lets me brush her teeth. In the mirror I see how dark the circles have gotten. How much less light is in her eyes. She grabs the towel from the rack and swipes at her mouth.

"Are you going to make me breakfast too?"

"Yes."

She looks relieved before remembering something. "I slept too much. I didn't have my tea party with Avie. I saw her bed is made."

"It's all right. You can do it later today. When she comes home from school."

Her face falls. "I miss school."

I gently turn her around and bend closer. "Tell you what. After breakfast, maybe we can pretend the playroom is school."

When her eyes light up, I feel my chest grow warm.

"And you can be the student. I'll be teacher," she adds.

"Sounds great."

She dresses herself in the clothes Livia laid out for her, and she sits in my lap as I detangle her hair carefully. She requests pigtails, and I sleekly part her hair. Two clustered twirls of hair sprout up on each side, and I secure each one with elastics, finished off with yellow ribbons.

"Wow! Radley, you're really good at it," Nina exclaims in the mirror. "Where did you learn to do hair like this?"

I stop while tying up the second ribbon.

"Oh. Well, I . . ." My fingers fumble with the ribbon, and I have to start over. "I did my own hair when I was a little girl," I say with conviction.

Nina whips around and whispers in my ear. A secret, even though we're alone. "You'll have to teach Mommy. Sometimes she doesn't part it very good."

"I'll be sure to say something," I whisper back.

Down in the kitchen, she instructs me step by step on how to make the cinnamon raisin oatmeal. *Not too much milk, and be sure to count in twelve raisins.*

I observe her slurp the bowl down, and a familiar satisfaction extends in the warmth in my chest from earlier. This isn't uncharted territory. This is muscle memory.

The sun peeps out when we enter the playroom, and Rabbit scampers in to join us. Nina stands with authority by the chalkboard, drilling me on my letters. She tells Rabbit to sit, and he dutifully does, panting up at her while she attempts to get him to tap letters with his paw. I pretend to falter on a few that she points to, and she tries not to giggle. When we're finished with that lesson, she moves on to selecting her favorite book to read—or, in our teaching scenario, for me to read.

I'm halfway through the book when she slumps into me.

"Nina?" I pull her up, alarmed.

She sits up straight. "I think . . . ," she starts and then yawns. "I think I want to lie down for a while now."

"Okay. Sure. Let's go upstairs."

We make it halfway up to the landing, with Rabbit following us, when Nina becomes too weak to continue. I pick her up and cradle her to her bed. I pull the covers up over her as she lies flat on her back. She reaches out and stops me.

"Radley."

"Hmm?"

"Will you stay with me? For a little while. At least until I fall asleep."

I nod and then lie next to her on the edge. Rabbit whines, and I let him hop in at the foot of the bed. Nina tucks her chin in and sighs.

"Everyone worries about me . . . don't they."

She doesn't say this like a question. She knows the answer.

I look up at the ceiling and blink a few times. "Yes. You're a smart girl, Nina. I'm not going to pretend and tell you anything different."

"Mmm," she murmurs. "I'm very sick. I can tell because Mommy is so sad."

"Yes, but we're going to get you feeling better, Nina."

"And Daddy. He tries to act like he's not sad. But I see it."

I feel her hand pat mine a few times. "Radley, can I tell you another secret?"

"Yes, Nina."

"I'm not afraid to die. Not really, anyways. But I would be sad not to see Rabbit again."

I glance at Rabbit, curled up in a ball. My chest tightens, and I feel if I stay any longer, it will rip.

"You're going to be okay, Nina. You're not going anywhere."

"Yes . . . ," she mumbles before falling asleep.

I slide out of the bed as silently as possible. I clutch my chest, clenching my teeth.

Why is this happening again?

After I make it into the bathroom, I fall onto my knees, and the edges of the tiles cut into me. As I shut the door with one hand, a single guttural sound slips out. I double over.

No. Not here. Not like this.

My hands cover my mouth, and I shake. Her tiny words repeat in my head. Repeating a pain in my core that won't go away.

CHAPTER 25

Whatever "talk" Livia had with Tallan earlier in the week doesn't seem to have stuck with him. He crossly makes his way out from the school entrance, backpack nearly dragging as he holds it by one strap.

"Hey," he mumbles as he gets into the car.

"Had a good day, huh?" I ask, putting the gear in drive.

"Oh yeah. The best."

He ruffles his hair out of his eyes and leans into his window.

At the intersection, I make a right instead of taking our usual route.

"Where are you going?" he asks, sitting up alertly.

"Not home. Not yet, anyway."

"Why not?" The smallest of smiles creeps over his mouth, but he banishes it with a sideways glance at me.

"Sometimes you need a pick-me-up," I say, glancing over slyly.

He lifts his head to look over the dashboard as I pull onto Fox Isle's main drag. We park in front of Lutz's Candy Emporium.

"Candy? I'm not Avie."

"Who said anything about candy?" I tell him as I get out of the car.

He follows me inside, and I take us past the fudge-making demonstration, rock candy displays in a rainbow of colors, and barrels stuffed with shovels to scoop out all variety of candies. In the back corner are a few high-tops. A man pulls out a paddle of piping-hot pizza from a wood-fire oven, tomatoes and peppers sizzling on top.

Tallan's eyes widen with delight. "They have . . . pizza here?"

I cross my arms, and I can't help but be smug. "Yes, they do."

"How did you know about this?"

"Andrea. She heard about it from a woman at church. She and Daniel ate here last week, and she swore it was the best pizza she'd ever had. She said to get the specialty with mushrooms."

He nods and I order one. We wait at a high-top. He kicks his sneaker against the pole a few times.

"Did Mom tell you to take me out or something?" he asks, fiddling with a straw wrapper.

I take a drink from my ice water. "No."

"Then why do this?"

I shrug. "Why not?"

He nods a few times and then turns his attention to the door. His cheeks redden, and he appears startled, mixed with something else.

I look over my shoulder, and I immediately recognize the boy he's spotted. One of the foursome from under the birches I'd seen at pickup. The boy with the bomber jacket and longish blond hair. He's by himself, though, browsing the barrels of saltwater taffy.

I look back at Tallan, and that's when I realize the "something else" that's also spreading across his cheeks. He's pleased.

The boy lifts his head from dumping a few scoops of taffy into a paper bag. He sees Tallan and grins. He gives him a wave. Tallan returns it, sliding his hands through his hair. The boy turns away to pay for the candy at the register.

I'm holding my breath as I watch it all unfold. When the boy exits, I exhale and lean toward Tallan.

"Who was that?"

"No one," he answers.

"No one?" I raise my brows.

"Well, his name is Colt."

"You guys friends?"

Tallan's mouth pulls into a sullen shape, but he doesn't answer. Once the pizza arrives, the hot metal plate landing on our table with a thud, he immediately takes a slice. The cheese strings out from his mouth, and I'm wise enough to know that until that first slice is down, it's useless to seek further communication.

I take a few bites, and by then he's halfway into his second. I hand him a napkin, and he takes it, swiping once messily.

"This is good, Radley. Thanks for bringing me here," he says.

All it takes is some pizza to get a kid back to human form.

"You're welcome."

He puts the rest of his slice down on his plate. "You know . . . I don't mean to be like this."

I pretend to not know what he's talking about. "Like what?"

"Difficult."

"It's okay." I dab at my mouth.

He slouches forward and puts his fingers on his temples. "No . . . it's not okay. I don't feel good when I get into it with Mom and Dad. But I can't help it . . . it just comes out."

I look at him with sympathy. "Tallan, you're not the first kid to be annoyed by their parents. Don't beat yourself up." I take a large bite.

He gives me an obligatory smile, and then it fades immediately.

"Tallan . . . you all right?" I ask while trying to finish chewing.

He swallows hard and averts his eyes. "What if I told you it's not just kid versus parent stuff?"

I put the pizza down, wipe my hands on a napkin, and focus on him.

"What if I told you . . . it was something else bothering me?"

His eyes meet mine, and I see dread floating in them.

"I would say, Tallan," I start carefully, "that you have parents who love you. No matter what. And it's okay to be honest with them."

I expect this to help ease some of the dread. But it's replaced with disappointment . . . maybe disappointment that I didn't get it. Or that I didn't ask the right question.

"Sure . . . I'll keep that in mind, Radley," he says, reaching for his slice. He returns to being sullen, crawling back into the shell he briefly peeked out from.

What have I missed here? Is it about that boy Colt?

We finish eating and return to the house to find Avie alone in the kitchen.

"Where is everyone?" Tallan asks her.

She punctures her juice box with her straw. "Daddy's upstairs with Nina."

"And Mom?"

She sits at the counter and sips through the straw. "Outside."

"Why?"

"She wanted to be alone for a little bit. So, I'm having my juice until she's done with that."

Tallan tosses his backpack onto a chair. "I'll go see what she's doing."

I hold my hand out. "No, it's okay. I'll go."

He doesn't protest. He falls into his chair and pulls out his books. I give him one final look before stepping out back. He seems unbothered by our discussion at the candy emporium. Focused on his homework.

He's a good kid. But something is troubling him.

I find Livia on the back steps, facing the guest cottage. She's hunched over, gazing out at its front door.

"We fought about that door," she says without looking at me.

She pulls her hand to her mouth, and it's then I realize she's having a cigarette.

"With who?"

I stand next to her, and she slides over and points to the newly free space.

"Beau. He didn't want a modern door. I did. Then we fought about it." She takes in a drag and blows out into the chilly October air.

"You won then." I stare at the door.

"Did I?"

We remain fixed on the door until she rotates her head so her chin meets the top of her shoulder.

"How's Tallan?"

"Tallan is fine. We went out for pizza after school . . . I hope you don't mind."

"No . . . not at all. I'm glad you two did that. He really thinks highly of you, you know."

I rub my kneecaps as if dusting off dirt. "Oh, I doubt he really does. What's there to like?"

She turns and wraps her hand around my wrist. "A lot. There's a lot to be admired, Radley."

I don't resist. When I look at her with coolness, she lets go gently and puts the cigarette to her lips. I expect her to inhale, but she taps it a few times before pulling it away. She examines it.

"You know, I never smoked. Not even in college. But every now and then I do this. To throw off the whole ecosystem, remove the balance. Maybe because I want to give back some of the chaos going on inside."

"Livia," I say once with a wary softness.

She puts the cigarette out. "Nina didn't have a very good day today." Her voice trembles. She wipes at her eyes.

"Is that why she's with Beau right now?"

"No, that's why I'm out here right now."

She pinches between her eyes. "You know they say being a mother is the hardest job in the world. But in the beginning, I thought that was a lie. It felt so effortless. To love and nurture that tiny, soft little body. I remember wishing each night for it to stay that way forever. That I could hold that precious warmth to my chest and stay there."

I watch her clutch herself, as if she's back there, in that moment of bliss.

Her hands fall to her sides.

"But now it's so damn hard. And my arms feel empty now."

She grinds her toe into the grass where the glowing bud lies. "Sometimes I think anyone but me would do a better job with these kids." Her face crumples like paper, and then she forces a smile. "Anyone else but me."

CHAPTER 26

"Tell me about the first time you met your husband," Dr. Edair asks me.

She has me lying down on the chaise. The room is dim. The curtains are drawn on the windows. There's no view of the sea for me today. There's no distraction of sailboat figurines or questions about her wife.

Today she isn't letting me escape.

"What is it exactly that you read about me, Dr. Edair?"

I sound like I'm accusing her of something awful. As if she's gone through all my things and found something I wanted no one to ever see.

She pauses before answering. No doubt selecting her words judiciously.

"I know you were married."

"And?"

Go ahead. Go ahead and say it.

"And that you had a child together."

"Why does any of that matter?" I speak slowly. There's a lull in her office. The air is thick, and I feel as though I'm talking through water.

"It matters because you're going to tell me a story, Radley."

"A story," I repeat.

"Yes. Sometimes it's easier for patients if they think of it this way."

"Easier to do what?"

"Acknowledge the reality of their past." Her voice grows stern. "You see, Radley, you live as though you have no past. That the traumas that happened to you don't exist. We need to dissolve that thought. We need you to accept what's real."

I shut my eyes. "And what if I don't want to. Accept it."

"Then . . . it will be difficult to move forward. Impossible to have any life of your own. Do you know why?"

I don't respond.

"Because you won't be able to stop focusing on others' instead of your own. The lives of others."

The last part of her assertion moves up my spine, and it stings. An irritation I want to remove but know I can't. The verity in what she has said to me.

"Are you ready, Radley?" she asks, softer now.

"Okay. I'm ready."

"Where was it that you met your husband?"

I open my eyes.

A story . . . she wants my story . . .

There's a kalguksu shop near Seoul's Namdaemun Market, owned by an eighty-year-old woman. She may still be there making "knife noodles," slicing at freshly made dough in her tiny one-room setup. The only place to eat your soup is on footstools stacked with old magazines and newspapers. She won't say anything to you but will take your money and nod.

This is where I met my husband.

We were married for eight years. Eight years of harrowing ecstasy. You can't have one without the other.

"Are you going to use that?" he asked me in Korean.

I shook my head apologetically. He pointed to the bottle of fish sauce. He had longer hair then, slicked back. So black and shiny it could've been a reflecting mirror.

"No. I'm finished," I responded in English, handing it to him. Like in any good Korean drama, our fingers grazed each other's when I passed it on.

"I'm Dae-Seong," he answered in accented English. "But you can call me Dane."

"Dane?"

"That's my Americanized name. I'm working on making my English better."

"Well, it seems to be working. Your English is great."

He poured a dash of sauce into his soup. "And your name? You don't seem to speak Korean?"

"Radley. I'm adopted."

"Ah. Staying long in Seoul?"

I remember feeling sad. We had only just met. But I knew I wanted him to be my friend. I don't know how to explain it, but I felt like I'd already lost a good friend.

"I'm leaving in a few weeks. I taught English for a year, but it's time to go back to the States."

He smiled and then poured a little more sauce into my bowl. "First have some kalguksu. Then we can talk more about you leaving."

And we did. And I never left.

He told me about how he worked as a lab technician, with dreams of doing more research in genetics. He loved science. He loved the millions of unsolved questions it posed, and he was eager to explore as many as he could.

I watched his eyes glow as I let my own ambitions spill out. I'd always been scared to say them out loud. Certain they sounded ridiculous. But with him, I felt free and safe. I wanted to travel and escape to other worlds. My first taste was in Seoul, and I acquired an insatiable appetite for more. Being so far away from where I'd started created a new Radley. A Radley who thought she deserved more for herself. I would write for travel magazines, having already had a few blogs published in my year in Seoul. I felt lighter. I felt fuller when I wrote my way through what I lived each day.

Nothing I said made him question my desires. Until he became a desire.

He was my first and only love. He set my body on fire even when we weren't in bed. We never once discussed having children. Why would we, with all that we had planned for the future?

I'd always assumed it would be only the two of us. I couldn't imagine bringing a child into this world. Not me. Not someone who was barely capable of staying above the surface.

Dane's parents were still quite traditional by Korean standards back then, so we didn't move in together. Instead, he'd stay into the late hours at my apartment. Eventually, we married. My parents didn't attend. His parents seemed indifferent but still satisfied that they had married off their only son.

We were both so young. I was only twenty-four, he twenty-six. I think it was our youth that shielded us from really grasping how hard life can be to traverse. How it can hit you with a force that knocks you to your knees.

We were oblivious to that. At first, anyway.

The four seasons caught us at each turn. Our hands ran along cherry blossoms in the spring, feathering petals with our fingers that swelled up in summer. A month spent on Jeju Island, the ocean salt twisted in my hair from swimming. After watching elderly women dive for abalone, we ate them fresh and briny with thick red pepper sauce. We returned to Seoul by autumn, not wanting to miss the nightlife and street food before winter took over. The cold didn't trouble us as we wrapped around each other in our first apartment, wondering if anything could be better than this.

The next year we planned for further travels. I'd gotten a temporary job at SeoWoo Tech, something to make an income until my travel writing took off. And Dane had been promoted to senior lab technician.

But change. Longing and wistfulness are inevitable. There's a Korean proverb that says the cold envies the flowers. Winter was not ready to move on.

How were we to know the next season would bring what it did?

I never asked for a baby. He wasn't looking to be a father.

This isn't real. We were so careful.

I felt numb when I saw the positive test result. It was a blessing that the numbness took over before the screaming of panic had a chance to break through.

Will I ever be enough for this baby?

Then a slow realization expanded over me, like a sponge taking in water. I would have to remain at SeoWoo Tech. We needed the money. Traveling would have to wait.

Of course the thrill of finding out I was pregnant was missing. This wasn't what we thought was in our cards. Neither was it thrilling to see my twenty-five-year-old body stretch and morph in ways I never thought possible.

"You look beautiful," Dane told me. But I could see him taking note of my puffy face, my thickening arms, and my acne.

Yet there we were in the hospital, holding hands as I panted, staring at one another, so unsure of why we were doing this. What was in it for us? Our lives had been cyclical, on point, and, to us . . . perfection. We needed only each other. What would this new being do to us?

I remember something ripping inside me. On that final push. It wasn't physical. It was a tear, breaking away from my former life and all the dreams I had. Because she had arrived. Silent at first, dramatic as we waited. A cry for the ages followed, and I will never forget how shiny and innocent her eyes looked when she stared up at me.

We named her Dove.

A dark, thick-haired, beautiful daughter who curled up into my chest. And in that moment, I was willing to give it my all. I'd only just met her and would jump through fire hoops for her. All the resentments that had built up, the fears and doubts, I let fall down into a hole. One that I covered up and pretended didn't exist.

In the weeks after we brought her home, the honeymoon period overtook us fast and furious. Furious in that we wanted nothing but to soak her in as she seemed to grow by the hour. Fast in that it was not to last. Her newborn calm was short lived.

She proved to be a difficult and fussy baby. Soothing her was an extensive chore and process. In the first year, I don't think I slept more than three hours straight at a time. Dove cried incessantly. Crying from acid reflux, crying because she was hungry all over again, crying for Dane instead of me.

I wasn't enough. The doubt from this. The seed was planted deep in me but forgotten for the time being.

There was no second-guessing for Dane. He slipped into his fatherly role so easily, I found myself envious of his ability. His effortless style in taking care of our Dove. Nothing ruffled his feathers.

She adored him in return. She obsessed over me. It was not a pleasing, flattering obsession. She wanted always to cling, to hold on, to need, to want, to take over every thought in my head. Every decision and move made for her, day after day, year after year.

I was too busy loving her, loving our family, to notice.

By the time Dove turned one, she was sleeping through the night, and our rhythm as a family of three steadied. I found myself enjoying our life again. Dane would go to work, and I spent the days playing with our laughing and content Dove. Our own bubble undisturbed, waiting for Daddy to return so we could resume our roles, energy pinging off one another. Our apartment had floor-to-ceiling windows. I imagined some other person, some other set of prying eyes, watching us. Wanting to be part of what we had together.

I eventually returned to the office—the transition was dreadful. But it was worth coming home to Dane and Dove. Coming home to the family I had created. Our faces beaming with wide smiles as we looked at each other across the kitchen table each night.

When Dove turned two, something even more marvelous happened. Her precocious personality shined in all sorts of delectable ways, bursting with inquisitive questions. Her way of looking at the world became my way of looking at it. Fresh. A lens beyond rose colored. Bright were all the shades in Dove's eyes. "Mommy, come look!"

Mommy.

I couldn't wait each morning to discover what she would find. Our hearts ready to burst over this little miracle we had created.

"We're so lucky," we would look at each other and say.

I thought it would never change, this complete devotion to my child. How could anything ever upend how I felt? The cogs in the wheels of each day, a repeated pattern I reveled in and wanted to stay in forever. Giving myself entirely to them was my life.

The sum of me. What was left of me.

We were a perfect family. We were the ones with the other life. The life that others wanted.

Until the day came that we weren't.

CHAPTER 27

I need a thicker jacket this morning, for these early hours at the orchard on the brink of October frost. The house is static and dormant, each of the family members still asleep in their beds. There's something about being the only one awake, the only one taking in what others will never see. I step out for a walk, the cold air startling my lungs at first breath. To be alone. To clear my head unbothered.

Which is why I'm surprised to see Chester and Sidney at work so early.

Chester tilts his flat, green herringbone cap at me. His gray knot seems to be missing.

"Good morning," he says. For him, an indication of a chipper start to his day

"Morning, Chester and Sidney."

Sidney waves and pulls a pink knit hat down over her ears. Her dyed blue hair has faded, and the combined light pink and blue hues make a cotton candy motif.

"What happened to all your hair, Chester?"

"Bah," he says, waving me off. "It was time. I'm not young anymore. Shouldn't be trying to hold on to my hair, thinning and all. At least that's what this one kept telling me." He juts a thumb at Sidney.

She smirks and rocks on her heels in triumph. I can only imagine what kind of battle that was.

"You both are here early," I comment.

"I was going to say the same thing about you. Up before the sun is fully up."

"I need a walk."

"Good for you," he says.

"Unless . . . you want me to help you two?"

He glances at Sidney. "No. I think we can manage."

"You sure?"

"Beau's been cutting our hours lately. We're trying to make up for it when we can."

My forehead scrunches in confusion. "Hours?"

Chester's shoulders raise, and he stuffs his hands in his jean pockets. "Over the years, we always worked the day, nights if we had to. Whatever it took to get it done, but . . ."

He steals a look at Sidney, whose mouth presses tighter.

"Beau started us logging hours last season. This season, well . . . been a little tighter on logging with an official system in place."

I'd never noticed either of them clocking or logging anything. No one had ever asked me to do that.

"Do Andrea and Daniel know about this?"

"Andrea and Daniel been doing the same. At the register."

What's happening in the business side of the orchard to make Beau do this?

"Beau or Livia haven't asked me to log my hours."

I start to wonder if this was an oversight, that they've forgotten to tell me this. Or maybe because I've been helping with the children and keeping busy with that on top of the orchard work.

Chester's gaze at me isn't exactly harsh. But it isn't kind either.

"Must be nice living with the owners," he says. He nods at Sidney, and they move away toward the barn stable. One of the horses whinnies, and a goat bleats. "Feeding time." He gives me a wink.

I walk fast, my head down. Trying to get as far as possible from anyone else who might rise earlier than expected.

Andrea must feel strange about it. But she's never said a word.

The Maine tree line looks so different from when I first arrived. Nothing escapes the fleeting nature of all that's around us, including the height-of-fall colors, saturated only last week. Faded from its glory, I see patches of empty space among the foliage, now just past peak.

I keep moving. Closer and closer to the horizon of the ocean, trying to catch it before the sunrise takes over. My breath quickens and the ground spins. Flashing lights invade my sight. It's hard to see anything, until I see Nina's small face, so innocent in how she spoke to me.

I'm not afraid to die. Not really, anyways . . .

I bend over, spreading my hands over my kneecaps. Wishing for every thought to leave my head. To leave behind an emptiness that I long for.

You can't escape. No matter where you go. It's there . . . ready to grab at you when you let your guard down.

"Radley," someone calls to me.

She wades through the tall grass I've stranded myself in. The ends of her coat are wet, and I look down to find mine is soaked.

"Are you all right?" Grace asks.

I stand up straight, brushing at my pants. "Yes . . . yes. I'm fine."

She's skeptical. "What are you doing out here in the wet grass?"

"Honestly?" I throw my arms up and let them slap down. "I'm not sure. I was going for a morning walk."

"So was I."

"I didn't mean to interrupt. Please, I'm okay. Taking a breather."

Grace doesn't budge. "I want to say I'm sorry to hear about Nina."

"Really? You didn't seem that sorry the last time I saw you." My words shoot out faster than I can even process them. Nina is not a topic I'm willing to be coy about.

"You're right," she answers right away. "And I'm sorry for that too. I truly hope she gets better from whatever it is that's ailing her. She's a wonderful little girl."

"Maybe you should be telling Livia this."

The sincere expression she was wearing slips off her face like a silk scarf on a hanger.

"Livia will be fine," she says curtly. "It's the little girl I'm apologizing for."

I step out of the tall grass with high knees. She reaches out to help, but I decline, hopping back onto a more flattened patch.

"Grace, she's only a mother. Trying to take care of her sick child." I look at her sternly, but she doesn't back down. Her agitation has actually increased.

"Yes. A mother. A lousy one at that."

I hold up a hand. "None of this adds up. You two were close. Very close, from what I understand. And to simply drop off like that . . . why? Why are you so hostile to her, Grace?" I expect her to rebut this, but she doesn't.

The corners of her eyes go lax. She looks weary. Tired of the long battle and ready to stop, even for a brief moment.

"Correct, Radley. We were close. Closer than most friends. I thought of her as a younger sister. We had the best times over dozens of cups of coffee. Wine some evenings, me and her laughing until our guts ached. She's really good at that, you know. Making you feel a certain way."

"Like what?"

Grace shrugs as if she has nothing else to lose. "She made me feel like I was one of them."

One of them. One of the perfect ones who shine.

"I know what I am and what I'm not," she goes on. "And I'm not a beautiful woman. And I know my husband can come off as odd. I'm not blind to these things. But . . . it didn't matter when we were friends."

I shake my head. "Then why stop being friends?"

She stares off past me at the skyline, which is growing deeper in red hues by the minute. She ignores my question.

"She was my best friend. Someone who shared the same values. Wanted to work and live for the same things."

"But you still do."

Her eyes flash. "No. No, we don't."

"Livia and Beau are good people."

"Are they?" She steps close to me, and for a second, I think she's going to veer into my face. "Yes. I'll admit it." She stares straight in my eyes. "I was jealous. Insanely crazy jealous of the children she was able to bear. The family she was able to create. Something I never can or ever will." Her voice breaks. "That's all I ever wanted . . . to have a child with Vaughn. Do you know how much love we have to give?"

She raises a finger and forces it down to her side.

"But *she* takes it for granted—that's what. She had no right to throw it all away like that. You think they're good people, Radley? Well, I'll give you one piece of advice."

Throw it all away.

I don't move. I don't utter another sound. I let her speak.

"Don't trust them."

CHAPTER 28

I'm still dirty from my walk. Mud is caked over my boots, my coat scratched with grass stains. As I approach the front doors of the house, Beau bursts through with energy, striding down each step with a bounce. He whistles an unfamiliar tune and then slows down when he sees me. The whistle dies down and fades.

"What happened to you?" he asks with concern.

"Wetter out than I thought it would be this morning."

"Walk far?"

I nod.

Beau looks out in the distance as if he can see what happened. "Be careful out there this early. You never know what animals you might run into by yourself."

Animals like Grace maybe . . .

I must be smirking as I think about this, since he peers at me with intrigue.

"You look like you did run into something?"

"Sort of." I tilt my head back and forth.

A grin follows. It's the first real one he's given me since I moved into the house.

"Well, stay safe out there." He adjusts his cap.

I take one step closer. "Where are you going?"

He halts and looks at the ground. "Picking up the new tractor. Really a used tractor. This one is in New Hampshire. I'll have to stay overnight, but the price is worth it."

"What happened to the one we have?"

"The one we had went kaput after all the hayrides."

I think back on what Chester told me earlier. I don't know exactly how much a tractor costs, but I can't imagine it's cheap.

"Have a good day with the kids," he says briskly.

He heads to his truck, and I give him a small wave. He stops and then places a hand on the hood. "Radley," he says, turning back to face me. "I don't want you to think I'm being too harsh. It's not like me to be like this."

"You're busy. I get that."

"I feel like I need to apologize."

"For what exactly?"

"For not being as available these last couple weeks. This time of year gets extra crazy, and there's a lot of equipment issues I'm dealing with, you see—"

"It's okay. You don't have to apologize," I interrupt. His explanation seems forced, and I don't want to prolong it any more than necessary.

"I don't?" His eyes grow large.

I shake my head. "I never told you this. But my brother, Jem . . ."

He nods softly and pulls his hand from the hood.

"You remind me of him. That's all."

I immediately wonder if I've shared too much. That perhaps it's unfair to Jem to compare him to anyone else. But it's how I feel.

Beau dips his head down and then circles back to look at me. "You think of me as your brother?" There's a strange expression on his face, a mixture of surprise and maybe displeasure.

"If that's weird for me to say . . ."

He pivots his feet awkwardly to the truck and then back to me. "I'm running a bit behind. The guy who's selling the tractor came off a bit anal on the phone. I better get going." He opens the truck door. "See you later, Radley."

I nod again, backing away. A movement in the front windows catches my eye. I turn to see a flash of Livia standing there, watching us. I can make out her loose curls, covering most of her shoulders. I try to see her expression, but the glare from the sun makes it difficult. The truck engine starts, and I get distracted. When I look back, she's gone. The window is now unoccupied.

—

Faye pretends to gobble up a cookie, causing peals of laughter from Nina and Avie.

"Again!" Nina commands.

She complies, and they laugh even harder. Once their uproar has died down, Avie places her chin in both hands, her elbows propped up at the tea table.

"I like having you around more, Grandma Faye."

"Me too," chimes in Nina.

Faye leans forward and smiles. "I wouldn't miss time with my chickadees for all the world."

She stands up to stretch. I notice a weariness in her eyes as she focuses on Nina and Avie. There's apprehension in the way she observes them.

"Everything okay, Faye?" I ask from the doorway. "Livia says supper is almost ready."

"Oh." She looks at me, fairly startled. "Yes. I think so, yes." She seems confused for a second and then looks back at the girls.

Avie pours another cup for Nina and reaches for a cookie. Faye steps forward and picks up the tray.

"I think that might be enough cookies for now. Don't want you to ruin your suppers," she says, biting her lip. She nudges me as she passes and seems unbothered now.

"Livia said she's making enchiladas. You know what goes good with enchiladas, right?" She winks and gives me her signature cackle.

After dinner, I take what's left of the strong peach margarita Faye blended for me upstairs. The slush slides around in the glass as I take each step.

The bathroom connected to the spare room holds one of the finest things in the house: a deep claw-foot tub. My shoulders ache, and I can still feel bits of mud cracking around my ankles that I missed wiping off this morning.

I turn the hot water spigot and let it fill the tub. Minutes later, the bathroom starts to steam. I pour in a few drops of lavender bath soap, and bubbles create a film on the surface. I submerge my body, and it melts in the soothing water. At the end of the tub, my face stares back at me in the cheval mirror. Tensions release, and I lean my neck on the edge of the tub. I close my eyes and feel weightless.

A knock raps gently at the door.

"I'm in the bath," I call out.

There's a quiet that makes me think the girls are trying to mess with me. I listen hard for them to giggle but hear nothing.

A few more knocks.

"You guys. I told you I'm in the bath."

This time the door opens. I freeze.

Livia steps inside the bathroom and shuts the door behind her. She holds two tumblers on a tray.

"Livia," I say, dipping lower into the water.

She sets the tray on the bathroom counter. The ice clinks in the tumblers. She lifts one of them and hands it to me.

I look at the glass in her hand, keeping my body submerged. "What are you doing?"

She smiles, and I see the glazed look in her eyes. The margaritas have done their duty. Strong and casting a spell on us all. I wonder if that's what Faye intended.

"Have a whiskey. Extra cold. That's how I like it." She extends the glass over the water.

I take it.

"Thank you," I say, managing to keep the rest of my body under the bubbles.

She retrieves her own glass and kneels next to the tub. Her head close to me.

"Cheers." She clinks her glass against mine.

I take a sip, and the cold whiskey suspends on my tongue like liquid mercury before I swallow.

"Look at us," she says, leaning her head into mine and placing a hand on my shoulder.

I'm afraid to look.

"Radley. Look at us," she says again.

I slowly bring my eyes up to the mirror, our faces side by side. Livia's lustrous skin next to my dull and pale complexion. When I see us together, my face looks like an afterthought.

"Do you like what you see?" Her cold whiskey breath blows against my cheek.

I say nothing. I take another drink in answer to her question.

"There's something"—she cocks her head and then traces an outline in the air around my reflection—"inviting about your face. Like I want to enter and find out what it's like inside. What's going on inside that head of yours?"

My body grows cold in the heat of the bathwater.

She sets her glass on the tile floor and returns to place her hands on my shoulders. She begins to massage them with gentle rolling motions. I stiffen under her touch.

"I think I pegged you wrong, Radley. From the moment I saw you, I had you all wrong."

I look at her image in the mirror. "How?"

Livia gives off a silvery laugh. "I thought you were so simple. And I mean that in an endearing way. How you spoke, dressed, expressed yourself. All straight and neat, like a perfectly packed suitcase. And you know what?"

"What?"

She puts her lips by my ear. "I adored you."

I bring the tumbler to my lips, but I don't drink from it. "Thank you," I say into the glass.

She simpers, her eyes half shut, and then runs her lips against the skin next to my ear. "It's okay, Radley," she whispers.

I draw the glass away.

"It's okay if Beau wants you."

I snap my eyes at hers in the mirror. They meet, and I see her expression has deadened.

"What . . . what did you say?"

"If he wants you. You can be with him if you want." She speaks faintly. I strain to hear her.

Her words swelter against my cheek. "I'll look the other way."

She rises from the bathroom floor and slips out as swiftly as she entered.

I stare at my reflection. I stare at the face she finds so inviting. So simple.

The skin her lips lingered on tingles. I'm unsure if it's from being touched or from disbelief. She's no longer here, but I can still feel her tantalizing stare. Why in hell does she want me to be with her husband? Is she testing me?

Is she testing Beau?

What kind of marriage am I living next to . . . this family that has swallowed me whole?

CHAPTER 29

Andrea flips the fried egg as it sizzles in her cast-iron skillet. She holds up the spatula at me like a scepter.

"Over easy or fried all the way?" she asks and blows her hair out of her eyes. Her kitchen is starting to get smoky and heated.

"Either one," I tell her as I stare out her cottage window. Rain again today. Wet leaves blow into the corner windowpane. One flattens against the glass. I reach out and trace its outline.

I touch my shoulder, where Livia massaged me in the bath. I feel warm and then embarrassed for both her and me. I wonder what Beau would think if he knew what happened.

If he knew his wife was trying to use me like a pawn.

Daniel clears his throat, and I hear him turn a page in his newspaper. I face forward in my chair to catch him glancing at Andrea and then hurriedly finding an interesting headline to read.

"All right. Over easy then." She eyes me suspiciously. "What's going on with you, Radley?"

I fold the napkin in my lap in half, straightening the edge with my nail. "Absolutely nothing," I answer and smile with added charm.

She squints her eyes at me with a lifted chin. "Everything going okay in the house?"

I look up at her quickly and then back down at my lap. "Yes."

She shakes her head and waves the spatula at me. "You know what they say about secrets, mi amiga?"

"What?"

"They make you sick." She points the spatula at Daniel this time. "Isn't that right?"

He brings his newspaper down. "Huh?"

Andrea widens her eyes forcefully.

"Oh. Right. Yes. Mm-hmm. Secrets make you sick, Radley." He rubs under his mustache and returns to his paper.

Secrets. Sick secrets that Beau and Livia hold together.

The egg starts to smell like it's burning. "Ay!" Andrea shouts. She quickly flips it. "I'll make a new one."

"No. It's fine. I don't mind crispy edges."

"You sure?"

"I'm sure."

She scrapes the overdone egg out of the pan and slides it onto a plate already laid out with cut-up tortillas and black beans. She sprinkles some chopped cilantro on top and ladles on a thick tomato sauce.

"Huevos rancheros, my dear. My abuela's recipe," Andrea says proudly. She sets the plate in front of me.

"Thank you. And for having me over for breakfast."

"Oh." She holds up a finger and then spoons over a few sliced jalapenos. "You can't have huevos rancheros without extra heat."

She pushes a plate of food at Daniel, then sets down one for herself and sits across from me. She digs her fork into the middle of the egg, piercing a jalapeño, and slides it into her mouth.

"Ahh," she says and kisses the tips of her fingers. "Almost as good as my abuela's." She sneaks a glimpse at my plate. "You're not eating?"

I've been too engrossed in her enjoying the first bite, watching it take her back to another time with her abuela.

"Right." I admire the colorful dish in front of me. I dig into the egg and scoop out a large portion.

The peppery sauce dances on my tongue as I savor my mouthful. I point my fork at my plate. "Amazing, Andrea."

She beams. "The sauce is feisty. Like my abuela."

I laugh. "You mean like you?"

Her eyebrows wiggle. "Daniel I doubt would disagree."

Daniel raises his head from his plate. "No trick questions, Andrea. Not while I'm eating this delicious breakfast." He stops and grins. "Which *you* so graciously made us."

"Your appreciation is noted," she says with mocking eyes. The corners of them crinkle. I noticed they were doing that a lot this last week. She constantly wore a broad smile.

It's late October and approaching the closing date on the laundromat.

"November is just around the corner," I comment, scooping another bite.

"Oh my. You don't have to remind me. Daniel and I are counting down the days."

Daniel gives her a loving look, and she returns it with an understanding only two people who truly know each other can.

Andrea stops eating and puts her fork down. She places both hands flat against her cheeks. "Sometimes I can't believe it's all happening. If my abuela were alive, she wouldn't either. She'd be so proud. Luna in college. Daniel and I owning our own business. We've worked so hard for all of this . . . so, so very hard. The sacrifices made daily . . ."

Her eyes well up full to the brim, and Daniel coughs, bringing a fist to his mouth.

I reach across the table and squeeze Andrea's hand gently.

"But you're here now. You did it," I tell her.

She wipes at her face with a napkin. "I think I'm extra emotional because we're getting so close."

"I want to hear more about the plans you drew up," I coax. "The ones you were starting to explain the other day."

"Well . . ." She sniffs and gives me a sheepish grin. She moves to a console in the corner and pulls out a file from the drawer.

I lean forward on the table as she spreads papers out.

"These are only preliminary drawings. But I thought we could expand the laundromat into a little café eventually. You see, we'd knock this wall down"—she points to her sketched-out plan—"and we'd have so much additional room."

Her eyes light up with excitement as she goes on to explain her other ideas and visions for the place.

"This is impressive, Andrea. I'm so happy for you," I say as I pick up one of the sketches to get a closer look.

"It'll be a nice change," she sighs.

"Yeah. No more logging hours either," Daniel inserts grudgingly.

Andrea casts a look at him but then shrugs. "Yes. None of that anymore."

I lower my gaze, not wanting to give away what I already know about this unwanted change at the orchard.

She turns her head in my direction. "We don't mean to complain. The Clarks have been good to us. I chose not to say anything to you . . . you being so new. But let's just say the last year or so, things have . . . differed. Maybe not for the better."

Daniel crosses his arms and leans back in his chair.

She taps his arm affectionately. "Two more months, Daniel. Only two more months."

Charlotte bleats at me as I feed her dinner. A few of the chickens cluck around us, and I rest against the barn wall, watching them all peck at the feed.

"Easy, ladies. There's enough for everyone."

I remain against the wall, not wanting to return to the main house. I'm unsure how to act around Beau and Livia. Afraid that being around them will somehow reveal to Beau his wife's strange desire. Or that I will somehow betray Livia if I give it away, this secret game she wants to play with me.

I'm unsure whether to be around them at all . . .

The chickens appear to be done; they're moving away from me and pecking at the ground by the entryway. I reluctantly lift myself off the wall and prepare to go back into the house. But I stop when I hear others.

Raised voices echo into the barn and then die down. I take cautious steps toward the stables. The voices grow louder, circling each other with heated whispers. I reach the opening to the stables and bend my body at an angle, remaining hidden but close enough to see two people I never thought I'd witness arguing.

"How could you do this to me?" Andrea accuses.

Livia places a hand to her forehead and rubs. "We don't have a choice—"

"To Daniel . . . to *Luna*!"

"This is the last thing we want to do. I wish there was some other way," she says more quietly.

"No . . . no." Andrea shakes her head furiously, escalating her tone. "Find another way. We've been nothing but loyal workers for you for how long?"

"Believe me. This hurts us as much as it is hurting—" Livia strains her neck out with desperation.

"You're not listening to me, Livia." Andrea's face looks red and frantic. "This isn't one small bonus to us. This is our lives. Our future! Please—"

"Andrea!" Livia shouts with both hands out. "There's nothing else that can be done." Her eyes glisten and she trembles. "I'm so sorry. Please believe me . . . if it wasn't for Nina's medical expenses and the business not doing as well . . . I'm so very sorry. We both are."

Defeat dulls over Andrea's eyes and then frosts into her response. "I'm sure you both are."

Livia reaches out and touches her arm. "We can talk later . . . okay?"

Andrea stares straight ahead, stiff. She doesn't respond.

Maybe sensing it's best she leaves, Livia brushes past Andrea and exits out the other gate to the barn.

I draw back into my shadow and wait. It feels like maybe a minute has passed, but Andrea remains silent. Perhaps she's already left. I bend forward again to see, and she's suddenly there, almost running into me.

"Radley," she utters. Her voice is flat and robotic. "How long have you been standing there?"

I look back at her with sadness. "Long enough."

"I see." Her jaw tightens. Rage is there in the line of it, all the way up to her temples. But it's the vacant stare she gives me that troubles me the most.

"Andrea . . . I don't know exactly what was said, but . . ."

She inhales deeply and then nods. "You want to know what was said?"

"Only if you want to share—"

"I'll tell you what was said. Livia and Beau have informed us that they will no longer be giving season bonuses. That includes this season. Right now." She points to the ground. "This land that Daniel and I have sweat over. Worked our fingers to the bone over. It all means nothing to them. Without the bonus now . . ."

She throws her hand over her mouth. It shakes, and she brings it back down to her side in a clenched fist. "Without that bonus," she says hoarsely, "we won't be able to close on the laundromat. Which means we won't be near our Luna. Which means . . ."

It's like watching a wounded animal blindsided and tortured. "You don't have to talk." I pull her into an embrace.

She shudders in my arms and then pulls back.

"No!" she yells. "This wasn't supposed to happen. Not after all that work. Ten years. Ten loyal years! Does that mean nothing to them?"

"Andrea. Let's try to calm down. Did Livia say exactly why?"

"Something about Nina's medical bills. And overhead costs. They've gotten too high. I should have seen this coming . . ."

"Maybe let the dust settle for a bit. And then you and Daniel can go to Beau—"

"Why bother? You heard how adamant Livia was. How stern she got. She's not like that. I've never seen her be so callous. So . . ."

She locks eyes with me. "They seem so perfect, don't they? The perfect couple. The perfect family, right? They aren't, though, Radley. I've protected them all enough." The corners of her eyes narrow.

"It's all an act."

CHAPTER 30

I sit up in my bed, wakened by sharp whines and barking.

Rabbit?

I glance at the clock. Why would Rabbit be up so early? His barks grow louder. My feet find the floor. I throw my covers off and run out to see why he's making such a commotion.

Rabbit stands in the middle of the hallway. He looks up at me and then wags his tail as if glad to finally see someone. He barks furiously and backs up.

"What's wrong, boy?"

Another whine, this one more urgent. Rabbit spins, and I follow him. He scampers into Nina's room, the door ajar. I feel for the light switch on the wall. He jumps onto her bed and nuzzles her as I flip the light on.

She doesn't react to his prodding.

"Nina," I say once. I place my arms on her shoulders and shake her lightly. "Nina, wake up."

Her eyes flutter, but she otherwise remains motionless.

"Nina," I say louder.

The lights go on in the hallway and flood the room. I squint my eyes. Livia sails in next to me.

"What's wrong? Nina? Sweetie?"

She elbows me aside in her frenzy as she scoops up Nina's small body. "Nina, can you say something to Mommy?"

Her head lolls back, limp. She opens her eyes. "I don't feel so good, Mommy," her weak voice answers.

Livia feels her forehead and looks at me. "No fever from what I can tell." She turns her attention back to Nina, adjusting her in her arms. "What exactly hurts, baby?"

Nina shakes her head. "Nothing hurts. I feel very tired." She closes her eyes.

Beau materializes in the doorway. He glimpses at us and wastes no time. He takes her from Livia's arms. "Get the truck ready. We'll take her to the emergency room."

Livia nods and dashes down the stairs as Beau follows behind her carrying Nina.

"Stay with the kids," he orders me over his shoulder. Rabbit trails him, panting anxiously.

Tallan opens his door as I pass. "What's going on?" He rubs one eye sleepily. He spots Nina in Beau's cradle at the top of the stairs and steps out into the hallway. "Dad . . . where are you taking her?" he asks, troubled.

"Go back to bed, Tallan. We're going to get her checked out, okay?" Beau answers rapidly.

Rabbit follows him. "Rabbit, stay," he commands. He points to me. "Radley is in charge while we're gone." He rushes down the steps before Tallan can respond.

Tallan glances at me in a sleepy haze. "Okay."

I reach for his shoulder and pat once. "Why don't you try to get a little more sleep?"

"What time is it?"

"Four in the morning."

"Is Nina going to be okay?"

I shrug, not wanting to lie, but I don't want to worry him even more. "I'm not sure what's wrong with her. But the doctors are going to take good care of her."

He studies me, and I feel like he has something he wants to tell me. Like something is stuck in his throat, and he's trying to expel it up and out for me to find.

"Tallan?"

Worry darkens his eyes, and he rubs the top of his head. "You should try to sleep too, Radley," he says and returns to his bedroom.

The images of Nina so limp and weak replay in my head.

A wet nose bumps my hand. Rabbit gawks up at me as if asking for answers.

"She'll be back, Rabbit. Don't worry."

He tails me into the spare room, and I sit on the bed, stroking the top of his silky head. Watching the minutes go by. Eventually Rabbit lies down on the floor by the bed and falls asleep.

Light from the dawn is sneaking in under my window shade when my phone rings.

"Livia," I answer. "How is she?"

"She's fine. She's fine . . . ," she says immediately. Breathily.

"What did they say happened?"

Livia exhales.

I hear Nina in the background asking for more juice. Beau murmurs something, and she requests animal crackers.

"Sounds like she might be doing okay?"

I can practically hear Livia nodding rapidly. "Yes, yes. Thank God for that. All her vitals were stable when we arrived at the emergency room. We had to wait awhile until she finally got looked at by a doctor."

"That must have been so hard . . . the waiting."

"It was. I just wanted someone to check her. But I guess her case wasn't urgent enough. Anyway." Her voice pulls away. "Yes, sweetie. You can have two packs if you want." She breathes into the phone. "She's more alert now. And starving."

She's okay . . . she's going to be okay.

I sink back into the bed. Rabbit raises his head at me.

"They ran her labs," Livia continues. "Her numbers were very low. That's why she was so incredibly weak."

"Do they know what caused the drop?"

"No . . . they couldn't figure that out," she answers more quietly.

"We would never have known. If it hadn't been for Rabbit." I look down at him, and his brow twitches. I motion for him to come up to the bed. He lunges up and circles into a ball next to me.

"I know . . . if it hadn't been for Rabbit . . . ," Livia says shakily. "They're going to release her late afternoon. Keep her for the day for observation. We'll be home then."

We hang up and I turn to Rabbit. "Did you hear that, boy? She's coming home today." I scratch behind his ears. "Someone's getting a steak bone tonight."

Avie wakes up shortly after and barrages me with a million questions about Nina, Rabbit, and when everyone will be back. I patiently answer her while making toast and scrambled eggs for breakfast. Tallan eats wordlessly at the counter, his silence more than making up for Avie's chattering.

"Tallan, can you please pass the butter?" she asks.

He turns his head and takes a bite of his toast.

"Pass the butter, *please*," she repeats touchily.

He gives her a strange look. And remains still.

"Why are you looking at me like that?" she whines.

"Tallan," I say. I reach over the counter and slide the butter dish to Avie. "Your sister asked nicely."

He stares at Avie again, a little too long, and then zeroes in on me. "Sorry."

Avie cuts off a pat of butter, oblivious to him now that she has what she wanted. When I glance back at Tallan, he's reverted to his toast.

I toss a blob of egg toward Rabbit, who catches it in his mouth.

Nina and the others return as promised in the late afternoon. Beau and Livia settle her in her bedroom with much shushing at Avie, who is off-the-walls excited at the homecoming.

"She needs alone time, Avie. She's been through a lot today," Livia scolds after the third time she's reminded her to quiet down.

"Avie. Why don't you come with me and help make dinner," I say, touching her shoulder. "Meatballs tonight. You can roll them."

Livia holds the skin between her eyes and then mouths a thank-you to me.

A hushed dinner follows, with Nina still up in her bedroom resting. Beau and Livia, like zombies, peck at their plates with forks. Tallan asks to be excused first, and it's an early bedtime for the children. They settle in quickly. The house requires a return to a composure lost the previous night.

Beau, Livia, and I clean the kitchen together. We're a muted threesome; only the clinking of plates and silverware penetrates through the uncomfortable dance we perform, sliding past each other courteously as we rinse the plates and load the dishwasher. No one utters a word. No one wants to move past the simple act of cleaning the kitchen.

The air is blemished and oily with our discomfort.

Livia goes to open the front door, muttering something about it being too stuffy. She marches through the foyer. I hear the door fling open. And then a startled gasp.

Beau and I share a millisecond of a look. We hurry to the front and halt at what we find. Two unexpected guests at the door, standing side by side behind the screen.

They hold hands and angrily stare through the black distorted mesh.

"Good evening, Andrea and Daniel," I hear Beau say.

CHAPTER 31

"How can we help you tonight?" Beau asks. He steps forward and leans into the door, holding the top of the frame.

Andrea holds her head high, the wind sweeping her curls across her face. "You talk to us like we're strangers, Beau."

Beau's chest expands.

"As if we haven't been in your home before," she continues. "Shared meals together. Cared for your own children."

"Andrea. Now let's be calm about this, all right? I hear you—"

"You don't hear me. And no. There's nothing you can *do* to help us, Beau. Not anymore."

Livia opens the screen door and slides to the side hurriedly. "Why don't you two come in. Have you eaten?" Her tone is chirpy and all wrong.

Andrea shifts her gaze to Livia with indignation. "Yes. We've eaten, Livia. How kind of you to think of us," she mocks.

Daniel lightly touches her wrist. "Let's tell them what we came here to say. We don't need to waste our energy doing any of this back-and-forth. We know who they are now."

His eyes meet Beau's, and a disappointed expression plays out over them. Beau grimaces as if Daniel has thrown a punch.

"Look. Daniel. Andrea," Beau starts with open palms. "We don't want it to be like this. Please. Come inside. Sit down. We can talk . . . we're here to listen to you."

Daniel shares a gaze with Andrea. They step inside together, still clasping hands tightly, drawing strength from each other. She catches my stare and gives me a flash of a tight smile.

I wonder if I should stay. Whatever disagreement they have is between them and not for me to be privy to.

I motion upstairs. "I can go and check on the kids while you all—"

"That's okay," says Livia. "I'd like you to stay, Radley. Please." She looks at me pleadingly.

Beau leads us into the kitchen. We all sit down at the table cluttered with the remaining few dirty plates.

Livia scans the mess. "Sorry about the dishes. We were cleaning up when you knocked."

"It's fine," Andrea says more civilly.

Beau straightens in his chair. "Okay. We're all ears. Livia and I are ready to listen."

Andrea shoots a quick look at Daniel. He nods once and keeps his eyes on the table, appearing to not want to engage any more than he has to.

Andrea's brown doe-like eyes that once carried so much vigor and energy are lackluster. She looks older, as if having drunk from a well that dries one out rather than replenishing. The rosy, opinionated, ebullient Andrea ready to reach for all the possibilities, the world a cushion rather than a trap, has faded away. In her place is someone I don't recognize.

Someone I twitch at knowing.

She presses her mouth closed and shuts her eyes tight. Breathing out, she opens them. Determined. Ready. Vengeful.

"We're leaving the orchard. Daniel and I. Tonight."

Stunned silence follows her announcement.

I keep my head bowed, not wanting to make any sudden movements. Daniel clears his throat and jerks his head to the side.

A wind gust blows the screen door open, and it flaps a few times.

Livia is the first to break the dead air.

"Why, Andrea?" she asks, barely audible. She spreads her hands out onto the table.

Andrea's brow knits into a scowl. "Why?"

"Yes. Why?"

"You honestly have the gall to ask why? As if you don't have a clue to the pain you've caused. To me and Daniel. To our family."

Livia sinks into her chair. Andrea is not here to spare anyone.

"A family you both once claimed was like your very own. Well." She crosses her arms. "'Family' must have a different definition in this house. Isn't it convenient now, when things are getting tough for you, to simply toss us to the side. Like garbage."

"You're not garbage to us. That's ridiculous," Beau says flatly.

Andrea tilts her head. "Funny. Sure seems like it."

"Andrea. That's not the case," he says softly.

She shakes her head. "You don't get it . . ."

"Livia tried to explain to you because we thought it would be better coming from her. But I'm here now." Beau puts his hand to his chest. "And I want you to believe me when I say, it's the last thing I wanted to do. On my father's life, we had no choice. The business doesn't run as smoothly as it used to. And it hurts me to even admit that."

Beau's face is pained; a line forms between his brows.

Andrea sighs. "You really don't get it. Do you?"

"Get what exactly?"

"You don't know what it's like. To be born into a position where you have to start in a negative space behind the starting line. Try that for a change, Beau, and then maybe you can get back to me about what really *hurts.*"

He blinks hard. "Andrea. You're being unreasonable."

"Am I?" she scoffs. "Couldn't throw your devoted workers a bone? Wonder what Daddy would say about that if he were here?"

Beau's jaw draws taut. He runs his hands through his hair and looks down at the ground, trying to compose himself.

Livia nervously touches his arm. "Maybe we should talk about this tomorrow. When we've all had a chance to sleep on it."

Daniel starts to get up. "Yes. Maybe that's for the best."

Andrea pulls him back down. "No. This ends tonight. We're leaving. Not another minute spent longer on this land than we have to."

"Andrea?" a small voice calls out.

All eyes shoot to the bottom of the stairwell. Tallan stands behind Avie. Her shoulders heave up and down as she holds in tears.

"You're leaving us?" she asks.

Andrea rises from the table. Tallan and Avie watch her with equally distraught faces, never taking their eyes from her as she goes to them. She puts her hands over Tallan's cheeks and then kneels to Avie and does the same.

"Yes. It's true. Daniel and I have to go. We have another . . . journey waiting for us."

Avie begins to cry, sputtering and shaking her head. "No, Andrea. You can't leave us!"

"But I have to, Avie. Luna needs me, and Daniel now . . . we need each other. More than ever." She gives her a kiss on the forehead. "But I will miss you children."

Livia covers her mouth. Beau's upper lip stiffens, and he looks away.

Andrea stands up. She pats Tallan under the chin. "Be a good boy," she tells him. His face scrunches up briefly, but he bites his lip with a nod.

"You too, Avie. Watch out for little Nina. She needs you."

She tears herself away and motions at Daniel to follow her. They've almost reached the door when Avie shouts.

"Wait!"

She runs to Andrea, who turns around and allows Avie to leap into a hug.

"Goodbye, Andrea," says Avie into her shoulder.

Andrea squeezes her eyes shut. "Goodbye, Avie."

When she opens them, she looks up to glare at Livia and Beau.

The look in her eyes flares, the flames of unforgiveness dancing in them.

Livia is too upset afterward to take the kids back upstairs. I hold Avie's hand and lead her up to her bedroom. She sniffs a few more times and asks for a tissue. I retrieve one, and she pulls her covers up high.

"Maybe they can visit? With Luna too."

This thought seems to satisfy her. I remain silent, not wanting to break her temporary consolation.

"Yes . . . that'll be fun," she tells herself. "But Nina will take this pretty hard when she finds out in the morning." She grows troubled again.

"You're right about that. So, let's be sure to comfort her when she needs it. Okay? But in the meantime, let's try to go back to sleep."

Avie snuggles deeper into her bed. "Okay. I'll try. Good night, Radley," she says as I shut her door.

I stick my head into Tallan's room on the way back to my own.

He's lying straight on his back. Staring up with wide-open eyes. His hands are clasped over his chest, and he blinks.

He barely acknowledges my presence.

"Tallan? You all right?" I ask, shifting in from the hallway.

He nods. "I keep thinking about Andrea and Daniel."

I sit on the edge of his bed.

"How fast it all happens. How fast people can just be removed from our lives," he says, pensive.

"I know it's hard, Tallan, but . . . people do come and go."

He doesn't respond at first, focusing harder on the ceiling, as if he sees something I don't. I get up to leave, and he finally says, "We were wrong to let them go like that."

I pause and watch him turn to his side.

"There's too much that's wrong in this house."

CHAPTER 32

I dream of a drum beating.

A wooden mallet striking over and over. The thick handle and bulbous head, meeting the skin-like sheath stretched thin, a vibration that I feel in the tips of my fingers. The beating gets louder as it speeds up.

What is it warning me of?

A pulse that matches mine.

I confront the drumming inside me, and I wake up.

The drumming continues. Once, twice, and then in quick succession. A knock downstairs. Incessant pounding at the door.

I'm alert. There's no fog of arousal, like a switch flicked on. I'm wide eyed. My legs carry me quickly, down the steps and to the front door. My thin nightshirt clings to me as I throw a sweater over my shoulders.

The beating hasn't stopped. Shouts from a male as I hurl the door open.

He's out of breath and hunched over. He points to the field behind him.

A wall of fire burns.

Ripping north with fierce winds blowing the firestorm onward. I hear the screeching of flames, seemingly delighted at the destruction it creates. The orchard stranded, her only choice to brace herself for what's to come.

She's burning. She's burning away into nothing.

Daniel launches himself past me. "Where's Beau? Wake him up!"

Before he has a chance to go search, Beau and Livia emerge behind us, frozen in place. For one second none of us can breathe. Nobody is ready to allow the apocalypse that rages on like a blazing light show to be a reality.

Denial comes easy with disaster.

Beau stumbles forward onto the porch, his fingers spread out by the sides of his head. Horror electrified in his eyes as animated flames reflect in them.

"No. Not here. This can't happen here," he utters, pulling a finger to the top of his lip.

Livia grabs his arm. "Beau," she says once.

He snaps his attention to her. "Call the fire department. I'm going out there."

"What?" she cries. "Are you crazy?"

"It hasn't reached the trees yet—"

"The winds are too strong! We don't stand a chance."

"Do you think I'm just going to sit here and watch it all burn?" he shouts back. "This is my land. *My* family!"

She tightens her grip. "Think of our children," she says through gritted teeth.

"I am," he growls.

Daniel races down the front steps, waving us all to follow him. "Come on. There's no time for this!"

Beau nods, rushing to him, and taps him on the arm. "Daniel. Thank you."

Daniel's expression stays neutral. He yanks his phone out of his pocket and starts to dial. He nods, and they bolt together, running in the direction of the barn stable. Rabbit appears abruptly, his fur brushing against my leg as he races after them and barks with alarm. The fire seems to grow larger as if reacting to their approach.

Livia watches them desperately; the farther they get, the more frantically she trembles beside me. She pulls me close to her face, our noses nearly touching. "We can't let them go alone. Please. We have to help them!"

I turn back to the field. The flames have grown more intense, the bursts of orange now flashing with bloodlike red.

I can't stand here, either, and watch it all vanish.

"Please, Radley," she begs.

I grab her hand and pull her down the steps. Our legs kick behind us, the grass ironically wet. But nothing can match the scorching beast we run toward.

We reach the guest cottage. Andrea steps outside, a shawl wrapped around her. A tight braid down her back. Her mouth hangs partly open. She turns to us like a robot.

"Daniel," she says, hushed. "Daniel . . . where's my Daniel?" Her eyes are wide with fear and realization.

"He's with Beau," answers Livia.

She hastens toward us, her hand gripping her shawl so tightly her knuckles bulge. "How could you let them go out there?"

"I didn't . . . I—I tried to stop them, Andrea," Livia stutters. "They're—"

Andrea snaps her head away, not wanting to waste any more time. She darts past us, running faster than I've ever seen her move. We follow her, trailing behind. Smoke fills our lungs.

She reaches the stables first. Pitching horse blankets at each of us, she drags one for herself and hurries to the orchard. We run down the rows of trees like children. But it's not a magical night for playing. It's a night for survival.

We find Daniel and Beau at the end of the orchard line, beating the encroaching wall of fire with blankets. Rabbit ferociously barks; the lower half of his body backs up, his front paws spread out in guard mode. The blaze roars back with great flames, growing impossibly higher and higher. Their blankets whip up into the air and down, rhythmic with each strike. Yet each repetitive beat seems useless against the inferno.

We join them.

We never stop.

An endless battle, fending off the sting of hot embers. Our chests grow thick with smoke, heaving in and out, struggling to raise our arms one more time—one more bid to beat back the monster.

The first tree catches fire.

Quickly it disintegrates into nothing as the fire spreads like blood through veins, channels going every which way through the branches until the entire tree is ablaze. A beautiful inferno and the star in the opening act of destruction.

A stick of dynamite lit, the flare spreads like a disease and illuminates the entire row. Flash after flash, each tree ignites. Orange erupts across the orchard field. Fire sizzles down each carefully planted row, tended to with such patience—only to become crackling bonfires in seconds. A whoosh of forceful air flares with each one, the tops of the trees dancing with flickering flames as they laugh with triumph. The fruitful field has turned into a pyre visible for miles.

We shield our faces and stagger backward. The orchard is engulfed in a sea of fire.

It's Livia who finally hears the first siren. She waves her arms, calling for help. The trucks from the nearest fire station have arrived. But the minutes tick by, and each tick of the clock is another piece of the orchard burned away. It feels like an eternity has passed when the first spray of water finally hits the firestorm.

It's too late. The wind, a fierce partner to the fire, has done its part in hurtling the flames through each branch, leaf, and blade. Burning, unstoppable at best, as futile attempts merely singe the blaze, angering it into roaring back with intensity. Hungry for more, insatiable and hardly satisfied. Not wanting or able to stop until it's all gone.

The entire orchard is gone.

Smoke fills the sky, feathery and slow. A dimly lit horizon does nothing to temper the devastation of the charred trees, soldiers all defeated after battle. The neighboring fire stations at long last join. Their yells vault through the air, voices echoing as we stand together in defeat. *There is no second water source . . . rapid brush fire . . . they didn't stand a chance.*

I look at Beau and Livia, dazed and numb, their faces darkened by soot and sorrow. Daniel begins to cough next to them and steps back, turning his head from the last of what the firefighters are attempting to salvage.

Andrea stands alone to the side, her shawl long abandoned. Hunched over and in a trance. She takes in the burned ruin, and a slow smile creeps over her mouth. It deepens with her tears. Her eyes are in anguish, yet her mouth says otherwise.

We sense the morning push in through the smoky air. An eerie quiet settles. And it's then that Livia turns around without warning. She runs back toward the house, breathless and arms clawing through the air.

The children. We forgot about the children.

I catch up to her as we approach the house. Two figures sit on the front porch. We scramble, fighting to get there faster to reach the children.

Tallan sits on the top step. He holds a sleeping Nina in his arms. He slowly looks up at us with hollowed eyes.

"She's gone," he says hoarsely.

"Who? Who is gone?" Livia demands.

"Avie."

She doesn't wait for an explanation. Tearing through the house, she calls for her. I follow suit, racing through each room, calling for Avie. Our yells repeating, the syllables of her name running into each other until nearly undecipherable.

Avie. Avie. Avie!

I stare at her empty bed. The sheets crumpled like a nest. I touch them and try to feel for warmth. For a sign of her.

And then I hear it downstairs. The realization in Livia's screams.

CHAPTER 33

"I had a f-feeling. I had a feeling in the pit of my stomach as soon as we ran t-toward the house," Livia stammers.

Tears run down her face, creating streams through the soot coating her cheeks. "I knew . . ."

The on-scene arriving officer hands her a glass of water. She takes a drink and swallows.

"I knew," she says again.

The officer takes back the glass with a somber face. He's young and hands me the glass as if I should know what to do with it.

"Here," I say, taking the glass from him.

He looks relieved. "The state fire investigator and her team should be here soon. Driving in from Portland. Fox Isle's department doesn't handle this kind of thing."

I observe his Fox Isle insignia, a red and blue stitched badge.

"What about for a missing child?" I ask. "I think that takes priority here."

"That's up to the sheriff. He's arriving soon. I don't know if it's been long enough since the child went missing—"

"We're not waiting." Beau's voice booms across the kitchen. He raises his head from his hands and lifts his elbows from the counter. "Avie wouldn't run off. She's not like that. She would never . . ." His voice cracks.

Tires squeal outside. A car door slams shut. A few seconds later, Faye bursts into the kitchen. She goes to Beau first, and he embraces her.

"I don't understand. How did this happen?" she cries shakily.

He shushes her with a kiss to the top of her head. "That's what we're trying to find out." He shoots the officer a hard stare. "When exactly is the sheriff getting here?"

The officer checks his phone. "Let me give him a call." He steps out to the foyer.

"Where's Tallan and Nina?" Faye looks to me and then Livia.

"Both upstairs in Nina's room. Tallan is with her. We don't want them to be around all this right now," Livia answers. But her eyes are blank as she stares in the direction of the refrigerator. They rove over to Faye. "How is it that she's gone, Faye? How is it that everything's gone?"

Faye's expression turns to stone. She sits next to Livia at the table and holds her tight, rocking back and forth, whispering quiet words in her ear.

The officer returns and slaps his phone a few times in his palm triumphantly. "Sheriff will be here any moment with our lead investigator. He'd like to question each of you individually, if that's okay."

Sheriff Sam Waters introduces himself ten minutes later. He's broad shouldered and stiff in his movements. A slender man with sharp, flinty-blue eyes and no hair on his head stands next to him.

"Detective Paul Fournier. He'll be taking on the investigation of your missing person report," Sheriff Waters explains. "We've got an unusual situation here with a dual investigation. I'll be working closely with the state fire marshal's investigation division. They've assigned Stacy Omidi, and I can assure you, whatever caused this fire . . . she'll figure it out."

Beau approaches them both. "I don't mean to be rude. But my daughter is missing. That's the only thing we care about right now."

"Yes, yes." Sheriff Waters clears his throat and looks to Detective Fournier. "You were going to start with questioning?"

"Questioning?" Beau's eyes dart between them. "Shouldn't we be dispatching a search team? There are miles of forest, not to mention the ocean—"

"We've already done that," Detective Fournier interjects with calm. "Two squads and two search dogs. Based on the description you gave dispatch, we're informing the teams. Now do you have something we can have the dogs sniff? Something that would have your daughter's scent? Avie's, I mean."

Livia stands up. "Yes. Avie has this stuffed rabbit she adores. She carries it everywhere. I'll go get it." She quickly exits to go upstairs.

Detective Fournier focuses his attention on Faye and me. "Apologies. You both are family members?"

Faye raises her hand. "Grandmother."

Understanding flashes in his eyes. He looks at me expectantly.

"Employee," I reply curtly.

Beau stretches his hand out sideways. "I'm sorry, but did you say how long until the teams begin searching? When will this start exactly?"

"Soon is all I can say." Detective Fournier doesn't seem fazed by Beau's urgency. "I'm not one to give false promises. You'll find I'm quite to the point. My job isn't to embellish."

"Yes. Your job is to find Avie."

"Correct. So, let's not waste any more time. Right now what we *can* do is start getting the facts. I need to know everything that occurred yesterday—that means daytime, evening, and everything leading up to the fire onward. No small fact is meaningless. It all matters at this point."

Sheriff Waters's phone chimes. He checks it and puts it back in his pocket. "Omidi is getting close. She'll want to meet with us first," he says quietly to Detective Fournier.

"Then we need to get started. Why don't you escort everyone but family outside for now," he orders, eyes flickering over me. "I'll start by talking with the father first."

Sheriff Waters motions, and I follow him through the front door. "You can wait here," he says, pointing to the porch swing. "Detective Fournier will come out if he needs you."

He walks back into the house stockily.

I sit on the swing as Rabbit scampers up the steps.

"Where have you been, boy?" I ask him softly. I massage behind his ears, and he whines, staring up at me with knowing eyes. "We'll find her . . . don't worry, we'll find her."

Please . . . let her be okay. Let her come home safe.

The shock of the last hours begins to make waves through my limbs. My chest tightens. I find my feet rising and search for the horizon. To breathe again. The skyline continues to smolder from the doused fire. Tunnels of smoke swirl up diagonally and dissipate. I make out the figures of firefighters still tending to the scene.

And then I think I see her. Grace. Standing in a cloud of smoke at the edge of the field as she takes in the damage. The haze conceals her, and then I can't make her out again.

"What in the hell happened?" Chester's voice blasts.

I didn't even notice Chester and Sidney approaching the house. I was so focused on what I thought I saw. Or perhaps didn't really see . . .

They gawk at me from the bottom of the steps.

"There was a fire . . . and Avie . . . ," I begin to say. And then I realize how late they are in coming to work.

"When did you two get here?" I ask.

Chester glances at Sidney. "Just now . . . why? And how did the fire start?"

Sidney keeps her gaze on the ground.

"Seems later than when you usually start."

They've been so eager lately to get every minute of work in. Even working before daylight touches the fields. But today they were unusually late.

"None of your concern when or why we start, Radley," Chester responds with irritation. "Now what is this about Avie? Speak clearly—you're talking all over the place."

Sheriff Waters swings open the screen door. "Radley, is it?" He steps halfway out, holding it open.

"Yes?"

"Detective Fournier wants to question you next." He notices Chester and Sidney and gives them a quick nod. "Morning."

They say nothing, side by side in their staring.

I follow Sheriff Waters inside, and he takes me back to the kitchen. Beau sits across from Detective Fournier. His face appears to have aged overnight, distraught with lines I've never seen before. Faye pats his back and looks up at me with hollow eyes.

"You're Radley?" Detective Fournier turns to me.

"Yes."

"Please. Have a seat. A few questions, if you don't mind."

Beau moves to get up. Detective Fournier holds up a finger. "We can continue with more questions once your wife comes back down."

There's no need to wait, since Livia rushes into the kitchen. "It's gone. I can't find it."

Avie's stuffed rabbit.

"Are you sure?" Beau starts to move to the stairs. "Did you check her closet?"

"I've looked everywhere. I turned her room upside down. It's not there. She sleeps with it every single night."

"What about the playroom?" Faye asks.

"It's not there."

Detective Fournier's expression sobers. "Did you notice anything else missing while you searched?"

Livia gazes at him, startled. "That's the thing. Nothing else is missing. Her room is untouched . . . except for her rabbit."

"Which means . . . ," Beau starts.

"It means if someone took her, it's likely they also knew to take the rabbit with them," Detective Fournier finishes.

CHAPTER 34

"How exactly are you employed with the Clark family?"

Detective Fournier looks over his reading glasses. We're alone in the playroom. The comedy in him sitting clumsily in a child-size chair is all wrong, given the circumstances.

"Orchard worker. I was a last-minute fill-in for Beau's cousin."

He waves his hand once in a circle. "You have much experience with orchards?" His piercing eyes give me a once-over that makes me want to cover up.

"I didn't have any. This whole move was to do something different."

He slides his pen under a note on his pad of paper. "But from what I understand, you also take care of the children?"

"Yes."

"So, you're their nanny?"

"No."

He pauses. "Then how would you describe your job as someone who takes care of other people's children?"

Other people's.

"I help out here and there. Mainly dropping off and picking up the oldest from school. You might have heard Nina, their youngest, has been very ill lately."

"And when did this helping out start?"

"A few weeks ago."

"So not long?"

"Not really. Almost a month maybe."

"But long enough that you moved into the house?"

He holds the question like a drop cloth, ready to let go and expose me for whatever he thinks needs exposing.

"Livia asked me to move in once it became apparent Nina would need to be taken to Portland for medical appointments."

Detective Fournier plops his pen down. "You've had quite the access to this family. Some would say a front-row seat."

Front and center.

"I've kept to myself for the most part."

"Really?" He furrows his brow skeptically. "Livia says you're close friends. That she trusts you implicitly."

"She did?"

"Dinners and glasses of wine together. I imagine intimate conversations."

I raise my head high. "If you're asking if I saw or heard anything unusual, I didn't."

Why are you protecting them? What's in it for you, Radley?

"Nothing at all, huh?"

"No."

He crosses his arms, lax. "Would you say Beau and Livia have a good marriage?"

A good marriage. A decent marriage. One everyone wants to have.

"They're both very busy. Beau manages a lot with the orchard. And of course, with three children, one of them sick, Livia has a lot on her plate."

"You know"—he leans closer—"usually when people say 'busy,' it's a euphemism for 'distant.'"

"Your word, not mine, Detective Fournier."

A small smirk emerges on his mouth and then flashes away.

"What about the children? Tallan, Avie . . . and Nina, right? How has their behavior been lately?"

I shrug. "Nina is very fatigued most of the time. And Tallan is your typical preteen. Moody, trying to figure out middle school."

"And Avie?"

"Bright. Big on pleasing. Loves her little sister . . ."

How is it that I'm sitting here answering these questions? How is it she's gone?

I hold my fingers under my nose. "I'm sorry," I say, shaking my head. "I want to help in any way I can. But I don't know what it is you're looking for here?"

He puts his hands up together in a point. "I'm looking for anything that would lead me to why an eight-year-old girl would be taken in the middle of the night."

"So, you think she was taken?"

He nods.

"And the fire? What if that has something to do with her kidnapping?"

"That certainly has not been ruled out. And we're going to do everything we can to find Avie."

He holds up a finger. "One more question."

"Okay."

"Do Livia and Beau have any enemies you're aware of? Anyone who would want to hurt them?"

I can think of a few as of late . . .

My stalling intrigues him. He peers at me. "Have they fought with anyone? Any arguments you may have overheard?"

I look up at him and hold his gaze. "They have neighbors, Grace and Vaughn Jean, who had a falling-out with them. And . . ."

A few disgruntled workers.

"Anyone else?" he asks eagerly.

Don't do it. Don't bring them into this.

"No. No one else that I can think of."

At the hospital, I squeeze Andrea's shoulder once as she sits by Daniel's bedside.

"Hey. He's going to be fine. The doctor said he'll make a full recovery."

She looks up at me with red-rimmed eyes. "I know . . . I know . . . but seeing him like this."

Once out of the haze of the fire, Daniel was short of breath. When it became apparent it wasn't getting better in the open air, he was sent via ambulance to the hospital for smoke inhalation.

She strokes the top of his head; his eyes remain closed as he breathes in and out of a cannula.

"I've never seen him so exhausted."

"Let him rest. You need to rest also, Andrea."

She rubs her forehead wearily. "Yes . . . I really do. But I can't leave him."

A nurse steps in to check his vitals. "I'm so sorry. I couldn't help but overhear. Visiting hours are ending soon," she says with authority.

Andrea lifts her head. "He'll be all alone, though."

She gives her a sympathetic smile. "He's in good hands. You can come back in the morning."

"Oh . . . I rode in the ambulance. I don't have my car."

I touch her knee. "I can take you home."

"Home," she mumbles. "It doesn't seem like it."

With further coaxing from me, and after promising a sleeping Daniel she'll return first thing, I manage to get Andrea to the car. She rests her head to the side, mostly quiet as we drive back.

"I can't believe it about Avie. I know I haven't said anything. But I could only focus on Daniel," she eventually says to the window. "Any news? I keep hoping she'll just show up and it's all a bad dream."

I turn the wipers on once it starts to sprinkle. "Nothing yet. At least last I heard."

She turns her head to me. "Maybe I should get a motel in town. I don't feel right going back."

"Why?" I give her a quick look. "It's where you live."

"Is it?" she asks tersely.

"Andrea. They don't want you to leave."

"Doesn't matter. Once Daniel is discharged, we're out of here. Luna needs us. She's worried sick about her father."

"You told her?"

"Yes. As soon as we got to the hospital."

I glance at her sideways. "You haven't told me yet what happened last night. Before the fire."

She twists her body back to the window. "What do you mean?"

"Daniel was the one who alerted us about the fire."

She doesn't answer.

"Andrea?"

"Interesting choice of a word."

I knit my brows. "Which word?"

She turns to me with purpose. "'Us.'"

The rain starts to pick up, and I increase the wiper speed.

Andrea doesn't move. "You. Beau. Livia. Quite the 'us.'"

"That's ridiculous, Andrea."

"It's not."

"There aren't any sides here. Avie is missing. I think we're all on the same side."

She exhales loudly. "I was asleep. If you want to know every detail. I was exhausted emotionally and physically, as you can understand."

"And Daniel?"

"Daniel sometimes has trouble sleeping. He must have gone outside like he does occasionally to get fresh air. I'm assuming that's when he saw the fire." She scoffs. "If it wasn't for him, you'd all be toast."

Her comment reeks of bitterness. I feel my body go cold.

I pull onto Clark Orchard land. The road doesn't seem as quaint and charming as when I first drove through it, the path rockier and the trees half bare. A picturesque scene gone ragged.

Police cars remain parked near the main house. Livia stands with Beau outside one of them. Detective Fournier appears to be leaving, his bald head ducking into the passenger side, Sheriff Waters holding the opposite door.

Livia watches us drive by from under an umbrella Beau holds for her. Something in her stare is unsettling. A predator ready to pounce. I slow the car, taken off guard by this unfamiliar energy she projects. She finds Andrea's eyes.

It's at that moment she strikes. Ambushing the car, she knocks on the passenger window.

"Stop the car, Radley," she demands. She continues knocking, never giving pause. "Stop the car!"

I slam on the brakes. Livia throws open the passenger door.

"You did this. You did this, didn't you?" Her face is an inch from Andrea's as she projects each word of her accusation with force.

Andrea sits stoically and stares straight ahead through the windshield.

Livia darkens. "I know it was you. You and Daniel. Who else would want to hurt us this bad?"

The rain dampens her hair, her shirt covered in dark wet spots. Andrea ignores her, which only fuels Livia further into a deeper rage. The anger changes her face into one I don't recognize.

"Say something!" she yells.

Beau comes up behind Livia, pulling her back, but she shakes him off in a violent twisting motion.

"You know . . . I can see it in your eyes. You know what happened to my baby!" she cries. Beau brings her into a bear hug, lifting her away as she flails. "Tell me. Tell me where my baby is!"

"Livia!" Beau barks. "This isn't the way."

Detective Fournier and Sheriff Waters step outside the police vehicles, watching with squinted eyes through the rain.

I move to drive forward, but Andrea's hand darts out and stops me. She whips her head back to face all of them.

"My husband is in the hospital because of you all after trying to save this godforsaken orchard. We had nothing to do with Avie disappearing or the fire," she says slow and growly through gritted teeth.

She sneers. "But that sure as hell doesn't mean I didn't enjoy watching everything around you burn."

CHAPTER 35

"The 'golden years,' you called them."

"Yes."

"I'd like you to tell me the story of those years."

Dr. Edair's voice soothes me. The tips of my fingers tingle, and I lay my arms above my head.

"There are some people who claim how blessed they are with their family," I start. "And maybe they really mean it. And maybe they're really right about it. But this family. My family. We were perfection and blessings."

"'Perfection,'" she purrs. "You have spoken that word a lot in this office. Why does it resonate so much with you?"

My eyelids shut halfway. When I think about the past, it grows heavy on me as I picture those lingering scenes. Scenes that play on 35 mm black-and-white film. Dr. Edair wants me to view the past again. A tunnel into what she thinks are happier times. But how wrong she is about that.

Dane and Dove. Dane and Dove.

We had our golden years. We had our chance at happiness. But it wasn't the "easy" that stuck in my memories. When a crack formed in the wheel, I kept spinning, never knowing when it would finally split. Finally breaking apart when I had to stop.

It's the "hard" we can't ever forget.

So pretty, Mommy. All for you.

I traced the tiny lens on the side of the golden bird's body. The charm hung on a delicate chain around my neck. I held the charm up to one eye and blinked through the lens at the projection of a photo. Dane laughed while he had Dove on his shoulders.

"Happy Mother's Day," I heard the two of them chime, Dove's high two-year-old voice like bells.

"I love it," I said, pressing the charm against my chest.

"Best mother ever," Dane said with an admiring smile.

"Best," Dove repeated, her eyes crinkled as she flexed her hands out.

Best mother ever. Best at what she does. Best at staying afloat.

I felt Dane's scrutiny. Wondering if I truly loved the gift. Wondering if I was forcing happiness.

"Where do you want to eat dinner?" he asked me later, after I'd put Dove down for her nap.

"You didn't have anything planned?"

I hated the way my voice sounded. Accusing and shrill. I hated the person I'd become. Unevenly tempered and fractious. I hated the way my tone must have sounded in Dove's ears.

Mommy so angry. Mommy so unhappy.

"I wasn't sure what you wanted . . . I thought maybe . . . ," he began but then shook his head. "I can never please you, Radley."

"What?"

Somehow, his sudden testimony of truth irritated me even more. As if it was dramatic and exaggerated and all kinds of wrong.

But he was accurate. Correct. He'd filled the right bubble on the answer sheet.

"All I want is for you to do something without me asking. You make me feel like such a nag," I said huskily.

He looked flustered. Panicked. And I felt sick and annoyed with him all at once.

"What about the kalguksu shop?" he blurted out.

"Which one?"

"The one we first met at."

I became calm. A calmed dragon no longer breathing fire. It was a sweet and nostalgic suggestion. He was quite good at that sort of thing at times. So we took Dove to the same shop. But the old woman wasn't there. It was her daughter.

"Where's your mother?" Dane asked.

"Retired," the worn-out daughter answered. Emotionless, she ladled out broth and noodles and slid three bowls at us. As the soup steamed into my nostrils, I knew right away the noodles were too hot for Dove.

"Be careful, let it cool—"

He was oblivious, too excited to give Dove a taste and already holding out a twirl of noodles for her. She bit into them hungrily. Immediately she began to cry. Red faced, placing her hands over her mouth like tape.

"Dane," I snapped. "Of course it's too hot! Why didn't you wait?"

He grabbed a glass of water, but she shook her head hard, more angry than hurt. It turned into a full-blown tantrum.

We left the shop after barely eating our dishes.

Dane suggested we stop to get ice cream before turning in. Dove lapped up the mochi flavor, and it cooled each of us down, a torrent of unrest and misery turned to happiness in one swoop. The boat we rocked back and forth from one extreme to the next was beginning to wear on me.

More than even I could have ever anticipated.

We made love that night, and afterward he whispered in my ear: "Let's make another one." He lay on his side as I looked up at the ceiling.

"Another what."

He laughed, but it wasn't funny. Not really anyway. "Another baby."

I stayed quiet.

He stroked the side of my arm. "Maybe another Dove. Or who knows. A boy this time?"

I didn't wait to contemplate my next words. I probably should have. Once I said them, it never was the same after that. Perhaps I knew that would happen. That's why I said them, spitting the words out like something bad-tasting in my mouth.

"There's not going to be another time, Dane."

His fingers stopped stroking me. Had I insulted him by not agreeing to his future plan? Or was it that I didn't want another child . . . with him. I'll never know. We never talked about it again.

My tolerance for rocking from one extreme to the next, for our family's daily torments, began to weaken after that.

What was wrong with me? Why couldn't I be happy with this blessing dropped in my lap? I had everything I'd wanted. Everything I thought I'd wanted, at least. And yet I couldn't keep up with them, two happy drifters contently floating far away from me. Farther and farther away. Was it only a matter of time before I was left alone?

The grind of working during the day at SeoWoo Tech and picking up Dove from day care was draining. *This* was a routine that didn't provide comfort.

Bit by bit, a rock getting chipped away at—the hole deepening with each tiring day. A job that was supposed to be a means to an end. Gorgeous travel posts taunted me as I scrolled on my phone during my lunch hour, reminding me of what I'd forgone. Yet as soon as I had Dove in my arms, her soft touch around my neck as she kissed my cheek, exclaiming she missed me, would immediately make me feel an ocean of guilt.

The tug and pull of my wants and her needs, the guilt versus the bitterness, was starting to tear my insides.

I blamed myself. I blamed my inability to be happy anymore, to find my happiness in Dove's giggles. In her tiny hand that reached out and wanted to hold mine. In her satisfied chewing when she ate something delicious. These things used to be everything to me. They used to fill me up to the brim and leave me always wanting more. It used to be that I could never get enough of Dove. Never get enough of our life as a threesome.

I had a broken part. And it wouldn't let me function. I resented myself for being broken. And the resentment began to fester. With each daily task. Each meal I had to prepare. Each counter I had to wipe. Each kiss on the head to soothe. Each return to her crib for one more tuck-in. My inadequacy became theirs.

Mommy, more crackers.

Mommy, play one more time.

Mommy, don't be sad.

Mommy, what are you doing?

Mommy, where are you?

I began to question myself until it became maddening. How was it that she'd gotten me as her mother? She was the most beautiful creature I'd ever laid eyes on. What egregious error had taken place? How had this happened?

The truth was I loved her more than myself. I loved her so much that I let the doubt take over. The doubt ate me whole and spit out an even less worthy version of a mother. Surely someone else could do better than me.

Surely someone else was far more deserving of her.

There was no single moment. No last straw. In its place, a buildup starting on her second birthday, her delight at the candles blown out as the smoke circled the room and sucked into my mouth.

I suffocated. My throat filled up with loathing. Flooded with loathing for all I still had left to do. For her. To teach her. I would fail, and she would suffer because of me. Because *I* was her mother.

I was a fool to think I could make her happy. I was a thorn in their lives.

Each day brought me closer to the brink. It was the day before her third birthday. I remember her laughing in the bathtub with Dane sitting by. They were so content together and pure.

It was all too perfect.

All too clear that I didn't belong.

I was tainting them. They would be happier without me. Being in their presence was hurting them. Because I was the piece that no longer fit. An urgency to lessen this damage took over, swarming me like hornets. I had to give them a chance.

I had to give my baby a chance.

I backed up, each step taking me farther away.

And then I left them. I shut the door behind me, sealing off their blended voices.

I didn't look back.

CHAPTER 36

Nina bounces once and then turns to me with a cheerful grin before she leaps into the pile of leaves. Rabbit jumps after her, startled, and then sniffs the pile.

"I bet you can't see me now, Radley," she says, muffled, her little body half buried. Her legs kick in the air.

"Nope. You're a magician. I can't see you, Nina," I say, playing along. "What's your trick?"

She pops up and giggles. "The leaves, silly!" She throws a few in the air. Most of them land in her hair, a crown of gold and red.

She's like her old self again. It's a miracle.

Livia sits motionless on the front steps. Her arms hug herself. A ghost. The last three days have slipped by achingly fast. Yesterday she was in a manic mode, unable to sit still, as if anything less than constant motion would be a disservice to Avie. The search teams paused after a straight forty-eight hours of combing the area. They are to resume early this afternoon.

So far they have found nothing.

No scent picked up. No evidence of a trail. The empty news makes it worse as each minute passes. But it's as if one child's bad fortune has been traded for the other's good.

I watch Nina as she runs across the lawn with exaggerated striding arms. She tilts her head back and twirls.

"Nina is doing so well today," I point out to Livia.

She nods, unfazed, vacantly staring out at Nina but not really looking at her. I can practically see her racing thoughts, the hurricane of worry and assumptions in her head. Rabbit pads over to her side, and she reaches out to pat his flank.

"I keep thinking this is all a nightmare, Radley," she says, her face remaining forward. "I keep willing it all to go away. This terrible thing that has happened to our family. Like I could ball it up in my hands and throw it out into the ocean." Her shoulders heave once, but she stops herself. "But then I go look into her room . . . and she's not there."

Nina stops spinning. She notices Livia. "Mommy?"

Livia holds up a hand and loosely waves. Her lower lip spreads out into a forced smile. "Keep going, baby. I'm watching."

Nina doesn't seem to buy this. But she spins to survey the road as a state-marked vehicle drives toward us.

The car parks, and a woman with an olive complexion dressed in a short-sleeved polo and slacks gets out. She puts a hand up as if letting us know we shouldn't be alarmed.

"Hello there. I'm Stacy Omidi," she calls out. "From the state fire marshal's office. I'm the lead investigator on the orchard fire case."

Livia stands up quickly. "Oh yes. Please come in."

Omidi walks closer and glances at Nina. "We can stay outside if you wish. I could see on my drive in someone was having some fun."

Nina stares at her inquisitively. "Do you like spinning?"

She nods. "I do. Sometimes."

"Want to spin with me?" Nina holds her skirt out as if she's about to curtsy.

"Not now, Nina. Ms. Omidi is here to talk with Mommy. Grown-up talk," Livia cuts in right away.

Omidi winks. "Another time then. But between you and me, I prefer spinning to grown-up talk."

Her face turns sober as she shifts her attention to us.

"Apologies. But I don't know who the landowner is here."

Livia wipes at her forehead. "I'm sorry. I'm so scattered. Of course you don't know who I am. I'm Livia Clark. My husband Beau and I own the property."

"And your husband? Where is he?"

"Down at the station. He's getting briefed by Detective Fournier. Frankly, I don't think he likes sitting around here waiting . . ."

Omidi frowns. "I've been informed as well. The search teams start up again shortly. I want you to know we're working closely with each other. We don't know if the two cases are linked. But at the very least, the situation is more than unusual."

She then darts her eyes to me. "You are?"

"Radley Asher."

Livia steps closer. "She works for us. Anything you say can be said in front of her."

"All right." Omidi examines me for a few seconds longer before continuing. "Well, Mrs. Clark, we've done our preliminary investigation of the fire."

"Call me Livia, please." She places a hand on her chest as if bracing herself. "And go ahead. What did you find?"

Omidi follows her instruction and doesn't wait. "We believe the fire may have been intentional in nature."

"Intentional," Livia repeats breathily.

"Yes. The fire does not appear to have started naturally."

I wait for Livia to respond. The news appears to have struck her with the realization that the fire was more sinister than previously thought. That the wind didn't carry a brush fire out over the orchard in some unfortunate mishap.

This was arson.

And whoever caused the fire may also have taken Avie.

Livia feels behind her for the front steps. Slowly, she sits back down and gazes out into the scorched field.

"Livia?" Omidi frowns with concern.

"I don't understand," she answers.

"I'm sorry . . . understand what?"

"Why this is happening to us." She clasps her fingers and holds them under her chin, tapping a few times.

Omidi looks over at me as if hoping I might bring some clarity to Livia's distressed behavior.

"How do you know it was arson?" I ask.

She shakes her head. "We're not officially calling it that . . . not yet, anyway. A secondary investigation will determine the final cause. But the burn patterns indicate there was an accelerant of some sort. In the north field."

The field closest to Grace's farm.

"What kind of accelerant? Gas? Lighter fluid?"

"Unlikely. There's no evidence at this time to indicate anything that strong. Something with less intensity. Like a cigarette or maybe a match."

She pauses and leans down toward Livia. "Were you aware that your property may contain underground passageways?"

Livia shakes her head, absent and detached.

"Passageways?" I ask with incredulity.

Omidi nods quickly. "This area has some of the oldest farms in the state. Some from before the Civil War. We think there might be something in the north field. I have a team member studying archived plat maps at the library."

And then it hits me.

"Stories . . . of the Underground Railroad passing through our land."

The mirage of her form through the smoke the morning after the fire. How she disappeared so quickly that it made me doubt what I was seeing.

She answers the door after the second time I knock. Her hair is unkempt, blond locks over one eye. She barely cracks the door open to greet me.

"Radley," she says, surprised.

"Hello, Grace."

I step closer, hoping she'll invite me in. But she doesn't and instead slips outside, rubbing her arms at the chill of the evening.

She arches a brow. "Can I . . . help you with anything?"

"Yes. You can, actually."

"Okay. Please tell me with what?"

She's all too calm. All too polite. Like she's trying to get rid of me.

"Do you remember the first time we met? When I wandered onto your land."

"Yes," she answers crisply. She looks back to the door. I think I hear something moving inside.

"You mentioned how old your land is. That maybe even the Underground Railroad passed through."

Grace crosses her arms and stares at me. "Yes. And like I said then, those are just stories."

"It doesn't appear to be a story. The fire investigator seems to think they're real."

She laughs. "Are you implying what I think you are?"

I don't say anything.

Her voice grows somber. "We're sorry to hear about Avie."

I close my mouth and swallow. It's gone dry.

Grace snaps her head back to the door as it swings wider. Vaughn towers in the entryway. I don't remember him being this tall and overwhelming.

"Grace," he mutters once.

"I'm coming," she answers, her eyes fixed on me until she turns to brush past him.

He leers at me and shuts me out.

CHAPTER 37

I'm already late picking up Tallan from school when an unexpected visitor arrives at the orchard.

Shai hoists a bag of medical equipment from the bed of his truck. The vintage one I first saw him in all those weeks ago. He turns to greet me, looking almost nervous in his stance.

"Radley," he says.

"I'm sorry, Shai. But I'm leaving to go get Tallan," I answer, holding up my keys in my palm as I step down from the house.

"Please, wait one second." He drops the bag on the ground and strides over, catching up with me easily.

I halt and place my hands near my waist.

He looks troubled, the lines deepened in his forehead, and he briefly touches my shoulder. It instantly feels warm, and the top of my head matches it, tingling.

"Hey," he says, leaning in closer. "I wanted to make sure you were okay. And I'm so sorry about everything that's happened. It doesn't seem real . . . any of it."

I nod at the ground and then meet his eyes. They're full of sympathy and worry.

"She's been missing a whole week." My words exit shakily. I didn't realize, until I began to speak, how his comfort affects me. How I immediately feel a warmth around me just being near him, hearing his voice. Maybe because something about Shai rings true.

He sighs. "I talked to Beau and Livia briefly earlier this week. I wish there was something I could do." He motions to his abandoned bag. "I'm here to check the animals. Making sure we didn't miss any injuries or illness from the fire."

"That's kind of you."

"Nah. It's the least I can do." He observes me again. "Are *you* all right?"

I shrug. "Does it even matter?"

"Yes. Yes it does," he tells me quietly.

"The house." I look back up at it; the windows seem to stare right back. "It's so quiet. Like the plug was pulled out. And every day that passes, it seems to get darker. When I stop and think about her . . . about Avie. Wondering if she's okay . . ."

"Shh." He pulls me in, and I let him hold me. For a few seconds I let myself be taken care of. But I step back, and a space forms between us. Any longer and I would give in.

"They'll find her. You can't lose hope," he says near my ear.

I fully release myself from his grasp. "There haven't been any new leads. The search teams have slowed down. How can a little girl disappear like that? Without a trace?"

"No news is better than bad news," he says, trying to reassure me.

I shake my head. "The more time that passes . . ."

A wave of grief begins to pull at my chest. Memories I thought I'd locked away. Clawing their way out.

If only time wasn't such an enemy. If only it really healed.

"Radley?" Shai says my name as if he's unsure of it.

I press my mouth closed and briskly turn to leave him. "I'm already late."

He doesn't move. He doesn't say anything. He lets me go.

I rush over to the school, trying to think about anything but the downcast look on Shai's face.

He's a good person. That's why you should let it be. It's for the best.

I'm late when I reach the front entrance, and I anticipate finding an especially irritated Tallan. I discover him sitting under the birches. They've lost their leaves, their silver-white trunks stark and naked.

And he's not alone.

The boy in the bomber jacket, Colt, laughs at something Tallan says quietly near his ear. I notice his braces as he grins with an admiring flicker at Tallan.

Tallan beams and then sees my car. He pitches his head toward me and pulls his backpack on. Colt, realizing I'm watching, gives me a cool tilt of his chin. I think I hear him say something about "catching him with texts later." Tallan gives him one final gaze before assuming his aloof pose, listlessly making his way to the car.

"Sorry for the wait," I tell him as he gets in.

His cheeks are tinged pink. "It's fine," he says.

I pull out of the parking lot. I wait for Tallan to speak, maybe tell me about his day, but he's determined to remain mute. We reach the part of the road with scenic turnoffs over the ocean.

I finally break the silence. "Your dad isn't home. He's at the station again."

He leans into the window.

"I think it's going to be you, Nina, and Grandma Faye for dinner tonight. Your mom wants to meet again with the fire investigator. She wants me to come along. So, what would you rather have? Leftover pizza or the—"

"Stop," Tallan interrupts suddenly. He lurches forward as he sits up straight.

"What's wrong?" I look back and forth between the road and him.

"Please. No more. Stop the car. Pull over."

"Are you sick?" I roll down his window before turning right into an overlook. Gravel and dust fly everywhere as I hit the brakes.

"No. Not sick." He scrunches his lips. He pounds his fist lightly against the dashboard a few times.

The ocean is full of caps today, white and rolling. I watch them crash themselves against the shoreline.

"Tallan," I say gently. Careful to tread with caution. "Why don't you tell me what's really bothering you."

He wedges his brows between his thumb and forefinger. "It's not that simple, Radley."

"It never is. But you've got someone here who will listen. No matter what it is you're afraid to say."

He allows both arms to fall to his sides. He pushes back into the headrest. "I don't know how to say this. I'm too scared . . ."

"Tallan. You are so loved. And your family, they're . . . did you know that?"

"Yeah," he says, nodding. "Sometimes."

"You don't have to be afraid."

He turns his head and then peers at me. "Do you know already?"

"Know?"

"I feel like you know already." I hear something accusatory in the way he says this. But also, a sense of relief. That finally someone gets it.

My cheeks are the tinged ones now. "Is this about Colt?"

His lower lip juts out in a bewildered frown. "Colt?"

"Yes, Colt. Isn't he the one you're hanging out with? The candy emporium . . . and when I picked you up just now. You were talking with him."

A half grin peeks out but disappears quickly. "I like Colt," he says bluntly.

"You do?"

"Yeah." He shrugs. "There's nothing big about that. I have feelings for boys and girls. And I'm happy with that. I love people for people. Anything else doesn't matter."

My face burns. Complete humiliation scalds my skin for assuming Tallan would be upset about his feelings toward Colt. That he would be anything but assured of himself. That none of this is an issue, nor should it ever be.

"Of course." I angle myself to him.

He wriggles in his seat impatiently. "I thought that you knew."

It's here when I realize, in the fear that flashes in his eyes, that he's talking about something else entirely. What is he so afraid of?

"Tallan. If someone is hurting you—"

"No one is hurting me."

"Okay, but if anyone is—"

"It's about Avie," he blurts out.

"Avie?" I reach out and grasp his arm. "If you know something about Avie that could help us find her—Tallan, you have to let me know."

"Of course I would tell you. I already told the police everything I remember and know from that night. But it's not about that night."

"Then what?"

"I saw something . . . more than once."

"You saw what, Tallan," I urge him.

He runs his fingers in his hair. "Avie and Nina." He closes his eyes and then squeezes them so tight it makes me flinch. "It doesn't matter anymore . . ."

I want him to open his eyes. I want to see what he saw.

"Because Avie is gone now."

CHAPTER 38

I find Livia cutting bell peppers at the kitchen counter. She barely looks up when I approach her. Tallan doesn't say anything to either of us before he thumps up the stairs to his room.

"Livia, have you spoken much with Tallan?"

She continues slicing in an automated fashion. "You mean today?"

"I mean . . . lately. Since the fire."

"He doesn't like talking with me anymore . . . remember?" There's an edge to her voice, and she chops the next piece roughly.

"Maybe tonight before dinner you could—"

"Will you go find Beau?" she interjects. She turns to me, pointing with the knife, and then looks down. "Sorry," she mutters and pulls it away.

I peer at her, confused. "Beau. Isn't he at the station?"

"No. He came back while you went to pick up Tallan. I saw his truck. But he never came inside. Do me a favor and go find him? Dinner will be ready soon."

She returns to chopping as if there's nothing left to discuss. No other reasons to give. I'm to go find her husband without question.

There's only one person who should remain in the kitchen. And according to Livia, that is her.

I drape my coat on again and walk out to the barn stable. I see no sign of him, other than fresh buckets of feed for the horses. I stroke Pepper along her snout, and she returns to eating.

The orchard is no longer a place to find solace. No shade to hide under or leaves to run my hands along. A smoldered and barren field is in its place.

It's here I find Beau.

He kneels on one knee. Rubbing ashen dirt between his fingers. When he turns to find me, he looks startled at first but then gives me a lopsided grin.

"Radley."

His grin weakens and settles into pain. Letting the rest of the dirt release back to the ground, he heaves in once and then clears his throat. Shaking whatever sorrow overtook him, he stands up.

"I still wake up hoping to find it back to how it was," he says. He wipes harshly at his face and squeezes between his eyes. "That all we need is a good night's sleep. And the trees will magically break through. And Avie will reappear."

When he looks at me with a tormented expression, I have the urge to console him. I imagine Jem. How he suffered alone in his body, never able to utter another word to me before he went. How I couldn't help him then and how much I wish I had the ability to help him now.

"Just because it's gone now," I tell Beau, "doesn't mean it's gone forever."

He lifts his head at me.

"Even if it's destroyed, it can grow again." I almost roll my eyes at myself. "Words not from a greeting card. I promise."

He cracks another half grin. "Well . . . thank you for them."

I hold my fingers together at my waist. "Livia sent me out to find you. She seems a little out of it . . . understandably."

He presses his mouth shut and nods, perturbed. "Of course she did."

"I think she's worried about you."

"She's not. I can guarantee it," he huffs.

My head shakes back and forth. "What do you mean by that?"

He rattles his fist as if getting ready to roll dice, weighing his answer. "It means Livia has shut me out . . . once again."

"Again?"

He dusts his hands and makes sure to lock eyes with me. "Livia and Beau. We're not the married couple that everyone thinks we are."

"I think given what's happened in the last week, you're not under usual circumstances."

A laugh nearly sputters out from Beau's lips. "You think this is a new problem?"

I carefully consider my words before answering. "No. I've . . . noticed a few things."

"Well, you're not imagining it. Livia has been upset with me for quite some time."

The woman at the Harvest Festival weekend. I certainly didn't imagine her or the look you gave her.

"Livia's upset with you. Because that woman showed up."

His eyes narrow with confusion. "What woman?"

"The blond woman. Sunday of the Harvest Festival. You saw her and you looked so . . . incredibly angry. And Livia, like she'd seen a ghost."

He stares at me with no reaction. If he feels any shame about the affair, he doesn't show it.

"Livia said there was an affair. That things were never the same because of it."

"Livia told you . . . that I had an affair," he says quietly.

"Yes."

I wait for him to admit it. For him to at least own his part in their marriage problems. But he covers his mouth and snickers.

"You think that's funny?"

He sighs and surveys the burned orchard again. "That's rich of her."

"I'm sorry?"

His face grows shadowy as he turns back to me. "Livia is the one who had the affair."

All this time . . . she's made me think it was him.

"With my college roommate. We were close, almost like brothers."

"But the woman—"

"That was his wife. I was upset because he showed up. It's the first time I'd seen him since . . . well, it all happened."

He's grown weary, the ache from the past sucking his energy away.

"When did this . . ." I find myself practically whispering. "When *did* this happen?"

"You mean when did Livia turn into someone I don't know anymore?" He's bitter now, and I wonder if reliving it is a good idea. "Before Nina was born. Before the miscarriage."

He looks at me sadly, and my heart sinks for both of them.

The miscarriage. Pain upon pain after being betrayed.

"You're saying this miscarriage . . . didn't involve you?"

He shakes his head. "Not likely. We were barely touching each other around that time. If I had to bet, that baby wasn't mine. But it didn't matter. For some sick reason it didn't matter. We were still incredibly excited. Because it was a chance at turning things around. But it made Livia worse."

When she turned into someone he didn't know.

He lifts his gaze up to the sky as if reaching for solace. "Livia's the love of my life. We were incredibly connected. I'd do anything to make her happy . . . I still would. But something began to change after having Avie. She was . . . restless. Distant. And the shock of finding her and *him*."

"Him" . . . you won't even address him by his name.

"I felt shattered. I didn't know how to make it right. Sometimes I still want to make it all okay again, but . . ."

"But?"

"We've done too much to one another. We're torn up versions of ourselves now."

I rub my arms as if feeling the chill of their marriage.

"You want to know the sick thing about all this?"

He doesn't let me answer.

"Livia and I discovered we're both very talented at pretending. No matter how bad it got, somehow, we could fake it together. Pretend that it was still as it was. And maybe we played these roles so well that we even convinced ourselves at times . . ."

You both fooled me . . . the Prince and Princess of Fox Isle.

"She wanted another baby, you know," he says faintly. "After Nina. But I didn't want to bring another child into this . . . this mess that had become our marriage. And me denying her . . . she was so incredibly angry. I didn't know she had it in her to be that angry."

I look at him with skepticism. "But you both seem so . . ."

"Normal?" He raises his brows. "I've tried. For the kids. God, for the kids I've tried so hard to keep things up. The orchard, being the perfect father and husband. But the truth is, I was sinking. But then . . ."

"Then?"

"You arrived."

There's a tenderness in his eyes that I realize I've seen before, but in a manner I hadn't even fathomed.

"You arrived, and for the first time in a long time, it felt like I could breathe again."

"Beau," I say once.

"I wasn't sure how to act around you. I struggled to put it away. I knew it wasn't right, but no matter what I did . . . even distancing myself from you. I couldn't make it go away."

"Make what go away?"

"I'm in love with you, Radley." He reaches for my hand. I look down, and somehow my fingers have entwined with his. There's hope and longing in his face, and I stagger back.

"No . . . no."

"Radley," he says again.

"No, Beau."

He reaches out to me once more. An unsettling feeling spreads in the pit of my stomach. The fact that I ever admired this man. Or his wife, for that matter. The fact that they both have an ugliness that has wrapped around me.

"It's okay," he says, speaking more softly. "Livia . . . wants us to be together."

I shoot him an astonished look. "How—how do you know that?"

He steps closer. "At first, I thought she was angry with me. Because she could sense my attraction to you. But then it became this *game* to her. Somehow twisting it around on me and making suggestions. We had . . . fights about it."

The night Livia pushed him . . . the rage they both had at each other.

"You may have problems in your marriage," I say, faltering at first. Disdain then fumes inside me and seeps out. "But you had everything you could possibly want. And now . . . you're going to throw it all away. Why? And for what?"

My anger catches him off guard. I back up more.

Who are you truly angry with?

He shakes his head. "Livia and I are never—"

"This isn't about Livia. It's about how you are a fool. For not seeing all that you already have right in front of you."

My lower jaw quivers. The disgust spreads through me, a geyser of tears that I cap off with one hard swallow. And it's right then I discover that Livia and Beau are not the ones I'm disgusted with.

You see yourself in them.

"I don't know what else to do . . . I don't know how to . . ." His head hangs.

I turn to walk away. I can't look at him anymore. But I stop for one more moment. "And I was wrong about something." I turn my cheek to the side. "You are nothing like my brother."

CHAPTER 39

"You left them," Dr. Edair says.

I left them.

I left my husband.

I left my baby . . .

"Yes . . . I left them," I force out in a whisper.

"For how long?"

She knows the answer. She knows from all that she's read in those notes about me. The harrowing details of my past that I wish would burn away. But she's making me say out loud what I did to them.

When I abandoned my family.

"One year," I answer.

"And how would you describe that year?"

"Describe it . . . you want me to describe an entire year."

I hear her click her pen. "Give me one word. One word for the one year you were away from your family."

I don't hesitate. "Happy."

If she finds my answer repulsive, I'll never know. And I wouldn't blame her if she did. She's good at her job in that way. No matter what she hears, she doesn't let on what she's feeling.

My year away. A shameful sabbatical from a life anyone would envy. I discarded that life. Wasteful and cavalier. I spent nearly 365 days being someone else. Someone I actually recognized as content.

How could anyone do such a thing? Who leaves their husband and child behind?

I don't blame anyone for thinking less of me. Or thinking I'm a horrible person, wife, and mother. Because in some ways I was. In some ways I wasn't, though.

But that's just the thing. Us mothers. We're two sides of a coin, twirling and shining in the air until we land on whatever we are in that moment. A good mother. A bad mother. A guilty mother. A beautiful mother.

Beautiful.

I wanted to feel beautiful again. I wanted to feel smart again. I wanted to feel all the things I felt before I gave every inch of my mind, body, and soul to another human. Because why should we feel any less than that.

Why should we feel like we aren't enough.

I had to shake away every thought that had taken over me. The voice that told me I was failing her. I wasn't enough for her. That suffocated any feelings of adequacy. It would have conquered me, leaving nothing behind.

I wasn't ready to be conquered.

So I did it. I shed this version of myself for an entire year. No one knew who I was. No one knew the precious daughter I'd left behind.

Here's the best part. The part that will make someone's skin crawl, their judgment of me sizzling like a branding on my forehead, forever marking me as a dreadful person.

I was happy. I thrived in my independence—yes, my delusions of being free again. I didn't let myself think about them. *They* didn't exist. Otherwise, I would have shriveled up, realizing what I'd done to them. The damage that could never be reversed after my abandonment.

I drank the potion of forgetting. This alluring elixir of misplacing all memories. I somehow traded my consciousness for a new one, a fresh mind that allowed me to be idle.

Without a past or any attachments, I could easily discover all that I'd never allowed myself before. I floated in this alternate universe because I was weightless.

I traveled throughout Asia. Spent all the savings I had. None of it to ever be spent on him or her. Kuala Lumpur. Bangkok. Kyoto. Manila. Shanghai. Hội An. I whisked up and down countries, tasting all, hearing all, and pondering nothing. The language barriers kept me a delighted outsider. No one needed anything from me, and I relished every second of that.

I stayed trapped in a coil of colors and sensations I'd never encountered, spinning down each second, minute, and hour of absolute self-regard.

One late evening in Hội An, I strolled the market paths. Steaming street food was being served at a rapid pace. An elderly woman cooking cao lầu smiled sweetly and held up a bowl of thick noodles with roasted sliced pork and greens. I handed her a wad of money, not taking care how much. She counted it, and her smile turned into confusion. She tried handing back the entire amount. I tried again to give her the money, but she swatted it away. Instead, she handed me a container of soup. I looked down at this kind gesture, her hand gently patting the top of mine. She said something to me. I will never know exactly what, but the soft corners of her mouth gave me an understanding. She waved me off. This woman who didn't know me. This woman who was acting motherly to me.

Somehow, this broke through the glass utopia I'd created, shaking me awake by the shoulders.

Somehow my ability to forget the past left me.

Somehow I needed to call home.

I shakily dialed the number. I'd erased it from my phone, but my memory came flooding back.

"Hello?" he'd answered. The familiarity of his deep, husky voice made my blood prickle. An itch I wanted to scratch.

I said nothing. Gripping the phone until it shook. Willing myself to utter at least one word. Something to let them know I was still there. That I hadn't really forgotten them.

"Daddy, who is that?"

I heard her voice in the background. She was almost four. She sounded so different, so grown since I'd last heard her silvery giggles coming from the bathtub. How could I think she would remain that way? She'd developed hard and fast, milestones and funny moments I'd missed.

I'd missed so much.

Every vessel and vein in my heart dropped to the floor, sinking with the force of anguish. Regret stormed through, surging like a biblical flood. I struggled to keep my head above water. To breathe and remember.

Remember your sweet baby girl?

The cost of my absence. How many days had my husband had to stay home from work? The monetary considerations aside, what damage was there to repair? Would she remember me?

I would return to them. I would reappear like an unwanted apparition.

And oh . . . how I would pay the ultimate price.

CHAPTER 40

I'm accustomed to leaving.

I'm all too familiar with it. Leaving people behind.

But I contemplate where it's gotten me. What it's done to those I've loved dearly.

The suitcase stares back at me. Half packed. Neatly folded garments. Most of the clothes I brought from Seoul unworn. Blouses and sweaters too nice to wear to work in an orchard.

An orchard that is gone. Extinguished.

But two children remain.

Are you going to abandon them like you did your own daughter?

I hear Beau return to the house downstairs. My bedroom door is halfway open. Muffled voices between him and Livia in the kitchen, his low and rumbling one no longer a reminder of my brother's. Instead, I'm bothered by it. Discomfort takes over, and I'm still baffled by his belief that he wants to be with me. All this time, he's harbored these feelings. Not the older-brotherly kind.

The kind who both betrays and unsettlingly pleases Livia.

What will Livia do if she discovers that Beau has confessed? Will she welcome it, seducing me into fulfilling her wishes?

I shouldn't assume she doesn't already know.

Or am I just a chess piece in their match against one another?

I'm on edge, unsure of how to behave around them now. As if one wrong move would send the three of us into torment. The idea of having to live with this nearly has me out the bedroom door with my suitcase.

But you can't leave the children. Not now. Not with them . . .

I hear Livia call Tallan and Nina to come down for dinner. Tallan's door hits the wall with a thud as he skulks through the hallway. I feel as though I can't move, a burglar caught with the owners at home. One hand still on the edge of the suitcase, the other resting on the edge of the bed. If I move, they'll know right away what I'm thinking about doing. That I'm ready to make my exit.

"Nina!" Livia calls again. What sounds like the oven slamming shut echoes up the stairs.

Nina doesn't answer. I don't hear the usual scampering of her feet and excited chatter.

The silence mimics the calm before a storm. I remain frozen. Afraid of stirring the air. But alarm bells begin to go off in my head.

Something isn't right. It's too quiet.

The suspicion of misfortune clouds around me. I snap to and slip into the hall and walk with hard steps to her room. Her door is shut. I open it quickly.

She lies on the floor, flat on her back. Eyes vacant, staring up at the ceiling. Her right arm twitches once.

I must have screamed or yelled for Livia and Beau. I don't remember doing it, though. All I know is I hold Nina in my arms as she spasms again. Those hazel eyes of hers zone in on the ceiling.

Beau lurches forward, and I rock back on my heels as he takes her from me. He shouts at Livia, and the word "seizure" pierces me. But the rest of the chaos I block out. All I can do is watch Nina, nothing behind her eyes.

Livia commands Tallan, who stands in the doorway with terror on his face, to call for help. He disappears so quickly, a flash of his outline seems to remain, and I blink it away.

Time isn't making sense. Time is passing with each blink. This child falling ill all over again.

Ambulance beams bounce off the walls, an unwelcome light show.

She's carried away in a stretcher, and there's no time to say anything else. Livia and Beau both attempt to climb into the ambulance with her. Livia arguing with the paramedic. "Only one guardian can accompany," he instructs her. She pushes past him, and both doors slam shut.

The ambulance veers away. Tallan stands on the porch, shivering.

Sound returns to me at a normal volume as the sirens begin to fade. I turn to touch Tallan on the shoulder.

"Let's get inside at least," I say.

He jumps back. Eyes wide as he looks at his shoulder and then at me. He darts inside without me.

I stay outside to collect myself.

There wasn't any life in her eyes . . . how can a child look like that and be okay?

I feel useless. Broken. I go over in my head what I should have done when I found her. I should have acted faster. My hopeless ruminations go on until headlights pour into my line of sight.

A Bronco parks hastily.

Tallan or maybe Beau must have called Faye. She tears up to the house. Her hand in a fist near her mouth with fright.

"I spoke with Beau. All he said was I needed to get to the house to be with you and Tallan. What's happened?"

I draw her hands into mine to calm her.

"It's Nina, isn't it?" she asks frantically. "What's happened to Nina?"

"She had what could be a seizure. They took her by ambulance."

Fear and then confusion spread through every line and wrinkle in Faye's forehead. "This doesn't make any sense," she says under her breath.

"I know . . . she was doing so well, and then suddenly—"

"No. This shouldn't be . . ."

"Grandma!" Tallan exclaims. He bolts outside and they embrace.

"Oh, my poor Tallan," Faye says into the side of his head. "You must be so scared."

She huddles him inside, and I follow.

We wait together in the kitchen. Faye begins to clean up, scrubbing the pans from dinner. I help her by wrapping up the food, first offering Tallan the dinner haphazardly left behind. He shakes his head and sits at the counter, still stunned and shaken.

It seems like hours later when Faye answers a call from Beau. She leaves the kitchen, glancing at Tallan, likely not wanting any news to upset him.

She returns five minutes later. A look of relief has washed over her. "She's stable. They have her in the children's ICU."

"ICU?" I repeat, alarmed.

"Beau says it sounds like out of precaution. But they aren't letting her out of their sight. I'm going to bring over some things for them." She rubs her face wearily.

"Of course."

"And you're okay staying with Tallan?"

Tallan makes no movement in his seat.

I nod.

Faye gathers a bag and gives him one quick peck on the cheek before leaving.

He doesn't look up at me. I'm cautious in speaking. Worried that a wrong word or movement will spook or anger him.

A pot that could bubble over.

"It's late, Tallan. We should get you upstairs."

He doesn't respond, only slides out of his chair and leaves the kitchen. I watch him take the first three steps up the staircase. He pauses on the fourth.

"I can't tell you anything, Radley," he says with determination.

I keep quiet.

"I know what you're thinking. That I told you I saw something before. With Avie and Nina."

"Tallan. Please."

"No. I can't. It doesn't matter anymore. Like I already said."

I break my composure. "Avie is missing. Nina is in the hospital. Please. Tell me what you know."

"I'm sorry," he says. "But if I do, it will only cause more hurt." He looks down at both feet on the stairs, pressed together. "We don't need any more of that."

CHAPTER 41

The manufactured sterile scent of the hospital intensifies my unease. I feel misplaced, a walking pathogen who doesn't belong as I float down the hallways to Nina's room.

I find Livia seated at her bedside, so close her body lies halfway onto the sheets. Nina is asleep. Her tiny chest heaves up and down, and my heightened angst about what condition I would discover her in drops somewhat. There's color to her cheeks. I swallow hard to keep the emotions from my relief in check.

Livia raises her head. "Oh, Radley. Thank you for coming. Nina . . . she's been asking for you." Her voice is hushed and sluggish.

"Of course."

"They're getting ready to move her out of the PICU. She did well last night." She looks back at Nina almost with a sense of pride. "Beau went to get coffee."

The intense worry of a mother has deeply blackened the circles under her eyes. Her skin seems dry and weathered, as if beaten from the searing winds of going through hell and back.

"What exactly happened? Did the doctors say?" I ask cautiously.

She adjusts the sheets, straightening them out over Nina's small figure. "Something caused her levels to drop so low it became acute. That's why she had a seizure. They gave her a transfusion, and that stabilized her."

I reach out and touch her arm. "That's good news."

"Yes. Yes, I suppose it's good." She strokes Nina's hand delicately, leaning in to scrutinize her before settling back into her chair. "Doing good, baby girl," she says with tenderness.

"You're being incredibly strong."

"Am I?" She lifts her face up to me.

"Livia. What you're going through—"

"Nina is going through," she corrects.

"She will pull through it. She has before."

Her face crumples and then falls into her hands. She sobs once and then shakes her head. "This can't be happening. Avie can't be missing. I feel this panic, a giant hole of panic in my chest. When your child is missing . . ."

She continues to shudder into her hands, and I let her be. What could I say to console her? Nothing would remove her from the horror she's standing in.

I watch this woman who I held up with a dazzled and bewildered regard. This woman who made me think her husband had tortured her with infidelity. But in truth, they deserved each other.

They deserved to torture one another.

Beau steps into the room, a sleeved paper cup in each hand.

"Radley," he says, stoic and caught off guard by my presence. "I didn't know you were coming. I would have gotten you one also."

"No, it's okay." I don't look at him in response.

It's okay. Is it, though?

The ordinary topic of coffee does little to remove the sting of where the three of us are. A hospital room with a child who could fall ill again without notice. A missing daughter. And a son who has fallen into a different kind of absence.

My face grows warm. I can't tell if it's from nerves or embarrassment. This man is talking to me about coffee, when less than a day ago he was professing a secret love for me. On all accounts it was more likely lust. He wished to get back at his wife. His attraction to me was cloaked in revenge.

And yet his wife sits less than ten feet from us both. A wife whose touch has been strategic. Each place on my skin she touched was part of her ploy. She was the guilty one, yet somehow, he had to feel just as guilty.

I feel like I can be seduced. Perhaps it's the feeling of being *wanted.* The vain reaction of being flattered. Like it would be harder to resist both of their plans for me.

But then I remember how sick I think they are.

I'm not sure why I agreed to be here in this room with them. A toxic pull stretches among the three of us, a game of cat's cradle gone too far, knots and twisted string that yank every which way until it hurts. Even if Nina wants me here, I need to stay as far from this pseudo husband and wife as possible.

"Detective Fournier called when I stepped out," Beau informs us tensely. "He's heading over to speak with us."

Livia sits up straight. "Did he say why?" she asks, alarmed.

"No. Only that he wanted to update us."

"Oh God . . . p-please," she starts to stammer.

Beau caresses her neck with a comforting grasp, bringing her head to his midsection. "It could be good news. Any news at this point . . ."

Their sudden meeting of the minds does nothing to stir any approval from me.

I have seen and heard too much for that to change.

Twenty minutes later, Detective Fournier leads us into a conference room on the same floor. He said he didn't want to disturb Nina. The room is all too large for the four of us. Beau, Livia, and I sit directly across from him.

I brace myself for what he'll share.

His flinty blue eyes appear as if they haven't seen much sleep over the last week. They're devoid of any emotion as he gathers himself to deliver news.

"As you've been made aware, we've received hundreds of tips about Avie. Local news has kept her story strong. This has been both a help and hindrance. It's difficult to weed through all of the tips. Most are fabricated by people wanting attention."

"Please. Just tell us what you've found," Livia begs and shuts her eyes. "I can't bear any more of the waiting . . . the not knowing."

Beau takes Livia's hand. My heart races.

Detective Fournier swallows as he nods. "We got a tip last night. Someone saw something on a popular hiking trail. About thirty miles north of Fox Isle. A patrolman scoped it out this morning."

"And?" Beau urges impatiently.

Livia puts her face into his shoulder.

"We found what we believe to be Avie's rabbit."

Her beloved stuffed rabbit. The only item missing from her room.

"That means she could be near!" Livia bolts up. "We have to search that area."

"We've already dispatched a search team and dogs to the location. They're currently on site. But I don't want to get your hopes up too much."

Livia's brief optimistic outburst dies down as she slowly takes her seat again. "Why do you say that?"

"The important thing is to remain calm. We are very much still in a search and rescue mode. However, we don't know how long the rabbit has been there. You provided some pictures that make us believe it's likely hers. But we need you to positively identify it yourself."

Beau leans forward on his elbow. "Can't someone bring it here? The sooner we can make sure, the better."

"Yes," Detective Fournier answers. "The forensic team is finishing their collection process. If one of you would like to come with me to the station."

"I'll go," Beau says right away.

Livia sits limp, her feet pigeon toed. "That's it? That's all that you've found?"

Detective Fournier grimaces. "It's a start."

"What about the underground passageways? The plat maps?" I speak up.

"We did survey the land based on those."

I lower my head. "You remember what I mentioned about Grace and Vaughn Jean?"

"Yes. We questioned them briefly. But the fire investigation is still underway. These things take time."

Time. What Avie doesn't have.

He sighs. "Unfortunately, when we found the entryway to the tunnel—"

"So, they do exist?"

He shakes his head. "They're caved in with debris. Soil and rock filled, mostly. Ground got too soft from farming. Nothing and no one could get through there."

"Where does this leave us, then?" Beau asks, biting his lip with apprehension.

Detective Fournier looks at Livia first, her face in her hands. He meets Beau's gaze. "We keep going. She's still out there."

Where are you, Avie? Where have you been taken?

The excess space of the conference room closes in on us all. Crushing us with the impossible task of finding one little girl in the vast Acadian forests. The thought of how far away she could be, how hidden, and how unlikely it'd be to get lucky with one search. But the worst of it all. The endless possibilities of what has happened to her. Countless scenarios of a gutting end to this. Tragedy or triumph.

"Hope" seems like a silly word right now.

CHAPTER 42

The house is empty.

Somehow, I'm the only one who remains.

Daylight does nothing to lessen the blight of the burned landscape. The harsh reality of what was once so exquisite, the vivacity of a season turning over, teeming with growth and the glossiness of fruit, the laughter of a family that once graced the air . . . all gone.

The fire did more than burn the orchard to the ground. It went deeper. Scorching the earth below to the core, leaving nothing for a rebirth. This was no setup for a phoenix rising from the ashes.

This was annihilation into silence. Smoky, with a finality that chills me as I sit alone on the porch.

I came here silently. But I lied. I came with a past.

Faint barking from Rabbit echoes through from the barn stable. I reluctantly get up to inspect what the ruckus is over. I find him in a stealth posture, trying to herd the chickens. They scurry around in annoyance at his repeated attempts to round them up.

"Oh, Rabbit. These ladies don't want to be told what to do," I tell him.

He trots over to me, ears back, and I slide my hand down the crown of his head.

Charlotte bleats at us as she basks in a spot of sun peeping through the rafters. She blinks, and the light hits her eyes in a peculiar way. I study her face. There's a glossiness to one of her eyes I can make out, even from where I'm standing. I go to her. She greets me with a turned-up snout and then bleats repeatedly, as if telling me to see for myself. Upon closer inspection, I notice an oozy substance glazing over her eye.

"Poor Charlotte," I say to comfort her, patting her flank. "Do you have another eye infection?"

She turns her head the other way, ignoring me. I rise from squatting and look around for supplies. In the corner I spot a storage trunk. I lift the lid to find a tray of medicines. A small turquoise bottle of eye drops I've seen before sits in the middle. I select it with my thumb and forefinger, pulling it out.

A figure abruptly darkens the corner of my eye, startling me. I step back, and the trunk lid slams shut. I spin around with the bottle still in my grasp.

Sidney stands with the daylight behind her, her face obscured by the shadows.

"Sidney." I clutch the bottle to my chest. "You scared me."

She takes two steps forward. Her usual silence doesn't bring with it any reassurance.

"Did you need something?" I ask. I tighten the grip on the bottle.

Her eyes blast me with alarm and a livid urgency that makes my heart race. She reaches out, trying to grab at me.

I turn my shoulder, shielding myself. "What are you . . ."

She swipes at me again.

"What are you doing?"

Her hand shoots out and grabs my wrist. She squeezes once.

"Drop it," her voice booms.

I've never heard her voice before. I've never heard her speak a single word. My shock from hearing robust vocals exit her mouth causes me to jump back.

I release the bottle, and it falls to the ground, nestling in folds of hay.

She looks down at it and then back up at me in a robotic motion. "You shouldn't be handling that without gloves," she says in a flat tone.

"Oh . . . I'm sorry. I didn't r-realize," I stutter.

Sidney's full cheeks redden, either from worry or embarrassment, I'm not sure. She gives me a quick nod and slowly turns around to walk out.

"Why?" I ask.

She stops midstep, one boot halfway off the ground.

"Why do I need to wear gloves?"

She doesn't move. Reluctance wilts in her sagging shoulders. It makes me think she regrets having spoken. That her apparent vow of silence wasn't worth breaking for me. She faces me again and brushes a strand of pink hair out of her eyes.

"Those eye drops. If you touch them, you can get sick . . . very sick," she answers. Her voice has quieted. But she stares at me with an urging few blinks, a forewarning behind her eyes. Eyes that have taken the time to see more than anyone else on this farm. The gift of observing is all she's ever had.

After she's left, I find a pair of working gloves in the storage trunk. After sliding them on, I gingerly pick the bottle back up and read the prescription label.

Chloroptic eye drops

chloramphenicol

PRESCRIBED BY: Dr. Shai Fin

The admonishment in Sidney's voice . . . for her to break her silence and speak out to me . . . but how? How do they make you sick?

Shai . . . Shai was the one who prescribed this drug.

I put the bottle back in the tray, rip off the gloves, and pull out my phone. I fumble my fingers as I place a call to him. My hands tremble, and I exhale.

Why is my heart racing? What is it about this that doesn't seem right?

"Radley," he answers on the third ring. "What's wrong? Is everything okay?"

"I don't know," I begin.

"What do you mean?" he asks, confusion drumming through the line.

"I mean . . . I think that—Shai. Please. Just listen to me."

He pauses. "I'm listening."

"Do you remember prescribing eye drops? For Charlotte."

There's another pause. "Yes . . . I think I remember. She had an eye infection. Why, is she ill again?"

"I think so . . . that isn't the point. The medicine in the drops. It's toxic to humans."

"Yes. They need to be handled with gloves. But Radley . . . how do you know this? And why are you asking me about it?"

"It doesn't matter. I need to know how. How do they make humans sick?"

His next words escape into my ear. His next words make me lose my grip on the phone.

"Bone marrow toxicity."

"What . . . what did you just say?" I whisper.

"As in severe anemia. But it would require repeated exposure. Did you touch it? I wouldn't worry unless . . ."

His voice trails off as the pounding in my chest beats louder. I stare back at Charlotte, lying in the hay. She blinks her marble eyes. I remember the first time those eyes looked at me.

"Radley?" Shai's voice echoes through.

I shake my head. It couldn't be. He would never . . . harm her like that.

My first moments entering the orchard. Entering this family.

The first time I saw the eye drops being used.

CHAPTER 43

At least Tallan is at school. At least there's that.

I wait in my room. I wait for their return to the house.

Whoever comes back first. It's either *her* or *him.* I need to ask. I need to ask if he hurt his child. If he knew what he was doing.

If he was the one making his little girl so sick.

The rumble of a truck engine turning off causes an iciness to crawl up my spine. Heavy steps make their way inside and pause in the foyer.

"Hello?" his voice calls out.

He must be making his way to the kitchen. "Anyone home?" I hear him at the bottom of the stairs. "Tallan? Faye?" He waits to say my name. "Radley?"

How can I ask him? How can I ask a father if he's hurting his child?

The staircase creaks, signaling his approach. Each creak a small yelp for me to abandon my task.

But it's too late. He stands in my doorway.

"Oh. You *are* home," Beau says.

I sit on the bed, my hands pushed down into the mattress. I look at up at him with what I think is disappointment. Perhaps a misery that it's come to this. His brow furrows once, swift to disappear. He presses his hands in the frame and leans forward.

"Well . . . I won't be here long. I can pick up Tallan on my way back. Livia wants him at the hospital. I came to grab a few things for her and Nina."

When he says her name, I can't hold it in any longer. Even her innocent name seems to be tainted by him. Like vomit I've held down for far too long, the accusation is acidic as it rushes up.

"I know what you did to Nina."

I feel air quickly coming in and out of my nose, my breath unsteady.

Beau's eyes narrow. "I'm sorry . . . what?"

"Nina. You made her sick."

He nods very slowly. "Yes. Nina is sick. She's in the hospital," he explains as if I'm the child. Confusion flickers over his face as he blinks at me.

Don't believe him. This is an act. An act he's been putting on for so long. The good father. The good husband. The good boss.

I swallow hard, my throat feeling like crinkled paper.

"Are you okay, Radley?" He tilts his head down to get a better look at me.

I ignore his feigned concern. "Charlotte. Her eye is infected again."

"How do you know?" He comes deeper into the room. Closer to me.

"Because I saw it. This morning. So I went to get the eye drops." I feel my voice getting stronger.

"You should have waited for me," he says, a sharpness in the way he speaks. Is he scolding me? Or does he realize what I've discovered . . .

"Why? Why wait for you?"

"Because the drops are quite toxic to humans."

"Yes. They cause anemia. Severe anemia." I throw my words at him, hurling them to see how they land.

Waiting to see what he'll do to me.

But his eyes soften. "Ah. I see what this is."

"You do?"

I slide back farther onto the bed, but he keeps moving closer, compensating for the distance.

"Those eye drops aren't what made Nina sick. No one but our old sheep takes them. We never let anyone else near them."

"How do I know you're not lying?"

He shakes his head and sits next to me. "I know it's hard seeing her sick. But this isn't going to make her better, Radley."

"What isn't?" My voice trembles. My body trembles. Everything trembles.

He reaches out and touches my chin and examines it as if I'm injured.

"Blaming. Being angry. I've been there."

Don't let him. Don't let him talk to you like a preacher. Like you need his help to understand.

"It can make it hard to think clearly. I get it. Sometimes it's easier if there's something to blame for all our pain."

"I'm thinking very clearly," I say with force.

Beau gives me a half smile. A sad smile. And I can see how much devastation lies in his eyes. "I love my children more than anything. And that's all that has to be said."

He brushes his lips on my forehead. I become lifeless and immovable.

"I think it may be time for you to be done working at my orchard."

CHAPTER 44

When I'm sure Beau has left the house, I finally move out of my rigid state. Every joint is stiff, as if I've been knocked around in my sleep.

You should leave. Now is your chance. He wants you gone.

Something inside melts with enticement at the idea of how easy it would be. To pretend I've never met any of them. Beau. Livia. The children. A foggy memory I could choose to ignore.

But there's something stronger . . . nagging at my core.

She keeps falling ill without warning.

I'm not sure if I believe Beau. He didn't wildly deny. He seemed to find the accusation ridiculous even. If anything rang true, it was that he loves Tallan, Avie, and Nina. That isn't something that's easy to fake.

And then again, he's lived with Nina's illness for far longer than I have. He'd know if the eye drops were hurting Nina. Or is he really that certain?

I feel myself drawn to the easy way out. The door to facing nothing but emptiness. When you're empty inside, there is less to hurt. Less to damage. But maybe I'm the one who's been lying.

Lying to myself that it would be easier if I left and pretended I'd never met the Clarks.

I resolve to make my way around the house. One last look. The only way to say farewell before I leave. I walk down the stairway, my hand tracing the banister.

Tallan's words seep into my head, as if he's right there whispering them all over again.

"I saw something . . . more than once."

The kitchen chairs are haphazard in their placement. A few pulled out as if I've just missed a gathering, a table of warm food and chatter now an afterthought. I tuck each chair back in, adjusting them so each is spaced evenly apart.

Light has assembled in the playroom, bright and beckoning. The door has been left open. I want to hear their laughter again. Their banter over their tea party. I close my eyes and listen for them.

It's the deafening silence that injures me the most. There is no greater quiet than that of missing children.

"Avie and Nina."

What was it that Tallan couldn't tell me about them?

I sit in one of their chairs. The tea set sits untouched from the last time they played together. A shrine to them until their hopeful return. I push forward a half-eaten cookie left on a plate, like a chess piece on a board. It slides easily, a few crumbs dusting the table.

"There's too much that's wrong in this house."

I wish Tallan could tell me . . . I wish he could tell me what he's seen. What's made this house so wrong to him. This house that I have to leave before it devours me and hides me within its walls. Urgency abruptly overtakes me with a wash of panic.

I rush to stand from the small chair, toppling over a teacup. It lands on its side, rolling in a half-moon pattern until stopping. Slowly, I set the cup upright. Streams of daylight hit the inside, revealing a dried sheen lining the bottom.

"I saw something . . . Avie and Nina . . ."

So many mornings of teacups. So many times, they drank from them.

I scoop my finger against the filmy substance. Placing my finger in my mouth, I taste it. Bitter and chalky particles dissolve on my tongue. *Medicinal.*

I've tasted it now. What harm tastes like.

I've watched this harm. Right here in this very room. I just didn't know it was happening. Every time she poured tea into that cup. Every time her little sister took a sip. Who would have thought a little girl could do such damage?

Did she know she was hurting her little sister? Or did she want to hurt her . . .

"You saw what, Tallan . . ."

Avie so eager to set up their tea parties. Avie always strong, and Nina so weak.

"It doesn't matter anymore . . ."

She knew how to hurt her.

"Because Avie is gone now."

CHAPTER 45

The tunnel of trees I first soared through, bright and celebratory that September afternoon, now stand half bare. Exposed. There is no hiding anymore. The ugliness has been uncovered.

I pass through them on the road from the house. Hollowed out and worn, matching what I've become inside. There's no turning back now. Whether Livia and Beau believe me doesn't matter. I can no longer stay silent. I drive fast, the bends in the road angling more sharply as my foot presses harder on the gas pedal.

An unwanted red glow lights up on my dashboard. I hit it out of frustration. I don't have time for this.

But I have no choice. The hospital is a good distance away. I would almost certainly risk running out of gas.

I feel as though I'm backtracking from how I first arrived here. The gas station is nearly vacant. The pumps are unoccupied. I run inside to pay, where the same red-bearded cashier leans behind the counter.

"Pump number three," I tell him hurriedly.

He's as eager for small talk as me, silently ringing me up.

Laughter floats from the back of the store. The pitch of it vaguely familiar.

The cashier glances at me. "Anything else today?" He hands me my receipt.

The laughter draws closer and travels down an aisle. I look up to see a tall man, the top of his head distorted between two mason jars. Another chuckle joins his, and they round the corner.

Pete and Jesse Shaw stand with linked arms, cracking up over something Jesse's whispering behind his hand. Jesse notices me first, his back straightening like an ostrich.

"Radley!" he exclaims. He shuffles over, with Pete in tow.

"We've been thinking of you all," Jesse says with his hand over his chest. "Been praying every day."

Pete shoots him a look and raises one brow. "You pray? Since when?"

"Since I started those meditation podcasts. I'm feeling more spiritual lately," Jesse sniffs back.

Pete rolls his eyes and then focuses back on me with a sympathetic expression. "How is everyone holding up? This is all so terrible. None of it makes sense."

"Apologies," Jesse says. "We haven't been around. Only found out about it all yesterday. We just arrived back in town. Took a trip down to New York City. Fabulous restaurants, a spa treatment, Broadway show, all on Faye. She felt so bad, changing her mind last minute like that, so she booked us a week away."

I part my lips for a few seconds before letting words fall out. "Faye sent you on a trip?"

"Yes, it was so nice to get out of Maine for a change. Since we're not taking the *Calypso* down south after all this season."

Pete shakes his head a few times. "Poor Faye. I can't imagine all this happening while she's on the boat. Has she made it back yet?"

I step back. "I don't understand . . ."

The two of them look me up and down before glancing at each other.

"Don't understand what, dear?" Jesse asks.

"I thought Faye was skipping this year. That you two were taking the *Calypso*?"

Jesse tilts his head. "Right. Didn't we just say—"

"She changed her mind. Last minute," Pete breaks in. He studies me as I take another rocky step back.

Faye told them she took the Calypso. *She's been lying to us all. But why?*

"Faye . . . Faye is on the sailboat," I falter.

"Yes," he answers. His voice softens. "Are you okay, Radley?"

"I don't know . . ."

She wants us to think they've taken the boat.

"Do you want to sit down for a moment, honey? Your face has gone white."

I stare at them both with an open mouth.

But she's taken the boat instead. And someone else with her.

CHAPTER 46

"Go on. Ask me," I whisper.

"I'm sorry?" Dr. Edair lifts her back away from her seat.

"Ask me what happened when I returned to them."

She slowly takes off her glasses. "Radley . . . perhaps we can stop for today. You've shared some very difficult moments in your past. I'm afraid if we continue—"

"You wanted to know. About my family. My perfect family. Right?"

I sound gravelly. I sound like someone else is speaking. Maybe that's what I want, to be someone else. Someone who never went through what I did. Less scarred. Less bitter. It's difficult to be anything but bitter if you've had it all and thrown it away.

Bitterness eventually becomes so sour that tasting anything becomes impossible.

Dr. Edair is quiet. I remain in the chaise as if my position defies her.

"I'm not sure we need to . . . go there today, Radley."

Go there. Where the end of the world exists. Where my whole world teetered on edge, and I was too late to stop it from falling. Because I wasn't there . . .

"But it's the best part, Dr. Edair."

She clicks her tongue, contemplating how to advance our session.

"I see you're trying to make light of it. How that can somehow make it seem unreal."

"I'm sorry . . . I don't mean to be rude."

"It's not necessarily rude. But I think we can leave the rest of your story for another time."

"You mean the end to my story?"

"Is it the end, though? Maybe there's more to your story after what happened. That's what I'd really like to explore more with you."

I utter a low laugh. It grows, and I hold my hands across my belly. "Come on, Dr. Edair. You're too good to throw that line at me."

I've silenced her again. Maybe I've pushed too far. But she finally speaks up.

"You don't need to do this, Radley. You don't need to punish yourself anymore. Sometimes the past can stay in the past." She's switched to an authoritative diction.

"What if that past never lets go of me?" I draw a shaky breath. "Am I done for?"

"Radley. What happened to you is more than traumatic. But you need to learn to not let it overcome you. Take over your whole life . . . as it has."

I shut my eyes hard, blocking what I can sense building up behind them.

"But I can't."

"Why?"

"If I let go . . . I let go of her too."

She's still there. I can feel her. I can feel her little fingers.

There was horrible turbulence on the plane. Suitcases shifting in the overhead bins, flight attendants wobbling like newborn deer and spilling drinks, forcing grins to reassure the passengers. I braced myself, knuckles popping out hard as I clutched both arms of my seat. The man next to me drew up the blind on the window and peeped out. Dark clouds filled our view, and I looked away. I checked the time.

Forty-five minutes. Forty-five more minutes until I can try to make it right again.

When I'd called, he told me they were leaving. He had promised her a trip to Jeju Island.

"I told her that Mommy used to love going to Jeju," Dane said with slight venom.

I'd begged him to not go. To wait for me to come back. That maybe we could go together.

"No . . . we're not waiting for you. Not anymore."

He'd hung up on me, and I panicked. I had to be with her. *My baby. My Dove.* Why couldn't I wait for them to come home from their trip? I think back on it now and realize it's because I knew.

I *knew* something wasn't right. Even an abandoning mother like me still had intuition. I'd learned a mother's intuition isn't reserved for only good mothers. Bad mothers can have it. That pestering tug in your chest.

Something didn't settle quite right.

The landing was rough; the back of the plane fishtailed, and after three hard bumps, it came to a stop. Eternity passed as all the passengers filed out.

He wouldn't tell me what hotel they were staying at. But I knew there could only be one. The seaside boutique hotel, the one with the abalone soup I'd eaten when pregnant with Dove. The one that took guests out on a little fishing boat to catch fresh mackerel for dinner.

I had been on that boat before. When she was inside my belly, eagerly craving the fish for a meal. The waves were calm then. The ocean a gentle rocker.

I didn't wait for the taxi to stop. I flew out, rain beating my head, and the driver cursed at me. The receptionist at the front desk greeted me with a bow and a smile. I asked with urgency if the boat had left yet. The stormy wind blew in through the open door, and a few newspapers flapped against my chest.

"How could they go out in this weather?"

"The forecast didn't predict it so early. They should be returning soon. Can I interest you in taking a seat in the lobby?"

So polite. So mild mannered. I ignored her and ran out to the beach. The waves were crashing hard. I pictured them out there in the high swells, and it made me ill.

They shouldn't be out in this. The waves are too strong . . .

Salt air stung my face. I waited and waited, watching a few beachgoers quickly come and go, scared off by the whitecaps. Soaked. My bones were drenched, wanting to feel the pain and punishment. Maybe if I endured it long enough, I would see my baby. But there was no sign of them. Minutes. Hours. I would never know how long. Eventually the woman from the front desk came out with a blanket, saying something about management dispatching the coast guard, and she led me inside.

I shivered. I rocked in the lobby and remained cold.

Whispers around me. *A lost fishing boat.*

But then the whispers grew louder, until they felt like a roar in my ears. Someone yelled that they had found survivors.

Survivors.

I bolted out onto the beach, racing toward the darkening horizon. A large fishing boat slid onto the sand, lights flashing from the coast guard in the distance. Two figures shuttled out, guided by the fishermen. The first figure floated toward me, and I clutched my fists against my chest. Please let it be her. Let it be her!

A man I'd never seen before, shaking from hypothermia, his eyes half shut, was ushered quickly past me. Shouts for the ambulance.

And then *he* staggered toward me. A life vest halfway strapped on. He could barely walk, each step to me a nuisance in my heart. Why was he returning without our daughter?

Where was she?

Then he caught sight of me. Dane. My husband. The father of my baby, whom I'd abandoned. His face was lifeless. And in that lifeless face I knew.

I screamed.

I ran at him, pummeling my fists against his chest. He shook his head. Over and over, he shook it. Whether denying what had happened or denying me, I didn't care.

"I'm sorry . . . I couldn't hold on to her. The boat capsized . . ."

I kept screaming until there was nothing left.

"She let go of my hand."

His face was a blur. I didn't recognize it anymore. Once she was gone, he became a stranger to me.

Her small body was found two days later. I didn't want to know whether it was found on the rocks or the sand. I didn't want to see her face. Just her hand. They let me see that part of her. A gentle sheet that revealed her tiny hand.

I held it. I felt her. I felt every other part of her with that small grasp.

When I let go, my heart frenetically clawed up my throat, captive with grief, and I vomited it out. The agony was too much to contain inside. It expelled itself.

And my heart never returned.

"Never returned?" Dr. Edair asks me now.

I reach up and touch my face, sure to find wetness. But it's dry and scratchy.

"Never," I answer.

"Radley . . . you're brave for telling me."

"No. I'm not."

"Why do you think that about yourself?"

I stare at her as if it's obvious.

"Because I deserve it. Every second of excruciating pain. I deserve to suffer through all of it."

Her eyes are round as they look back at me. And I think I see a glimmer of confirmation in them. Maybe I want to believe she agrees with me. That of course a neglectful mother like me deserves all the suffering.

I'm the reason my daughter is gone, after all.

"Radley," she says once.

There's silence between us.

"It's okay, Dr. Edair. I don't fault you for judging me. I would too."

She shifts, and I can tell she's ready for this session to end. Perhaps she's afraid the grief will cling to her if we go on any longer.

"Dr. Edair?"

"Yes." She remains patient. Bless her.

"Can I ask you one last question?"

"Of course."

I stare at her with pleading eyes. "My entire life. No matter what has come my way. I've been able to reason everything. But why then . . ."

I catch my breath. And then it comes. The last bit of my heart left to dissipate. A lump lodges, and I can barely speak. Shuddering and tearful.

"Why . . . oh why, then, can't I find the reason for the death of my daughter?"

CHAPTER 47

I select a bench in the harbor. Watchful of any boats docking or leaving, I have blurry vision from focusing hard. The tide is steady tonight. I dial Faye's number. A baiting signal.

Come on, Faye. I know you're out there.

One ring. Two rings. Three rings.

"Hello, Radley?" she answers with a question. She isn't loving my call.

"Yes. Hello, Faye."

A pause. The line breaks and then comes back in. "Everything all right?"

"Where are you, Faye?"

Another pause, this one longer. "Do I need to come out to the hospital? Beau texted earlier saying Nina was stable and improving."

"No," I lie. "I'm at the hospital."

Liars can be lied to.

"Oh? What's happened?" Alarm picks up in her voice.

"She's not doing well. Beau told me to call you. You need to get to the house. Someone needs to stay with Tallan tonight."

"I'll be there," she tells me quickly.

I hang up and wait. I sit back and watch the marina settling down. Most of the boats are tied in for the day. A thin orange line hovers above the horizon as a few fishing boats drift back into their docks. But I'm waiting for a different sort of catch. This one will be the biggest of all.

There's a sliver of sunset left. But I can make her out.

The *Calypso.*

She glides in at the quiet end of the harbor. Trying to be discreet. A figure with a long braid down her back stealthily slips out, tying up the sailboat. I wait patiently, tucked in my vantage point. She walks down the main long dock and takes the steps up the marina's hill.

This is my chance. She'll come back when she figures out the ruse.

I hurriedly make my way down, the ocean air getting stronger the closer I get to the dock. Running toward the closing rays of the sun, chasing after what's left for me to see.

The *Calypso* floats gently. I feel as though I shush her as I climb aboard. After tripping over a coil of rope, I fall onto the floorboards.

The lights have been turned off. I crawl to the stairway going belowdecks. Peering around one more time to see if anyone has spotted me, I make my way down the stairs. There's no sound. Only the thumping in my chest and the distant rolling of waves.

Not a single seagull squawks. If there's anyone else on board, the silence isn't promising.

I step past a miniature rolltop desk, scattered papers and a seashell paperweight on top. The kitchenette appears recently used. A pot lined with dried cheese sauce inside, a few noodles stuck to the bottom.

An empty glass of milk on the table. A child's dinner.

"Avie," I say once.

She doesn't answer. Because Avie isn't here.

Maybe I'm wrong . . . maybe this is just Faye simply changing her mind.

I turn back to lift the empty glass. The last bit of milk circles the bottom.

The *Calypso* tilts forward as a small rogue wave hits the harbor. I hold on to the kitchenette table, stumbling farther toward the bow.

The berth. Where Livia put Nina down for a nap.

A narrow door separates me from the end of the bow. I hesitate to open it. If what's beyond this door is what I think . . . then what I suspect about Faye is true. A scary truth I'm not sure I want to meet.

I wrap my fingers around the knob. I swing it open.

A small curled-up figure lies in the bed. Familiar waves splay out on the pillow.

"Dear God," I utter.

"She's sleeping," a voice says behind me.

I whirl around to find Faye sitting at the kitchenette.

"You might want to close the door and let her sleep," she instructs.

I obey her without thinking, only wanting to separate Avie from her in whatever way I can.

"How long . . . I m-mean why?" I stutter.

Faye scoots out of the kitchenette booth. So casual in her movements, as if I've popped over for an evening sail. As if I'm not the person who's just discovered that she's kidnapped her own granddaughter.

"You seem to be confused, Radley. I started to get in my Bronco, but then Beau texted me, saying Nina was awake." She stares at me pointedly. "Ordering pancakes for dinner at the hospital."

"I guess I lied then, Faye," I answer back. I position myself closer to the door. "But we both know I'm not the only liar."

She's calm as she gazes back at me. "Yes. I'm a liar too. So what? I'm protecting my family."

I shake my head. "How is this protecting them? How is this—"

"Avie needs to be protected. From herself." She steps back and grips the kitchenette table, unsteady for a second. "More importantly, she needs to be away from Nina," she says firmly.

Away from Nina . . . she suspects it too.

"Nina is sick because of Avie," I say.

Faye's eyes shift up at me, round and surprised. They retreat then into resignation, a sadness. Perhaps other people knowing makes it all the more true.

"I didn't want to believe it at first." Her voice has grown softer. "My Avie. Capable of such a thing. But the sicker Nina got, the more I began to suspect something else was at play. They spent so much time together, all those daily tea parties. At first, I thought I was being paranoid . . . delusional even. But then."

She places a hand over her mouth, unable to finish.

"But then . . . ?" I urge her.

Her hand falls to her side. "Then one morning I saw it with my own eyes." She shivers as if seeing it all again. "Dropping something in Nina's teacup. I didn't believe it. I couldn't sleep. I thought for sure I was seeing things." She stares at me, eyes shiny. "How does a child know how or even want to do something like that? To their own sister?"

Her shoulders shake, but she stops herself. "And then it hit me."

"Hit you?"

She nods hard once. "If I said anything. To Beau. To Livia. To the authorities. *Anyone.* I would ruin Avie's life. She would forever be branded as a psychotic child. Locked away. But I *know* my Avie. I know she only needs to be talked to."

"Faye." I step closer to her. "That's not for you to decide. Avie needs help. Help neither you nor I can give her."

"No!" she snaps. "I've lived my life. It doesn't matter what happens to me. But Avie still has her whole life ahead of her. She just needs time. Time away from Beau and Livia. From that house. I can talk to her . . . I can talk some sense into her," she says, tears welling in her eyes this time.

Time . . . she just needs time.

"You made time. You created time for you and her. To be alone together."

She wipes her tears harshly and meets my scrutiny. "Ah . . . I knew you were a sharp one when I met you, Radley." She half smiles.

"The fire," I say, speaking boldly.

"Yes, yes . . . the fire." She closes her eyes and sighs. "All it took was a single match. To distract everyone so I could take Avie with me. But mainly . . ."

There's something in her voice. Dropping an octave, low and growly. "This land and family needed a renewal."

"Jesus, Faye." I swallow hard.

She stands taller, straightening her back as if to defy my judgment of her. "Enough talking. It's time to go," she announces.

Go . . . she's still going to sail away with Avie.

"And the Shaws?" I ask, stalling her. "You sent them away for a week on purpose."

"Yes," she answers, peering at me. "It gave me time to avoid questions. Slip in and out of the marina when I needed to make appearances."

Keep pressing her for details . . . stall her even more.

"The rabbit . . . Avie's rabbit. Was it you?"

"Of course," she answers as if it's obvious. "I tipped the police to where I left it. Led them in the wrong direction."

"And fooled the rest of us."

She abruptly waves up at the stairs, unfazed by me. "I don't have time for any more of this." She stares at the ground with her arm up like a scarecrow, pointing. "You need to get off the boat. I'm taking Avie with me."

"You're not taking her anywhere, Faye." I move back in front of the berth door. "She needs medical attention."

"No, she doesn't. She's sleeping, like I already told you. The insomnia medication I use is safe. I checked the dosage."

"What?" I exclaim. "You drugged her?"

She looks up at me coolly. "I had to find a way to keep her quiet. At least until the time was right for us to get away."

"I'm not letting you in there, Faye," I say sternly.

"Fine. Have it your way. I'm setting sail regardless."

I widen my eyes. "This isn't some sailing trip. You *kidnapped* Avie."

"No," she says rashly. "I'm *saving* her." She turns and quickly makes her way up the stairs.

I follow her as fast as I can. When I resurface on deck, she's already turning the motor on.

"Faye. I don't know what you think you're doing, but it doesn't have to be like this," I plead louder.

She ignores me and moves to get the mainsail up. The motor grows noisier.

"Faye. Stop!" I shout.

Get Avie. Get her off the boat.

The singular thought pierces through me, and I scramble back down, tearing through the space I so carefully tread through before. I fling the door open and place my hands on Avie.

"Avie, Avie. Wake up!" I shake her arm.

She doesn't move at all, and panic strikes my chest.

But a few seconds later, she groans once and curls up even tighter.

"Please, Avie," I urge. I pull her up with my hand behind her neck, and she goes limp.

She's not just asleep. She's been put to sleep with whatever Faye's given her.

I scoop both arms under her and lift her out of the bed, her head cradled on my shoulder.

"You're going home," I tell her, dipping my chin into her hair. She squeezes her eyelids and nuzzles into my neck, wanting nothing more than to sleep.

I rush up the stairs and climb above deck a second time. The night air hits me, and I feel alert, adrenaline coursing through me.

Faye stands at the helm, ready to steer the boat, and looks over her shoulder.

"Put her down," she orders.

"I'm not letting her go until you step away from the helm," I say, fighting back.

She turns her whole body and faces us. "Think about it, Radley," she says with a tilt of her head. "You're going to ruin Avie's life—our entire family's lives—if you don't let me take her."

I wearily place one foot back toward the side of the boat. "I'm not family," I correct.

A sad smile appears on Faye's mouth. "No. You're not."

My fingers grip Avie harder. I slide another foot back, careful not to fall. "But I did have a family. Once."

"Once," Faye says with disbelief. Her eyes follow me as I back up against the railing.

"Yes. I had a husband. And a beautiful baby girl." I turn my head to look at the water below. The jump wouldn't be that far down. But I would need to hold on to Avie and keep her afloat . . .

"And what happened to them?" Faye asks, inching closer with her arms stretched out as if ready to catch us.

"I left them," I utter shakily. I realize then my face is wet. Two tears glide down. "I left them for a whole year. And then it was too late."

She speaks softly. "Too late."

"She drowned. My daughter. And I drowned with her that night."

Jump. Jump now before it's too late.

I suck in air, preparing to lunge and hurl our bodies over the side. But Faye is suddenly there, storming forward, knocking me over with an incredible force. I fly onto the deck and hit my head hard, letting go of Avie. She wakes, crying as Faye picks her up. I reach for her futilely, still lying on my side, the sky spinning above me. The stars brighten as I feel myself slipping away, temples pulsating.

Get up. Get up, she needs you. You can save her this time.

The boat begins to shift away from the dock. The water slides underneath, the bow a dial turning counterclockwise.

I pull one knee under me, raising my head groggily. I make out Faye's figure behind the helm. Avie slumps near her feet.

"Avie," I whisper.

I stumble up and fall back down. The boat picks up speed. Too fast for the harbor. Faster and faster it gets, dizziness and nausea taking over.

You left her . . . you abandoned her. And now she's gone forever.

I shut my eyes, and I feel her tiny hand holding mine.

Why didn't you save me?

Grief. Unleashed raging grief stirs in me. Lifting. I stagger to my feet and charge with everything left inside me. The distance between Faye and me closes, and I thrust both hands into the side of her body.

The wheel veers to the left. For a second the boat feels weightless.

I grab Avie from the floor. As I lift her into my arms, her head flops onto my shoulder. I look up, and terror flashes through me. The side of another boat appears, looming like a wall.

We're going to crash.

There's no time to think. No time to punish myself anymore. My body moves before anything else runs through my head. I clutch Avie's small body, pressing her against me as we dive vertically into the water, my feet breaking the surface first.

For a while it's darkness. Cold and quiet. We resurface to what sounds like the world ending.

The screeching and slamming of the bow colliding with the hull of another boat at full speed thunder crudely. I tread water, holding Avie's head against my chest, her body floating outward. Smoke fills the air. But this smoke smells electrical, growing stronger each second, until fire bursts up, blazes flashing in every direction.

I feel myself drifting away with the faint distant sounds of sirens. But nothing will release my grip on her.

I've got you. I've got you, baby girl . . . I came back.

The glow of the fire in the sky comforts me.

I came back to say goodbye.

CHAPTER 48

The first face I see is Nina's.

My eyes flutter from the overhead hospital lights.

"Hi, Radley," she says cheerfully. She sits in a chair next to my bed. There's color to her cheeks, and her eyes are bright.

"Hi," I answer hoarsely. I bring my hand to my head. A throbbing rings from the core.

"You have a concussion," Livia says from the doorway.

"How long have I been here?"

"Two days."

I sit up and wince.

"Take it slow. You've been through a lot," she tells me softly. She nods toward Nina. "She's been waiting every minute to see you."

Nina scoots forward in her seat. "You're so brave, Radley."

I raise a brow. "Am I?"

"Yes. You found Avie." She swings her legs with pride.

"Wait . . . Avie." I turn my head to Livia. "Where is she? Is she okay?"

Livia's expression is exhausted. But the deadening worry has lifted from the darkness under her eyes. "Two floors up. She's doing great. Thanks to you." She smiles and bites her lip, holding in what I think are tears.

Avie . . . how do I tell her the truth about Avie.

"Faye was treated for minor injuries, if you're wondering," Livia goes on, this time colder. She meets my dazed stare. "The police took her straight from the hospital. She's in custody, being questioned by Detective Fournier."

I nod. "And Beau?"

"He's at the station. I suppose he still feels some loyalty to his mother," she says dryly. She looks back at me for a moment. "How did you know?"

"Know what?"

"That it was the *Calypso*?"

"I ran into the Shaws," I answer flatly. "It didn't make sense. Her lying about it all."

Livia shakes her head. "She could have killed her," she mutters angrily before glancing quickly at Nina. "Anyhow . . . Nina wanted to see you. I'll give you two time. I should go check on our other patient."

She pivots to her right and almost runs into Tallan. He holds a cup of coffee out.

"Oh, thank you, sweetie," she says, kissing him on top of his head. "Look who's awake." She waves the cup at me.

Tallan's eyes widen, and he grins. "Radley."

"Hey there," I answer from the hospital bed.

Livia taps the side of the doorframe. "Well, I'll leave you kids to watch over Radley for a bit. I'll be back soon."

"Where are you going?" Tallan asks.

"Just up to see Avie."

"Oh . . . is she coming home then?"

"I'm not sure. They might keep her for another day or so."

Tallan remains stoic.

She smiles and tousles his hair. "She'll be back home soon enough. You're a sweet big brother to worry."

He nods a few times, ducking out of her hand with a faint grimace only I notice.

Nina points to a vase of deep-blue dahlias set on the end table to my right. "Did you see? Aren't those pretty, Radley?"

I reach out and lightly brush my fingers against a few petals. I already know who they're from.

Livia smirks. "Oh yes. I should have mentioned. Shai dropped those off. He waited for you to wake up. But I finally told him I'd let you know he came by."

She walks out into the hallway as Tallan comes farther into the room.

"Take a seat, mister," I tell him, pointing to the recliner in the corner.

He strides across the room and sinks in, assuming his slouched position.

Nina wiggles in her spot. "I'm so glad Avie will be home. And then we can have a tea party."

Tallan's eyes shoot up at Nina and then to me.

"Nina." I clench my teeth as I sit up higher. The pain in my head pulsates. "When you and Avie play together . . . does she do anything to hurt you?"

Nina stops wiggling. "What do you mean by 'hurt'?"

"Does she do anything that seems funny. And I don't mean the funny laughing kind. But anything that doesn't seem . . . right."

She shakes her head emphatically. "No."

"You sure?"

"Avie doesn't hurt me."

I watch as she pulls on my patient wristband. "Hey, I had one of these." She holds up her bare wrist. "But I don't need it anymore."

I smile. "That's good. That's a good thing, Nina."

She chatters about what I should order for lunch from the hospital menu as I glance at Tallan. He sits with his face to the side, staring out the window. One hand nervously clenched, his thumb rubbing against it.

CHAPTER 49

The house has been occupied again since yesterday. A familiar rustling of bodies, creaking of floors, Rabbit's barking, and noises from the kitchen. Minus Avie. She'll remain in the hospital for one more day until discharge.

Nina laughs as Livia tickles her at the kitchen table.

"Another bite of oatmeal, sweetie." Livia nudges the bowl toward her. Nina plants her fists at her waist and shakes her head from side to side.

"More blueberries, please."

Livia sweetly pokes her cheek. "You bet." She gets up from the table as Beau walks in.

"Any news on Faye?" she asks discreetly, barely audible.

He shakes his head. When he meets my eyes, he looks away quickly. I'm unbothered. His embarrassment is beyond warranted from his behavior toward me and his blindness to what really mattered.

I sit directly across from Tallan. He doesn't touch his cereal. I observe him as he fidgets with the place mat and then looks at the white owl clock.

"Not hungry?" I ask him.

He doesn't respond. When he looks at me, I think I see a nervousness in his face. But he flashes a quick smile. A plastic smile.

"Not really." He turns to Beau, who pours coffee at the counter. "Can I be excused?"

Beau nods absently. Tallan sits up hurriedly and takes his full bowl of cereal to the sink.

"Here you go," Livia says, returning with the blueberries. She plops them in the oatmeal.

Nina gives her a lopsided grin with her tongue sticking out, and she wiggles her brows and takes a bite.

Livia turns to me. "Radley. Is there any way of convincing you to stay?"

I hinted to her last night at my need to leave once Avie has her homecoming. I have no place here anymore. Not among them. Not once I tell the truth about what her daughter has done.

I've been around enough pain to last a lifetime.

"I don't think so," I answer quietly, forking a bite of egg. Rabbit bumps my knee under the table, and I toss him a piece. "Detective Fournier is having me come down tomorrow to give my official statement."

"And then?" she probes.

"It's time for me to move on. The season is almost over."

Livia sighs. "It's not going to be the same without you," she laments.

I look up at Beau, who clears his throat and directs his attention to Nina.

Nina has managed to escape her chair. She skips toward the playroom.

"Where you going there, Nina? You haven't finished your breakfast," he says.

"Getting the tea set. Avie will be home tomorrow," she announces.

Livia gets up from the table and picks Nina up, cradling her. "Silly. You need to finish your oatmeal. I put in extra blueberries, remember?"

Nina squirms with determination. "Avie will want to have a tea party ready."

I look at her sadly. Her shiny face, excited for what can never happen again. What *should* never happen again. "Nina, I don't think Avie will be getting your tea party ready . . . for a long time."

Livia cocks her head at me quizzically. My comment a barb that has shot through the air.

"That's okay," Nina exclaims with cheer. "*Mommy* used to always get our tea set ready. She showed Avie how to do it." She looks up at Livia, still holding her in her arms. "Isn't that right, Mommy?"

Livia freezes. A glitch that lasts for maybe a millisecond.

But I see it. A preview of her deceit.

Her eyes. Slowly she brings them up to meet mine. Beautiful and tawny. The light in the kitchen hits them so perfectly. In this perfect house. In this perfect family. For the first time I see the ugliness in them. The exhaustion of holding up a facade with the weight of a thousand tons. Perhaps she's done. Perhaps she's willing me to figure it out.

She showed Avie how to do it. She showed her daughter how to hurt. A daughter so eager to please her.

I stare back with pity. Because it's all I have left to give.

"Please . . . don't," she mouths at me.

A faded sound rings in the distance. A blare that perks up Rabbit's ears. Sirens grow closer, screeching and grating.

"What's going on?" Beau asks, alarmed, the windows flashing with red and blue. The color bleeds into the curtains as the sirens get louder.

Tallan stands in the kitchen doorway, his head down, as Rabbit's barks pierce the air. Loud, aggressive raps at the door.

"Fox Isle Police Department!" The door crashes open. "We're entering the premises!"

Footsteps clatter into the kitchen. I don't see their faces as they swarm us. Because all I can see is a mother. Holding her child. Slumped with her on the floor.

Livia buries Nina into her chest. Sobs muted in the top of her sweet head of curls.

She rocks back and forth. Over and over.

"I'm sorry," she cries, stroking her child. "I'm sorry . . . I'm sorry . . . I'm so sorry."

CHAPTER 50

The guest cottage I first stayed in seems abandoned. I walk through one last time, making sure I haven't left any traces of my being here.

I wish that were the case. That I had never come here.

Clark Orchard. Clark family . . . farce.

It's been one week since Livia was arrested. She's to face arraignment tomorrow. A multitude of charges, but the leading one is attempted murder.

Mother. Murder. It's sickening how close those two words sound, like relatives who should never have been related.

It was Tallan who called the police that morning.

He explained to me later, crying into my arms as I held him. After the police had handcuffed his mother and led her away, head hung and heaving with anguish. Beau demanding an explanation and being sternly told to calm down.

"I thought it was Avie. I thought it was Avie this whole time," Tallan said, shaking through tears. "I was so afraid. For so long I was afraid. I didn't know what would happen to her if I said anything. But then when we got home last night . . ."

I shushed him then, telling him he didn't have to speak, but he shook his head, refusing. Finally, he was able to say what he'd been holding inside, a secret that had given him his own kind of sickness.

"I saw her . . . *Mom*. Putting drops in her dinner. We'd been home for less than a day, and already . . . ," he sputtered through his rising chest. "And I couldn't sleep. All night. But by morning I decided. I had to do it. I had to call for help. Please tell me I did the right thing, Radley, please! I had no choice . . ." He sobbed, and it killed me.

He, too, was just a child, after all.

A child as innocent as the one I'd lost.

And it hit me right then as his crying died down into muffled breathing: Livia had done the unthinkable. She had intentionally harmed her child. All three of her children suffered the consequences. Yet a small sliver of me felt the weight that she carried.

That's how I felt her pain. Because I had been right there.

Somewhere on the road she traveled as a mother, long and unyielding. Each turn unpredictable. Frightening. Thrilling. Consuming. She lost herself. Unable to take it, to find the air again, she chose to cling to a past that could never be brought to the present.

Because that's the price of motherhood. We want it all back, just when we finally understand how beautiful it all was.

I understood her plight.

A horse neighs in the distance now. I climb up into the loft and look out the ocular window to see Pepper running in the barren field. She paces and then turns, restless. I watch for a while, her snorting puffs clouding into the frigid morning air. November is well underway and with it the turn of a season. Autumn has ended.

My time here has ended.

I've slipped off the window ledge and landed near the bed when something catches my eye. A white rectangle on the pillow. Expertly camouflaged. I'm amazed I caught sight of it. I pick it up and open a trifold letter:

> Dear Radley,
> By the time you hopefully find this and read it, Daniel and I will have long left Clark Orchard. I don't regret leaving. But I regret not being able to speak to you beforehand. You didn't deserve that kind of goodbye.

> From the minute you stepped onto the orchard with that undecipherable expression of yours, I felt like we had been longtime friends.
>
> To be completely honest, I sensed a sadness in you. Something deep seated. But I never had the courage to ask you. So, whatever it is that causes this sadness, I hope you find a place of healing someday.
>
> Daniel and I are going to try that. We're still going to Boston to be near our Luna. We aren't going to give up on our dream. Not just yet. If you're ever there, please look us up.
>
> All the best,
>
> Andrea

I fold the letter back up and place it on my chest. I sit on the bed for I don't know how long. Wondering if people—good people like Andrea and Daniel—ever get their happy ending.

I can only hope that's the case.

When I exit the cottage, I jump, startled. My hand still on the knob, I swing the door outward.

Grace stands with her head down. She raises it and holds up a hand as if to surrender.

"I'm sorry. I didn't mean to scare you," she says. There's something delicate about her . . . softer.

I close the door behind me. "It's fine."

She twists her hands together. "I came here to offer my help."

"Help?" I raise a brow. "Now you want to help?"

"I know this all seems too late. But when I heard what happened with Livia and Faye. What they had done to Avie . . ."

I cross my arms. "Town talks fast, huh."

She shakes her head. "I don't mean to gossip. What I mean is I realized I was wrong."

Wrong . . . does it matter? Who is right or who is wrong . . . does it ever?

"I'm not sure that makes a difference," I say harshly.

"No . . . no, it doesn't." She sighs. "But I'm here now. As a neighbor. As a friend. And I want to help out with the children. In any way I can."

I nod a few times. "That's gracious of you. But I won't be here for any of that."

"You won't?"

"I'm leaving tomorrow."

She glances at me wistfully. "Well, I'm sorry to hear that."

I take a few steps away from the cottage. "Before I go, can I ask you something?"

"Sure."

"What was it that caused the falling-out between you and Livia?"

Her face falls, and then regret goes down with the corners of her mouth. "At the time it seemed important. But now . . ."

I remain silent. It's Grace's turn to tell the truth.

"I found out about the affair Livia was having," she blurts out. "It rocked me to my core that someone who had everything could just risk it all . . . and for what? A fling?"

"How did you know it was a fling?"

She sighs. "I wasn't positive about that, I guess. But when I confronted her about it, she acted like it wasn't a big deal. That she deserved to have her fun. I was so angry at her for not caring. For not being the friend I thought she was."

Livia's affair has damaged more than one relationship, it seems.

"I suppose it's time to let the past go. To move on," Grace says, quieter.

"Yes . . . yes it is," I answer.

She looks at the ground and digs her toe a few times. "I . . . I started taking up photography again. A few nature shots to start out with."

"That's wonderful, Grace."

She grins.

I peer at her. "Just out of curiosity . . . what does Mr. Jean have to say about all this?"

Embarrassment flushes her cheeks. "He's not a bad guy, you know."

"I didn't say he was."

"When the fire happened . . . he got scared. Paranoid that we were next. His land is everything to him. That's why he wasn't happy when you showed up."

She shrugs. "Fear. Grief . . . it does funny things to a person."

That I understand . . . that I can agree with, Grace Jean.

And for a brief moment, I felt Grace and I were the same woman. We had both suffered loss. She lost something she'd never even had. Me . . . someone I would never get back.

There's no immunity to any of it.

CHAPTER 51

Livia walks in, flanked by two guards. The dull gray prison jumpsuit hangs on her, a size too big.

She wants to see you. Before you go. Please.

Beau implored me as I finished packing this morning. Barely making eye contact with me but needing me to grant his wife this one request. I agreed.

But for her sake, not his.

I was curious more than anything. Curious to know if she could somehow be a worse mother than I was. A competition no mother should ever enter.

She sits across from me, glass separating us.

"Ten minutes," one of the guards says, handing her the receiver. He steps back and nods at me. I pick mine up and hold it to my ear.

Neither of us says anything. She squeezes the metal cord once and releases.

I wait. She is the one who invited me here. She is the one who needs to speak.

She looks up at me with blank eyes. "I'm not a bad mother."

I want to tell her that's a lie. That it couldn't be further from the truth. But instead, I lie. Maybe because I know she's already suffering a punishment worse than the one I'm living. Her children are out there. Growing up. God willing, thriving eventually.

And she will always remain in here.

"I know," I tell her.

A strange, satisfied smile spreads out on her full lips. But it disappears as fast as it showed up.

"Do you want to know why?" Livia asks.

"Why you're not a bad mother?"

She shakes her head slowly. "No. Why I did what I did . . . to Avie."

I glance at the guard. "I don't think it's wise to speak about that . . ."

"It doesn't matter," she says almost angrily. "I'm not hiding anything. Not anymore."

I lower my voice, as though that will make a difference. "Livia, you're being arraigned tomorrow. For criminal charges. Do you understand the seriousness of this?"

"Yes," she answers. "And I'm going to plead guilty."

She's not going to put up a fight.

A duty tugs inside me, telling me to try to change her mind, to do everything she can to see her children again. But then I remember how sick she made Nina. How her own daughter suffered a seizure, and she had the gall to pretend to be surprised and concerned. Even though a small part of me understood her in some terrible way . . . her actions were premeditated.

I keep forgetting who Livia really is. Perhaps it's too difficult to sustain that thought. No one wants to believe a mother could really inflict that kind of pain on her own child.

"We were very happy once. Beau and me," she says, a far-off look in her eyes. "Sometimes I think that's all we are owed in this life. One instance of happiness, if we're lucky."

If we're lucky . . . if we know to recognize that instance.

She leans on her elbows. "But then . . . we became two people that didn't know how to be happy. Like we were so skilled at it and then forgot how—never relearning it. But Beau was exceptional at one thing."

"What was that?"

"Pretending to be good."

"Good . . ."

"The good husband. The good father. The good son." Livia nods with each phrase.

"So were you," I tell her, grimacing.

A small taut laugh comes out of her. "Yes. I suppose I was too." Her expression goes stern. "But I wasn't pretending with Beau when I told him I wanted one more child. One more baby. That's all I wanted. If he had given it to me, then maybe none of this . . ."

"None of what?" I ask. But I know exactly what she means.

She ignores my question. "When it became clear it wasn't going to happen, I had this emptiness. A hunger in me that couldn't be satiated with anything but the thought of another baby. I was holding on to what used to be. I was holding on to what was in the past, everything else around me changing. It was unhealthy. The thoughts and this longing I had."

The guard moves closer. I notice him looking up at the clock.

Time never changes. Past or present. We always run out.

"And then Nina got ill. She was weak and she truly was anemic. That's the irony in all of this . . . it was the truth. At first, anyway. It was during this time she became clingy, needing me—infant-like. She was never a very affectionate child until this happened."

"You enjoyed your child being sick."

"No," she hastily corrects me. "I enjoyed taking care of her. For once she *let* me dote on her. She was my baby all over again. For the first time, my hunger was met. It felt so good to feel whole again. It felt like . . . we were back to a time when we were once so happy."

Yes. But at whose expense?

Livia sighs. "When she started to get better . . . I didn't want it to end."

"So you drugged her," I say flatly.

"No . . . not the entire time. I had Avie assist me."

"Why? Why bring Avie into it?" I demand.

Her lower lip quivers. "Because I couldn't bring myself to do it anymore." She covers her face. Her voice chokes up. "But I still needed my fix . . . I still needed my baby."

I lean in close to the glass. "You see, that's where you're wrong. She never stopped being your baby."

The guard steps forward and announces that our ten minutes are up.

Livia puts her hands against the glass. "I just wanted more time. Is that a crime?"

She stands up as the guard takes hold of her arm. She stares at me with a hollow look I'll never forget.

"Why do they have to grow up? Change on us? I need to know the reason for taking it all away. Why, Radley . . . *why* does time eat away at us?"

CHAPTER 52

Warm ocean air finds its way over the curves of my face. I sit back on the bow of the *Calypso*, the water crashing up and soothing my legs, tan and heated from the southern sun. The boat has run into some rugged waves. But it doesn't bother me . . . not anymore.

I'm bound for Marathon Island. Another place where no one knows me. No one can see my past in my face . . . not yet, anyway. But this time I don't hold any secrets. This time they don't own me.

I hear Jesse and Pete playfully bickering over their afternoon margaritas. A game of cards and Jesse accusing Pete of cheating.

"You think you're so sly, but I caught you sneaking a look," Jesse jabs with a chuckle.

"Absolutely not true," Pete answers, exasperated. "You're boring me now."

"Fine. I guess I win by forfeit," he sings.

"You wish," Pete mutters. "Hey, Radley!" he calls.

I look over my shoulder.

"I have a margarita with your name on it." He holds up a frosty glass.

I squint one eye and grin. "All right. I'll be over there in a minute."

My hair blows over my face and then slides away. The margaritas make me think of Faye. Wondering if she'll ever heal from her own wounds. She took a plea deal for child endangerment, the kidnapping and arson charges dropped in exchange. As to whether the judge will be so kind in sentencing, that is still up in the air.

Her lawyer called me to relay a message. One simple sentence: *"Take the boat with the Shaws and live your life, Radley."*

At the time, I wasn't sure what to make of it. What life was there for me to choose? To even take on.

My farewell to Nina, Avie, and Tallan wasn't a long one. I'm not one for dragging out goodbyes. I made it brief for my own sake. Those three beautiful faces that had somehow brought me back to life. If I held them any longer, I'd be drawn back in. Thrown down a funnel, living someone else's life. I miss them, though.

I always will.

Shai met me at the dock before we launched our winter voyage. He kept it simple and open for me to decide. A warm, quiet voice in my ear when he leaned in. And in that offering, I felt safe. Free.

"If you ever return, I'm here."

But right now, it's my time to set sail. My time to be done burning in the memories of my past. To be done looking at the lives of others.

ACKNOWLEDGMENTS

This book is for all the moms out there. We play many roles each day, and sometimes we fail at them all. Sometimes we feel on top of the world. But mostly, we just want to love our children. And it's okay if that's all you have at the moment.

That's all that matters.

I'm not one for long, drawn-out acknowledgments, so here we go.

Thank you first and foremost to my parents, Jung and Kyung Won. I wouldn't be here—I wouldn't be anywhere—without your love, sacrifice, and support.

Thank you to my sister, Jennifer Grilli, for her constant guidance in all things in life. You are the best sister ever.

Thank you to Liza Dawson Associates and my amazing, superb literary agent, Rachel Beck. Your steadfast guidance over the years means everything, and I can't wait to see what else we do together!

Thank you to the entire team at Lake Union and certainly to my fabulous editor, Nancy Taylor Holmes. You've been an enthusiastic beacon from the start; your eye for storytelling has been invaluable to this book, and it means the world to me that you love this story as much as I do!

Thank you to my incredible dev editor, Jodi Warshaw. Wow. All I can say is wow! Your editorial talent and insights are phenomenal. You helped carve this story into the best it could be, and I'm forever grateful.

Thank you to my friends and family for all their continued cheerleading.

And finally, thank you to my A.J. for always being there for me. And to my baby boys, Preston and Archer. My three guys: I love you all, always and forever.

ABOUT THE AUTHOR

Photo © 2022 Caitlin Bielefeldt

Ellen Won Steil is the bestselling author of *The Lives of Others*, *Becoming Marlow Fin*, and *Fortune*. She grew up in Iowa in a Korean American family and earned her BA in journalism from Drake University and law degree from William Mitchell College of Law. She lives in Minnesota with her husband and two young sons. Ellen believes most good stories have at least a hint of darkness. For more information, visit www.ewsteil.com.